PRAISE FOR GARRETT LEIGH

"Emotional and brilliant..."

ALL ABOUT ROMANCE

"...tastefully erotic...more smart than smutty..."

PUBLISHERS WEEKLY

"Powerful and compelling..."

FOREWORD REVIEWS

LUCKY

GARRETT LEIGH

Cover Art: Garrett Leigh @ blackjazzdesign.com

Editing: Victoria Milne

Proofing: Con Riley & Victoria Milne

For my foxes, as ever, with love

AUTHOR'S NOTE

Throughout the book, you will see Lucky mentioning *drone* or *bubble* when he refers to getting high. This drug is mephedrone, which was —staggeringly—legal in the UK until so-called "legal highs" were recently criminalised. Mephedrone is far more common in the UK than crystal meth, which international readers may be more familiar with. In fact, crystal meth is pretty tough to come by over here, so it's far more realistic that Lucky would use mephedrone instead.

ONE

Dom

"In point two miles, the destination is on your left."

I shuddered; excitement and dread battled for space in my screwed-up soul. *This fucking place.* There was something about downtown Dalston I could never escape, even when months and months passed between visits. Maybe it was the smell—the Turkish restaurants, and the grotty meat market. Sizzling chargrilled lamb mixed with raw chicken flesh that was well past its best.

Or perhaps it was the haze that descended on me every time I cruised the streets, searching out an address I'd tapped into my GPS, cut and pasted from Grindr. The brutal tunnel vision that wouldn't lift until I'd paid someone to drain me dry.

Yeah, that's right. 'Cause it wasn't enough to chase down a stranger on a hook-up app, I was going to pay that motherfucker too—for his time, his silence...for the privilege of indulgence.

I rolled down my blacked-out window and another shiver passed through me. Indulgence. Something else I couldn't seem to escape. In my world, it was a lifestyle, a given...even now, when every part of me, except my dick, was screaming at me to turn my souped-up wank-mobile round and go home.

But I didn't go home. I squinted at the numbers and names on the blocks of flats and parked my car in the street next to the one I wanted, 'cause I was a fucking ninja at this shit, and knew by now to keep hook ups as far away from my car as humanly possible.

"Nice wheels. You some kind of billionaire?"

I shivered again at the memory. Not quite, but the attention was dangerous, so I avoided it...like I avoided everything else.

Dickhead.

I locked my car and took the long way back to the nondescript block of flats I needed. Crossed the road a few times. Lingered outside a dodgy chicken shop and pretended to talk native on the phone.

Fucking charade. But it calmed my nerves. Like putting on a show for the people around me who couldn't give two shits what I was doing in their postcode could make everything right.

The block of flats was dodgier than I'd expected. My hook up—LCK£_98—buzzed me inside, and I jogged up the grimy stairs to the type of landing I hadn't seen since my mum sold her Thetford council place for big bucks a decade ago. Back then places like this had been home. Now it felt like I'd been dropped on the moon.

I wandered the corridor until I came to a grubby front door. There were no numbers on it, but powers of deduction led me to believe it was the right one.

That and the fact that it was on the latch—left open for any old closeted queer to stroll in.

I shut the door behind me, hard enough to announce my arrival, and hopefully convince whoever was behind that profile picture that I wasn't a fucking target. I'd survived a dozen Grindr encounters, but rocking up at some rando's house didn't get any easier.

Footsteps sounded from within the flat, and nerves started a new rave in my stomach. I glanced at the stained walls and broken floor-boards. By now I'd had my dick sucked in worse places, but the vibe tickling my belly right now was ambiguous enough to kick-start my already-thumping heart.

"Wow. You're not what I was expecting."

I jumped and whirled around to face a doorway I hadn't noticed to my left. Blinked. And did that shit all over again. *Fucking hell. Are you kidding me?* LCK£_98's profile picture had been a pale, slim torso, and in our private message exchange he'd sent me a snap of his full lips pressed together in a teasing pout, but there'd been nothing else to giveaway the streak of fae-like beauty that stood before me now. Dark skinny jeans clung to his long legs, and a ripped vest hung from his slender frame, showing swathes of milky skin, all set off by piercing blue eyes, a ton of weathered leather bracelets, and sandy hair tied into a messy knot at the nape of his neck.

Long hair was my kryptonite. *Damn. Did I dream him?*

"Okay...so you're not a talker?" The young man leaned on the doorframe and twirled an escaped lock of hair around an elegant finger. "That suits me. Do you want to come in, or do this in the hallway?"

"What?"

"You're here for a blowjob, right? We said fifty quid, but looking at your flashy skids I might have to raise my prices."

Reality kicked me in the nuts, clawing me back from wherever my renegade imagination had been about to take us. I dug deep for my apathetic hook-up mask and plastered it on my face. "Charge me whatever. I don't care."

"Definitely rich then."

"Does it matter?"

"Not to me. I ain't gonna rob you, mate."

I ran my gaze over his slight frame again and sneered a little. "I'm not worried about that."

"Then you're an idiot. Now, are you coming through, or getting your dick out right here?"

Getting sucked off in the dilapidated hallway didn't ring my bell, so I followed him through the door he'd emerged from into a bedroom far cleaner than anywhere I'd seen since I'd got out of my car. There wasn't much to it—a bed, a chair, and an artfully placed mirror—but the normality of it eased some tension, even if the soft light from the single lamp drove me to pull my baseball cap further down my face.

"Relax." The young man appeared in front of me, close enough that I could smell the cigarettes he'd clearly tried to mask with toothpaste. "You can keep your hat on for a blowie, you know."

"Thanks," I said dryly. "You want me to pay you first?"

"Obviously. Seventy-five, wasn't it?"

I rolled my eyes. This kid was good, but I was too intrigued by him to haggle. I pulled a folded bundle of notes from my back pocket and passed him two fifties. "Call it a hundred and skip the small talk. Is there anyone else here?"

"No. I'm all alone, if *you* were thinking of mugging me."

"I'm not." I gestured to my belt. "I want you to suck my dick."

And fuck if it didn't feel amazing to say that shit out loud. Liberating. Sometimes it seemed like my sexuality was nothing but a demon dancing around my brain, reminding me every ten minutes that I was living the worst kind of lie, but in moments like this it was real.

I was real.

The young man leaned closer still. I wondered for a heart-stopping moment if he would kiss me, but of course he didn't, and my virgin lips mourned his mouth as he bent his neck to look down at my crotch.

He reached for my belt and began to undo it. My breath caught in my throat and an age-old battle warred within me: to make him stop, or to put my hands on him to urge him to go faster. To cram my cock into his mouth before I lost my nerve, or—

"I—"

He glanced up. "What?"

I shook my head. "Nothing."

Something flashed in those big blue eyes, but was gone before I could decipher it. He looked down again and freed my belt from the buckle, and then he unbuttoned my jeans, pushing them down my hips.

"I'll say it again," he whispered. "You really aren't what I was expecting."

"No?" I choked out.

"Your Grindr name is Perignon55, so I kind of figured you'd, uh, *be* fifty-five."

I'd sent him a couple of pics of my body, so I was kind of offended he'd pegged me for an extra quarter century, before I remembered we were talking about Grindr. "My pictures were genuine."

"I can see that." Cold air hit my dick and I realised my underwear had joined my jeans stretched around my thighs. "I recognise your cock."

"That a good thing?"

"Fuck, yeah. It's so pretty down here."

Coming from a bloke with a dude bun, I almost laughed, but there was nothing funny about the delicate finger ghosting along my shaft.

A strangled noise escaped me. My cheeks burned, but he didn't look up. Just flattened his hand against my stomach and urged me towards the bed until I hit the edge and sank down.

"I'm glad you decided to come in the bedroom," he said.

"Yeah?"

"Yeah." He grinned wickedly and dropped into a crouch. "That floor in the hallway is a bitch to my knees."

The reality that I wasn't the only man he'd blown in this flat—that he'd blown even tonight, maybe—threatened the barricades of my blinding arousal, but the charge didn't last long. The young man's smirk disappeared and he buried his face between my legs. He closed his mouth around my cock, and for the first time in months, the stars aligned.

"Fuck!" The curse tore out of me, and I fell backwards onto my hands, arching up from the bed as much as I dared. We hadn't discussed how physical I could be with him, but instinct held me back. His mouth was fucking beautiful...precious, though outside of common respect, I didn't know why that made me hold back.

"What's your name?" I gasped out.

He gazed up at me through long lashes, swirling his tongue around my tip, like he was gauging if I was serious. If I was really attempting conversation while he was trying to blow me.

"Please," I whispered. "I want to know."

He pulled away and wiped his mouth with the back of his hand. "Lucky."

"What?"

"My name's Lucky," he said. "Like you're going to be if you let me get on with sucking your dick."

I took the hint and went back to staring as I turned the name over in my head. *Lucky*. It sounded like Grindr bullshit, but I liked it.

Lucky brought his tongue back to my cock. More swirling set me on fire, but then, without warning, he closed his lips around me, and swallowed me whole.

"Fuck!" The second exclamation hurt my chest, but I ignored the scratchy sensation and lost myself to the forbidden ecstasy of sliding my dick down a man's throat. Instant release bubbled in my groin, but I fought it like a starving man fighting for grain. *Not yet*. I craved oblivion, but I craved this more—the touch, the smell—everything about a man whose primary occupation in this moment was to make me feel like this.

And damn if Lucky didn't make me feel some type of way. I leaned back on my hands for as long as I could, but it seemed like no time at all had passed when my hands found their way to his head. My fingers drove into his hair, and I thrust up gently into his mouth. "Fuck, yeah. So good, so good."

Lucky's answering groan vibrated through me, and one of his hands disappeared. The crunching sound of a zipper being lowered reached me, but I was too far gone to contemplate what it meant. I fucked his mouth, losing myself in his tight grip and steady moans, as my hands roamed what little of him I could reach. One remained tangled in his hair, twisting around the soft strands, while the other gripped his slender neck, scraping blunt nails over silky skin.

It was too much, and nowhere near enough. I thrust harder, but he made a noise of protest, and I backed off.

He pulled off my cock and glared at me, but the aggression in his eyes held more challenge than rebuke. “Lie down.”

I shuffled back on the bed as he yanked my shoes, socks, and jeans off and tossed them aside. Naked from the waist down, my dick jutting up to meet the cool air of the unfamiliar room, I should’ve felt vulnerable.

But I didn’t.

A low growl rumbled from me as Lucky crawled up the bed, and I lay back, ready for him, like we’d done this a thousand times. The only thing wrong was that he was wearing far too many clothes. “Let me see you.”

“No.”

“Please?”

“*No.*” Lucky nudged my legs apart and placed himself eye level with my dick again. “This isn’t about me.”

Wasn’t it? I’d signed into Grindr to silence the monster dancing on my shoulder. To find a blank and willing mouth to scratch my itch. But this was more than that—so much more. “I’ll pay you extra.”

“I know.”

Lucky took me in his mouth again, this time asserting his control. His hand on my hip kept me still as he worked me, and the gentle pressure felt like a ten-ton weight pinning me down.

I was so fucking done. Ragged cries fell from my lips, rising in pitch with every pass of Lucky’s tongue. I thought I’d reached the jackpot, but then he did something else. A drop of saliva slid down my balls and lower. Lucky’s fingers traced it...and then pressed inside me.

Crying out, I reared up from the bed, my hands reaching to throw him off me, but then sensation took over and fear of the unknown, of an unwelcome intrusion, turned to something I’d never felt before. A dam of white-hot bliss burst somewhere deep inside of me. Orgasm hit, and my dick exploded in Lucky's mouth. "Oh god, Jesus, I'm coming."

More nonsense fell from my lips, but I barely heard it as pleasure charged through me in waves. Everything I'd repressed for months and months drained out of me and into Lucky, and I was powerless to the rush of it. Entranced by the double-edged pleasure of his mouth on my dick, and his finger stroking a magic spot inside me.

I sagged on the bed as it faded. Lucky slipped his finger painlessly from me like it had never been there at all, and sat back on his heels, a tiny thread of come hanging from his lips.

Smirking, he caught it with his tongue. "Good?"

"Fuck off."

"I'll take that as a yes."

I shook my head, but couldn't help grinning back a little. "How much are you going to charge me for the finger?"

"Nothing. And for what it's worth, I'm sorry. I should've asked you before I did it—I don't know what came over me."

I sat up on my elbows. "I wouldn't do anything to *you* without asking."

"I know."

How he could be so sure, I had no idea, and I wasn't sure I wanted to. As fast as the glow of the craziest orgasm I'd ever had faded, the harder reality set in that I was half-naked with a stranger in a grotty Dalston flat—a stranger I'd paid to suck my dick—and the longer I stayed put, the more chance this had of blowing up in my face. *Get in, get off, get out.*

But I wasn't ready for this to end.

Lucky turned away and reached for my jeans. I grabbed his hand. "Wait. I'll give you another hundred if you let me suck you."

TWO

Lucky

"Stay in control."

"Don't let them call the shots."

"Stick to the plan."

The advice Simone had given me when she'd lent me her pad to do this echoed in my head, mingling with what I should've said to this bloke's blurted, breathless request:

"Blowing me is a hundred and twenty."

"Just your mouth. Keep your hands to yourself."

"No."

But I didn't do anything Simone had told me to. Didn't say anything I should've said.

I just swallowed and nodded, praying he wouldn't figure out that I'd never blown a dude for cash in my whole damn miserable life. "Okay."

The dark eyes peering at me from beneath the man's low cap widened, like he'd expected me to refuse—like I had when he'd asked me to take my clothes off. "Are you sure?"

"Are *you* sure?" Jesus. What the fuck was going on here? Simone had warned me about tricky johns when I'd convinced myself that taking advantage of the trendy cash-fuelled Grindr kink was some kind of fucking masterplan—that it wasn't real hooking because I wasn't standing on a street corner—but she hadn't said anything about picking up blokes that were clearly too nice to be paying for blowjobs.

The man sat up further, and I belatedly realised he was still clutching my hand. "I'm sure," he said. "I mean...if you're okay with it? I don't want to pressure you."

I laughed—couldn't help it—and reclaimed my hand. "You think I'd let anyone do that to me?"

"No. Um—" And then something changed. Like the man realised his mask had slipped. His earnest gaze faded like it had never been there, and apathy took its place. "Look, there's an extra ton if you want it. Either way, pass me my jeans, yeah?"

I missed the nice guy. I couldn't see much of his face, but his eyes had been kind when he'd stopped thinking so hard. When he'd let his desire get the better of him.

I liked that.

Leaning back, I retrieved his designer jeans from the floor, but instead of handing them over I plucked the cash from his back pocket, and peeled off another two fifties to shove in my own back pocket. "I'm sure I want to take your money to let you suck my dick, and seeing as we're skipping the small talk, I suggest you get on with it."

The man shrugged out of his leather bomber jacket. The label inside caught my attention and I tried not to cringe. He'd paid more for his coat than he had for me. What did that say about either of us? That I was desperate and he was a kinky bastard?

Or maybe he was the desperate one and I was just a whore.

Not that it mattered. How could it, when having his dick in my mouth, sliding it down my throat, had made my cock so hard that I couldn't contemplate a reality where he didn't return the favour?

I scrambled to my feet, my legs stiff from a prolonged period on my knees, and stepped towards him, fumbling with my jeans as urgency stole over me so suddenly I felt dizzy. Barely ten minutes had passed since I'd refused to take my clothes off for him, now I couldn't get my dick out fast enough. My *hard* dick. 'Cause, yeah. I wasn't oblivious to the fact that this bloke was gorgeous, despite how hard he was trying to hide behind that damn baseball cap. Sultry eyes, full lips. Smooth skin and dark stubble. What I'd seen of his bod was killer, and his dick was fucking beautiful. Clean, cut, thick, and long. The moment I'd seen it I'd wanted to ride it, but I'd settled for sliding an uninvited finger into his tight hole instead, because life happened that way sometimes. Upside down, inside out. His startled cry flashed through my mind and arousal throbbed my every nerve.

Fuck. I'd have blown this guy for free any day of the week.

I wedged myself between his spread legs and he leaned forward enough so my crotch was level with his face. "You might have to take your cap off to deep throat me. Don't worry, I won't look."

Silence. The man didn't move a muscle. Then...slowly, he reached up and pushed his cap from his head, letting it fall away to the bed.

Keeping my promise, I fixed my gaze on the opposite wall, and finally freed my aching dick from the confines of my super-tight jeans. A sharp intake of breath pierced the air, but I couldn't tell if it was mine or his.

He put his hands on my thighs, resting them there at first, and then his grip tightened, and he tugged me closer.

His breath ghosted over my cock. I shivered, anticipating his lips and tongue, but then a compulsion overcame me and I seized his shoulders. "Wait. I want to know your name."

"Why?"

"Because you know mine."

"Lucky?"

"Yeah."

More silence. I chewed my lip. Had I blown my load without even getting my dick wet?

Some professional I was gonna be if I ever did this again. Still, I had his money, and I was in enough of a bind to fight him for it.

"Dom."

"What?"

"My name. It's Dom, and if you use it against me, I'll kill you, got it?"

I got it, even if I couldn't bring myself to believe that a man whose eyes could be so gentle would ever hurt me.

Idiot. But the time for thinking was over. *Dom* wanted to suck my cock, and I was so far beyond gagging for it I could hardly stand up.

He tugged me forward again. A wet, feather-light tongue grazed my tip, and a shuddery moan escaped me. I clung to his shoulders and squeezed my eyes shut. "Shit. Do that again."

Dom obeyed, though whether it was because I'd asked him to or he was going to do it anyway, I had no idea. And I didn't care as teasing strokes became more purposeful, and then he sucked me into his mouth.

I stumbled for real, crying out as my dick slid down his throat. *Fuck.* What was it about this bloke that turned me inside out? This wasn't how this was supposed to go down.

Dom steadied me, but didn't let up his rhythm. He worked me with his tight lips and slick throat, and hummed around my cock, throwing petrol on a fire that was already well lit as I clung to him and tried not to hump his face. But after a while it became clear that perhaps he fucking *wanted* me to.

He took my hands from his shoulders and placed them on the back of his head. I fought the urge to look down at him, but gave in to the feverish craving for friction. He had short hair, so I clung to his strong neck and thrust my hips, fucking his mouth as hard as I dared, all the while trying to block out the cautious beast on my shoulder who warned me over and over to be careful. 'Cause Dom wasn't my boyfriend, or even a casual fuck buddy. He was a stranger who'd paid me to be with him. A stranger who had half a foot and several stone on me, even if I did fight like a psychotic Inspector Gadget.

His rumbling voice bothered me too. I was vibrating with the need to come, to shoot down his throat, in his face, or even in my own fucking hand, but his groans as he swallowed my cock were deep enough to set my teeth on edge. To remind me of someone I'd come to London to forget.

Not that my arsehole father had ever sucked my dick. He wasn't that kind of cunt.

Like Dom heard the chaos swirling around my brain, his moaning cut off. He brought his hands back to my legs and reclaimed control.

The slight change in angle sent white dots dancing in front of my eyes. I was gonna come soon, and come hard, spilling out everything I had wherever he'd let me.

I wondered if he'd try and finger me like I had him. The notion made me clench up, like he was already there, easing inside me, curling and teasing, and my time was up. "Where do you want me to come?"

Dom squeezed my thighs and kept working me with his mouth.

I took that to mean he wanted it down his throat, and my climax rushed up, shocking me with its violence. Heat spiked my blood, and my legs seized up, muscles contracting. A loud groan ripped from my chest, and I started to come, spurting into his mouth so hard I couldn't see how I'd ever stop. "Fuck, fuck, *fuck*."

It seemed like forever slipped away as Dom drained my dick, still working it even as it softened. Eventually, it was too much. My frazzled nerves couldn't take it. I pulled back enough to slip from his mouth, and then gave him a moment before I opened my eyes.

He was already jamming his cap on his head and reaching for his jeans.

I couldn't make sense of how that made me feel, any more than I understood our entire encounter. My pockets were stuffed full of his cash, I'd swallowed his gorgeous dick, and had the best orgasm of my life—so why did watching him prepare to leave me seem like the end of the world?

Fucked if I knew, and I pushed the weirdness aside and heeded Simone's advice to get myself back together as quickly as possible.

I stepped away from him and pulled up my jeans, patting my back pocket to check the money was still there.

When I looked at Dom again he was dressed and heading for the door.

"Hey, Dom?"

He stopped and turned, but didn't look at me. "What?"

I didn't know either. So I stared at him and held out the packet of tobacco I'd reflexively reached for. "Smoke?"

"No, thanks."

He stared at me, treating me for the first time to the full view of his face. Like I hadn't already known he'd be a fucking knockout: high cheekbones, chiselled jaw, and dark, troubled eyes.

"Are you okay?"

"What?"

It seemed to be his knee-jerk response to everything, so I stepped back into his personal space, even as he leaned away from me. "Are you *okay*? You seem a little freaked."

"I'm not freaked. Just got somewhere to be."

Somewhere that wasn't a scuzzy flat with a paid-for Grindr hook up.

I took the hint and let my unconsciously reaching hands drop. "Fair enough. Have a good night."

Dom said nothing. Did nothing. Just kept staring, as though now our eyes had met, he couldn't look away.

I knew that feeling, but I had a scraping of pride left. Fixing a sneer in place, I turned away. "Shut the door on your way out."

"Wait."

"Why?" I rolled a cig with one hand and stuck it in my mouth. "No small talk, remember? Sorry I forgot the rules for a moment. I'm over it now."

The thorns in my voice surprised even me, but I didn't look at Dom as I lit my smoke and took a deep drag. This whole thing had been a mistake—no money was worth the whiplash he was giving me, or the churning in my stomach as I couldn't work out if I wanted him to ask for another round, or just get the fuck out already—

"Hey." Dom gripped the hand that wasn't holding my fag and it forced me to look at him. "I'm not okay, but that's on me. I had good time...I got *Lucky*, right? Goodnight, mate."

And then he was gone, slipping out of the borrowed flat like a shadow, and leaving me to wonder if he'd ever truly been here at all.

THREE

Lucky

"You bloody idiot!"

I ducked as Jamila swung at me, escaping with a glancing blow. "What? I told you I was doing it—it's not like it's a fucking surprise."

"That's not the point. Why didn't you tell me when it was actually happening? So someone knew where you were going? Shit, Lucky. What if you'd been murdered or something? Who'd have known?"

"Simone knew, but thanks for reminding me you're the only one who gives a damn about me."

"Don't be a dick," Jamila retorted. "Simone's not your friend—you barely know her—and it's not my fault you don't have an address where the police could've gone when they found your body, or a job that would miss you when you didn't turn up. What am I supposed to do when you disappear for days on end? Assume you've got your hands on a big bag of drone? Or that you've snuffed it on Grindr?"

The crude words were all wrong falling from her pretty mouth. In the past I'd have kissed her to shut her up, but we weren't doing that anymore. Kissing was too intimate—too complicated—for our unique brand of friendship. And as much as I wanted to deny it, she had a point. Simone had known I was using her flat, but we weren't close enough for her to bother checking up on me. I hadn't even seen her, just left her key and a ten-bag under the mat.

Sighing, I lay back on Jamila's bed. "Sorry, mate. I didn't think."

"You never do. That's what's got you into this mess in the first place."

"Not fair," I protested. "I didn't ask to get kicked out of the YMCA."

"No, but you knew not to take drugs in there, and you did it anyway."

I tuned her out and closed my eyes, wishing I'd bought a bigger bag of weed with the money I'd earned from my encounter with Dom, though a bigger bag of weed would've meant less cash in the box I kept under Jamila's bed, and even longer before I could afford a dungeon of a room at the halfway house up the road. I didn't have enough for a deposit yet, let alone a first month's rent.

Jamila nudged me. "Don't sulk. It's only because I worry about you."

"I know." I kept my eyes closed so she wouldn't make me cry. "And I know you're right too...I just—I can't see a way out. I'd rather kip outside Debenhams than get a room at the Bay Centre."

"Not in this weather, you wouldn't. It's freezing."

Freezing to death sounded better than the terrifying hostels I sometimes slept in when Jamila's mum wasn't working nights. The only good thing about those hellholes were the drugs, but a friendly warden had turfed me out for being off my nut, and I'd wound up right back where I'd started. Scoring some bubble and walking the streets till dawn was an alternative, but drone comedowns, despite urban myth that they didn't exist, sucked donkey dick, especially when you had nowhere to curl up and die.

"So..." Jamila poked me in the ribs. "Are you going to tell me about this old minger you sucked off for cash? Was it horrible?"

I opened my eyes slowly, searching for the words to describe Dom. "It wasn't horrible. It was...hot."

Jamila arched a perfect brow. "Did you do it with the lights off and pretend it was someone else?"

"No, though I reckon *he* might've preferred the dark. He was pretty fucking skittish."

"Married?"

"Dunno. Didn't ask." And I hadn't even thought about it until now. Hadn't checked his fingers for a ring. Or considered that the obvious guilt weighing Dom down meant anything, because it *didn't* mean anything. I needed his money, and I didn't care who he'd hurt to give it to me.

Right?

As I recalled the rare flickers of warmth in his liquid gaze, I wasn't so sure, but Jamila had ways of distracting me from most things, and after a while, Dom left my mind.

Tick tock tick tock.

I squeezed my eyes shut, trying to block out the old clock in Jamila's hallway. If it wasn't for the fact that her grandfather had brought it with him on the boat from Grenada a bazillion years ago, I'd have set the fucking thing on fire by now.

Tick tock tick tock.

Fuck my life. I opened my eyes and sat up, mindful of Jamila sleeping soundly beside me. Her share of the duvet was bunched around her waist, exposing her back to the chilly night air. Her smooth skin was marked by my fingernails, barely there indents that were a perfect echo of the light and gentle orgasm she'd drawn from me with her soft hands.

I'd returned the favour with my tongue, but my mind had been elsewhere as she'd writhed beneath me, and she'd known it too.

"You've got Grindr brain again. How are you going to pity-fuck me when you're thinking about dick?"

Only a fellow pansexual could make jokes like that and get away with it, and Jamila—my faithful BFF-cum-fuck-buddy—had been making them for years, ever since we'd ditched school together to mess about behind the cricket pavilion. It was nights like these I missed our old lives in Brighton. Things had been simpler then.

She was right about the Grindr brain, though. I slipped out of her bed, snagging a stray condom wrapper as I went, and padded through the silent flat to the cold kitchen. The dinner she'd saved for me was on the side, but I ignored it and opened the cereal cupboard.

I chose the cheapest brand and poured myself a small bowl, adding the bare minimum of milk. Jamila wouldn't mind, but sharing her bed with me five nights a week was enough without rinsing her mum's cupboards.

With my bowl of frosted flakes, I retreated to the living room, and huddled up on the couch with an old blanket and my phone. I logged into the Wi-Fi, and then opened Grindr, scanning the grid of profile pictures for the torso shot Dom had used—a torso a phone camera hadn't nearly done justice to, if the scant inch I'd seen of his abdomen the other night was anything to go by. The image attached to Perignon55 seemed pale and nondescript, but the real-life strip of flesh I'd seen was hard, sculpted, and dusted with just the right amount of dark fuzz...the kind you only saw when you got up close and personal.

The kind that kept you up at night a week after you'd buried your face in it.

Is he thinking about me?

I doubted it. Next to a man like Dom, I was so skinny and pale I was practically transparent. Unless he had a Milkybar fetish, he'd probably forgotten all about me.

But even as I thought it, my gut told me it wasn't true. I didn't know Dom from Adam, but I recalled every sound he'd made—every gasp and moan—like he was coming in my mouth right now. His smell and taste had left me dizzy, but more than that, the way he'd come with his whole body, like he'd been waiting his entire life for a man to touch his cock, would stay with me forever.

I couldn't see how *he* could forget it either, unless—

His torso pic wasn't on the active grid. My heart skipped a beat. *Fuck.* What if he was one of those ghost profiles that disappeared? I felt weirdly sick at the possibility, but couldn't quite bring myself to believe it. He'd left without asking to hook up again, and I hadn't heard from him since, but coming as hard as that? Nah. No way he'd leave it as a one-time thing.

There were a million reasons why I'd be wrong, but when I checked our brief message thread, his profile was still there—just without the misleading snap. And he'd been online in the last few minutes.

My fingers hovered over my cracked phone screen and anticipatory warmth pooled in my groin. Simone had lent me her pad as a one-off thing—a favour for some cheap sniff and cut of whatever I made—but I'd left her good bubble...good enough to persuade her to let me borrow her bed again if she wasn't using it to blow desperate motherfuckers herself.

The heat in my blood faded as quickly as it had come. *Desperate motherfucker*. Did I really think that of Dom? That he was so hard up for blokes he had to pay for that shit? I'd been over and over it in the seven days since that night and I still couldn't decide. I clicked out of the message thread and scrolled through some others, scanning the dudes who'd practically begged me to take their money before I'd settled on Dom. One bloke had bombarded me to the point where I'd blocked him and wondered if I was out of my fucking mind. 'Cause that was the other thing. For all I knew, paying for sex was just Dom's kink, which left *me* with the label of desperate motherfucker.

A label I couldn't see myself shaking anytime soon. Still. Even without the cash burning a hole in Jamila's mattress, and my dick rock hard with the memory of what had put it there, a different itch in my blood wouldn't quit. I shut down Grindr and finished my cereal, washed up my bowl and put it back in the cupboard, crawled back into bed with Jamila, and set my alarm to wake me up an hour before her mum came home.

Then I swallowed my last Valium and knocked the fuck out.

Dom

The dull thud of leather on leather was giving me a fucking migraine. Late nights and early mornings didn't fit a full training schedule, but I didn't have time for a pity party as I ran sprint drills with my teammates under the hawkish glare of Fernando—the head coach from hell.

Half an hour later, my training group took our turn on the football pitch, honing ball control and skill enhancements, and despite the company of my long-time training partner, Maldano, I was bored out of my tiny mind. Football had been my life for as long as I could remember—the only thing in the world I was actually good at—but any passion I'd had for it was long gone, drowning in the monotony of testosterone-fuelled bullshit, fag jokes, and casual misogyny. I was so over this crap.

Maldano slapped my back. "Time's up, Dom. Let's get naked."

"Twat."

He danced away to give someone else the benefit of his juvenile humour, and I hit the showers. Nude men in peak condition surrounded me, but I ignored them and stuck close to my locker, dressing quickly with my head down.

Out of habit, I glanced at my phone, but didn't dare open Grindr until I was safely in my car, loitering behind the blacked-out windows.

Another habit—a new one—took me straight to Lucky's profile, but he hadn't been online since the night before, and nothing about his profile had changed. The subtle pound sign in his username remained and there was every chance he was hooking up with someone right now—

Stop it.

I knocked my fist against my forehead, like I had done so many times since I'd slunk home from Dalston a week ago. Since I'd realised my usual cure for the beast that kept me awake at night had failed spectacularly.

Yeah, that's right. It wasn't enough that I'd spent the last decade burying myself in a black hole of self-loathing so deep I couldn't see how I'd ever climb out, now my antidote to the crippling pain was broken. Gone. If anything, hooking up with Lucky had widened the crater.

I need to touch him again.

For fuck's sake STOP!

At this point, punching myself in the face seemed my only option, but with my entire body aching from a full-on training day, I settled for starting my car and leaving the club grounds, keeping my cap low as I passed the usual clutch of paparazzi hanging around the gates. I wasn't one of their favourite players to stalk—too fucking boring—but they'd still stick their cameras in my face if they saw me looking, and I wasn't in the mood for that shit today.

My mind still on Lucky, I made the short drive from the club to my Greenwich flat. Some days after training, I hit the gym, but not today, 'cause I wasn't in the mood for that either.

At home, I dodged the doorman and slipped into the lift, keeping my head down until I was through my front door, but even then, I wasn't safe. My housekeeper, used to me being gone most of the day, was still in the apartment, scouring a kitchen I rarely used.

"Constance, you don't have to do that." I dropped my keys on the counter. "I didn't even know that shelf belonged in the oven."

Constance carried on scrubbing. "It's on the list, Mr. Ramos. I'll get into trouble if it's not done."

"Not with me."

"Not today maybe, but you wouldn't like to open a dusty oven."

The chances of me noticing were less than zero, but I left Constance a tip, and let her finish her work in peace. Of all the housekeepers who'd passed through this particular building, she was the only one I entirely trusted not to root through my stuff. How many times had I come home to find something private not quite where I'd left it?

Too many to count.

Paranoia licked at me and my phone felt like an unexploded bomb in my pocket. I changed the passcode every week, cleared my history every couple of hours, but the fear of someone getting their hands on my phone scared the life out of me.

I locked myself in the bathroom and sank to the floor with my back to the door. My thumb hovered over the Grindr app—buried deep in a folder of game apps—torn between deleting it for the tenth time this month alone, or opening it up and following through on the fantasy I'd carried since I'd left Lucky in that grimy flat: the one where I pinged him with a request, he came back with a price, and a few hours later he had my cock in his mouth again.

On cue, my jeans were suddenly too tight. I loosened them, but didn't touch myself. Hadn't since that night with Lucky. But no matter how hard—*heh*—I tried to ignore the heat sluicing through me, I just couldn't do it. I deleted the Grindr app and reinstalled it ten seconds later, praying no one ever hacked into my Apple account and saw my daily homo-seesaw struggles. One download from years ago could be bluffed out, but five times a week? I was so fucked up.

I tapped on Lucky's profile and clicked through to our message thread. He still hadn't been online today, but I was growing used to just missing him. It was like he knew when I'd given up and hidden my phone under my pillow...like he didn't want to cross my path again.

Common sense said I was being fucking dramatic, and my treacherous imagination recalled the ragged sounds he'd made as he'd spilled in my mouth. You couldn't fake that shit, right? He'd come hard, and behind his insolent stare, had seemed as wrecked as me.

Besides, even dick blind, I hadn't missed how he'd looked at my money—like it was the only thing between him and the end of the world. Even if he didn't want to see *me* again, I was pretty sure my wallet could persuade him.

Don't be an arsehole.

I came back into myself with a start, and the creeping burn of shame began to corrupt the tickle of arousal buzzing in my veins. Sucking in a shaky breath, I stared at the pouty selfie Lucky had sent me before we'd hooked up, at his soft lips and young face. I—

My phone buzzed in my hand. Startled, I nearly dropped it, and it took me a moment to realise it had come from Grindr—that it was the vibrating alert I'd been waiting on for seven long days.

I gazed down at the screen. A grinning emoji winked back at me, accompanied by two little words that set my world on fire.

LCK£_98: *how's tricks?*

FOUR

Lucky

LCK£_98: *how's tricks?*

Perignon55: *gud. u?*

LCK£_98: *same old shit. did u wanna hook up again?*

I regretted the bluntness as soon as the message hurtled off into the stratosphere, but I couldn't take it back so settled for chewing my nails down to the cuticle instead, a tic I could usually ignore when I was floating down from a Valium buzz.

Dom didn't reply straight away. I stared at my phone for as long as my poor nails could take, and then got up and left the greasy spoon I'd been nursing a cup of tea in for most of the day. On my way out, the owner stopped me—a moody Polish bloke I'd thought was hot until I'd met Dom.

"You can't come back tomorrow," he said. "I don't mind you hanging out when the weather's bad, but if I let you in every day, I'll have to let everyone else in who's got nowhere else to go."

I accepted the dismissal with a shrug and moved on. Rumour had it the cafe was changing hands in a few weeks anyway, and I'd been scuzzing it around the city for long enough to know that the sexy Polish dude and his easy-going grandfather were rarities.

Lacking any better ideas, I got on a bus and rode it back to Dalston, leaving Vauxhall behind. There was a bookshop in Stoke Newington that let people sit down and read. Perhaps I'd do that.

I was half-asleep when Dom finally returned my message.

Rubbing my eyes, I stared at his response, and blinked awake as it sank in.

Perignon55: *yea*

LCK£_98: *when?*

Perignon55: *tonight work for u?*

I licked my lips. Tonight would be near on impossible. It was Friday night—Simone used her flat at weekends, and Jamila's mum was home too, meaning I had nowhere to clean up before letting Dom anywhere near me.

LCK£_98: *i'm free but can't accom, can u?*

Another long silence stretched out, and I'd used Grindr enough to know what it likely meant: that Dom's end of things was as impossible as mine, but for very different reasons. He couldn't accommodate me because he had a whole world to hide from. Wife, kids...who the hell knew?

Me? No one cared what I did and I had no life to protect, but that had inconveniences all of its own. I had no home to invite him to, and no means to rent a room for the night. Unless he fancied a quickie in an alley, no one was getting any dick tonight.

Or, at least, I wasn't getting his. It wasn't like I could be sure I was his first choice.

Or even his second.

Perignon55: *can u get to shoreditch*

LCK£_98: *maybe. what u thinking?*

I expected another long silence, but Dom pinged me straight back as I was getting off the bus.

Perignon55: *hotel. i can get a room*

My pulse quickened and my fingers flew over my phone screen.

LCK£_98: *that could work. u want same as last time?*

Perignon55: *that okay?*

LCK£_98: *yea. let me know deets*

Perignon55: *talk later*

He went offline, and I went into fucking meltdown. Even if he came back to me with a late-night meet, I still had no way of making myself presentable before Jamila's mum went back to work tomorrow evening, and a glance in a nearby car window confirmed that I looked like absolute shit.

Panic lancing my chest, I called Jamila. "I need your help."

"Of course you do," she said when she replied on the second ring. "But you won't take it when I give it to you, so why do we have to play this game all the time?"

"It's not a game," I said. "And I'm not talking about borrowing a tin of beans for my dinner. I've, uh, got a date."

"A date."

It wasn't a question, she knew me well enough to see through me, but I rushed to perpetuate the bullshit anyway. "Yeah. I'm seeing someone."

"You're seeing someone from Grindr for cash, aren't you?"

"Yes."

"Who?"

"Same guy as last time. He wants to hook up again."

"For the same stuff? Or does he want more?"

"The same. I checked before I agreed."

The sound of running water trickled down the phone, and Jamila closed a door wherever she was. "So what do you need my help for?"

"I need a shower and to wash my clothes. He wants to meet at a hotel, but I'm a mess, J. I can't show up like this."

"Thought you said it was the same as last time?"

"It is."

"But it's at a hotel."

"So? How's that worse than a skanky flat up the road?"

Jamila had no sensible answer to that and agreed to smuggle me into her flat to use her bathroom, which luckily wasn't too hard as her mum took sleeping tablets on her days off.

"I still think you're nuts." She stood in front of me, holding out a clean towel.

"No, you don't," I whispered back. "You know why I'm doing this —I need the money."

"So sell ten-bags then, like you used to."

"Ten-bags? You got any idea how many of those I'd have to shift to make the kind of money I can get from this bloke in one night? Besides, shifting bubble is just as risky these days. The old bill is all over that shit."

"Getting nicked isn't the same as some douchebag trick murdering you."

"Dom's not a douchebag."

"Dom?"

Fuck.

"...if you use it against me, I'll kill you."

"Um—yeah, that's what I call him. Don't know his real name, though."

"Super." Jamila reached for a comb and started to pick the knots out of my straggly, damp hair. "So you don't know who he is, just that he likes to pay younger men to get him off."

"I'm not that much younger than him, actually. I reckon he's about twenty-seven, maybe? It's hard to tell."

"Well that's something, I suppose."

"Why? Are older men more likely to be murderous?"

"Shut up." Jamila shoved my head forward. "Just don't get killed, okay?"

Dom

I paced my apartment, watching the clock, my stomach churning with equal parts terror and exhilarating anticipation. *Seriously? Fake names and prepaid credit cards?* It couldn't get any more tragically ridiculous, but still, I did it anyway—*had* to—before the yearning in my gut drove me off a cliff.

That or I died a slow death staring at my phone, willing it to vibrate with the Grindr notifications I usually disabled.

LCK£_98: *what time?*

Despite waiting on Lucky's reply for more than an hour, I jumped out of my skin. Then I took a deep breath and placed the last piece in the convoluted puzzle I'd created just to get my dick wet.

Perignon55: *9ish room 239*

LCK£_98: *k. u want me to bring anything?*

Perignon55: *just u*

The message was gone before I considered that I'd made it sound like we were lovers. That all I needed in the world was him, the paid Grindr hook up I'd spent a total of twenty-six minutes with my entire life.

Loser.

But I didn't have time to berate myself too much. I had a meeting with my agent before I could drive to Shoreditch, and I was already running late.

I took a shower, ignoring the half-chub I'd been sporting since Lucky had confirmed his availability, and washed myself at light speed. Dressing, I noticed my hands were shaking. I held them out in front of me, trying to still my quivering fingers, but it was no good. Nerves were playing havoc with the bone-deep excitement spiking my blood, and my chest was so tight I could barely breathe.

It was in moments like these that I longed for the freedom to knock back a few beers, a couple of shots, or even smoke a joint with my buddies behind the church in Thetford where I'd grown up, but my life wasn't that simple anymore. Booze and dope were forbidden, and my childhood buddies were long gone, swallowed up by the isolation I faced in adulthood. These days, there were only two men in the world I called friends, and lucky for me, one of them was waiting in the Greenwich bar down the road from my place.

I slid into a seat opposite Ishmail Malik in the quiet booth he'd secured at the back of the bar, and admired, as always, what little I could see of his lean, dark frame. Isha had been my agent since I'd turned seventeen, managing my rise through the ranks of lower-league clubs until I'd hit the jackpot. He had a few more clients now, but I'd been his first...and he'd been my first crush.

Not that he knew it. As far as he, and anyone else, was concerned, I was simply too focussed on my game to give a shit about women—too pious and boring, which was ironic, considering that picking up blokes on Grindr had become my favourite hobby.

If you could call something you craved and detested in equal measure a hobby.

"Dom?" Isha snapped his fingers in front of my face. "You in there, mate? I haven't got all day, you know."

I blinked, forcing away the choking cloud of guilt that left me nauseous. "Liar. You always schedule me last on your list 'cause I'm on your way home."

"No, I schedule you last because you're kind enough to buy me dinner."

It was true. Isha's other clients were mainly young twats fresh out of academies and had more money than sense, and no fucking manners. He was probably lucky to get a beer out of most of them.

Lucky. The word stuck in my mind, lodged in my brain, and played on a loop until I realised Isha had started the meeting without checking I was actually in the room with him—mentally speaking.

I shoved my hands under the table and scraped my nails down my thighs, like fidgeting could tie me down to the world, but as hard as I stared at Isha and tried to compute what he was saying, I was so fucking lost.

He rolled his eyes and poured me a glass of iced water. "What the fuck's up with you? You're usually the one client I can count on to give me their undivided attention."

"Sorry." I swallowed some water, letting the cold shock me back to the present. "I'm just tired, man. Long day."

Isha raised a thick eyebrow, his face as unconvinced as his trademark impassiveness would allow. "All your days are long. What's so different about today?"

"Nothing."

"Sure about that, because you look like you're sitting on something sharp."

"Fuck you."

"Right. You ready to talk business?"

I rolled my eyes, but gave Isha the courtesy of hearing him out as he explained the latest endorsement deal I'd been offered over a dinner I couldn't stomach.

As usual, I turned it down flat. "I'm not interested in fucking shampoo adverts, mate. You know this."

Isha eyed my uneaten plate of food. "Course I do, but as your agent, and your friend when you're not being a pain in my arse, it's my job to sell you this shit."

"Why?"

"Because..." Isha pointed a fork at me. "*I* need to earn a living beyond your transfer fees, *and* you can't play football forever. Sooner or later, you're going to have to think about what comes next."

"I'm twenty-six."

"Exactly. You've got five years tops—seven if you're extremely fortunate—and they won't be top flight. Your contract's up at the end of the season, remember? You need to use that pretty face of yours while you've still got it and take one of these deals. Shore yourself up, mate, before the ship sails."

It was nothing I hadn't heard before. I earned ridiculous money kicking a ball around a field, but I was no Teddy Sherringham. My left knee was already falling apart, and besides, my enthusiasm for the game was at an all-time low.

That didn't mean I was about to put my name to some shite shampoo endorsement, though. Isha was right about the need to plan ahead, but what he didn't know was that I'd saved more than half of every pay cheque for the last decade. I'd bought my London flat, and a few houses up north that I rented out, but aside from that, my only purchase beyond regular necessities had been the wank-mobile I'd gladly sell once I was away from an environment that demanded excess to fit in.

I slid the endorsement contract across the table. "I'm not doing *this*. Find me something that matters and we'll talk again."

An hour later, I left Isha in Greenwich and drove the eight miles north to Shoreditch. I abandoned my car in a secure underground car park a street away from the hotel, and made the rest of the journey on foot, head down, shoulders hunched, my faithful cap pulled low over my face, as my heart pounded and blood roared in my ears.

I half-expected Lucky to be waiting outside, and pictured him lounging against the shiny wall, engrossed in his phone, a cigarette dangling from his perfect mouth, but he wasn't, obviously. I was an hour early so I could scope the place for paps and be sure my fake name and ghost credit card had given me the veil of privacy I needed to make this work.

And there was no guarantee Lucky would even show up. I'd paid him two-hundred quid last time, but with a face like his, I couldn't imagine he was hard up for paid hook ups.

My stomach gave an uncomfortable flip as I slipped into the room I'd checked into under an assumed name. Lucky wasn't the first bloke I'd paid to meet me, but I'd never thought about any of the others beyond what they could do with my dick, so why was I so fixated on Lucky? On what—or who—he'd done before me? On what he'd do after? What was it about this kid that had me pacing a Shoreditch hotel room like a caged lion?

Fucked if I knew.

I just knew I had to touch him again.

FIVE

Lucky

The last time I'd been in a hotel was when my dad had taken us to an away match in Northampton. We'd stayed in a Travelodge. My brother had scored the winning goal and I'd slipped over in the mud and banged my head on the goalpost.

My father hadn't spoken to twelve-year-old me the whole way home and the bewildered disappointment in his weather-hardened face, like he couldn't understand how his genes had produced such a disaster, played on my mind as I wandered the hotel corridors. After my spectacular failure to become a carbon copy of my brother, he'd predicted my life would be lost to a future of poofy endeavours. If he could only see me now, roaming a Premier Inn, searching out room 239 so I could suck the dick of a gorgeous man with a full wallet. He'd be so fucking proud.

Imagining his reaction distracted me from the nerves that were somehow worse than last time, and carried me to the second floor. I found the right room and knocked, and the door opened a millisecond later, like Dom had been stalking the peephole.

He stood back, half-hidden by the door, and waved me in.

I crossed the threshold and the door slammed, the loud click echoing in the otherwise silent room as I turned to face Dom.

He was blocking my exit, his arms folded across his strong chest. "Hey."

"Hey yourself." I dropped my bag on the floor, resisting the urge to mirror his pose. "How are you?"

"I'm good. How much cash do you want? Same as last time?"

"Depends what *you* want." Already, arousal was licking at me. "It's still seventy-five for a blowjob, but if you want to pay my bus fare, I won't complain."

Dom rolled his eyes like we were old friends, and I kinda liked it until he reached into his back pocket. The bundle of notes was technically why I was here, but somehow, watching him count off the fifties seemed all wrong. Was it too much to expect a conversation?

He didn't ask you here to talk.

The devil on my shoulder was bang on, but I didn't feel like conceding just yet. I took the money from Dom and crouched to tuck it safely into my bag. "Is this how it's always gonna go down? I name a price and you round it up? 'Cause if it is, we need to start hooking up on the regular."

Dom stared at me, his eyes liquid suspicion beneath the bill of his cap. "You think I'm an easy mark?"

"That's not what I meant." I stood and took a cautious step forward. Dom didn't seem the type to go psycho on me, but what the fuck did I know? "I was kinda trying to say thanks without sounding like a desperate loser."

"What are you desperate for? Money?"

I shrugged, denial caught in a net on the tip of my tongue, but what was the point? Besides, despite needing the fucking money, I couldn't deny the thrill that had run through me the moment my fingers had closed around the cash. The exchange meant we were one step closer to the other reason I'd hyperventilated all the way here... the one that had kept me awake all week long, wasting the nights I'd been lucky enough to score a bed: I *wanted* him.

Dom accepted my non-answer with a shrug of his own and folded his arms again, watching me, the steel in his dark gaze giving way a little to the agitation I'd seen in him last time. The restlessness that had clued me in to the possibility it had been a good while since he'd last slid his thick cock into a man's mouth. Since then, I'd bounced back and forth between picturing him as a master player and some kind of closeted virgin, but right now?

Yeah. I was leaning more towards the second.

I took another step forward. Dom leaned back, subconsciously, maybe, I couldn't tell, but it didn't matter, because I was on him a second later, up in his personal space before he had a chance to protest.

Biting my lip, I unfolded his arms, and tentatively pushed his cap off his head. It had been dark and dingy in Simone's flat, full of shadows we couldn't avoid, but the hotel room was bright and airy, and I realised his hair was longer than I'd thought—long enough to weave my fingers into and hold on tight.

Dom didn't protest to me exposing his face, but he avoided my eyes, his gaze fixed on something behind me.

I didn't mind—much...at least, I tried not to. "So...you want me to suck you off, yeah?"

"No—um, I mean. I do, but now you're here, I, uh—" Dom rubbed the back of his neck. "I can't stop thinking about sucking *you.*"

A jolt ran through me. His mouth around my cock had turned me inside out last time. I swear it had taken *hours* before my legs had stopped shaking. The idea of a rerun had played on my mind more than I cared to admit, but I hadn't truly considered it likely, especially at the expense of blowing Dom.

I sucked in a breath. A yearning deep inside me cried out for me to drop to my knees and taste him again, but the prospect of coming like a motherfucking train down his throat won out. "You can suck me if you like—I'm not going to complain about your sweet mouth. Where do you want me?"

Dom swallowed harshly. "On the bed, but take your clothes off first…I'll pay you extra."

"You don't think you've paid me enough?"

"That's up to you."

It shouldn't have been—it was his money burning a hole in my grubby messenger bag—but I appreciated the sentiment, even if it prompted me to drop my guard far lower than it should've been on our second hook up. "I don't need extra money to take my clothes off. Just mind your manners, yeah? I'm a fucking gentleman."

A ghost of a smirk flickered across Dom's chiselled face. "Me too."

"Sound." I shrugged out of my coat, dumped it on the floor, and I kicked off my boots. "But if I'm going nekkid, I'm kinda counting on seeing some of your skin too. That's fair, right?"

Dom made a sound low in his throat, but I couldn't tell if he was giving me permission or not.

Either way, I didn't stop to look as I stripped my way to the bed, leaving my clothes trailing behind me until only my jeans and underwear remained.

At the bed, I spun around and faced Dom. While my back had been turned, he'd shed his bomber jacket and hoodie, leaving him in a fitted T-shirt and dark jeans, his belt buckle undone.

"Getting there," I said. "Want me to help?"

"I'm supposed to be getting your dick out."

"We can do both."

"Both?"

"Yeah." I unbuttoned my own jeans and beckoned him closer. "I wanna see you so bad."

The words were out of my mouth before I could stop them. Heat flashed up the back of my neck, and I dropped my gaze to Dom's crotch to avoid his reaction. Perhaps he'd think I was pretending, or playing him, but it was so fucking true.

He closed the distance between us. His hands hovered over my hips, but he didn't touch me. "I want to see you too, Lucky."

"Yeah?"

"Yeah."

In answer, I loosened his jeans enough to shove them down a little. Then I grasped the hem of his T-shirt and lifted it up, revealing inch after inch of the most gorgeous body I'd ever seen. The strip of flesh I'd seen last time hadn't done Dom's abs justice. Ripped and oh-so-lightly furred, his treasure trail was fucking delicious, even if I was tracking it in the wrong direction.

His chest was glorious too. Not too big, but cut. Once I'd ditched his T-shirt, I couldn't resist running my hands over him, absorbing his shiver. "You're so fit. Why are you here with me when you could have anyone?"

"Maybe I don't want anyone."

Valid, but I doubted it. The more I touched Dom, the more obvious it became that he liked it—*needed* it—even if it wasn't unique to *my* hands gliding over his warm skin. "Try again," I whispered.

"Okay. Maybe I'm an arsehole."

That, I could halfway believe, because even if it wasn't entirely true, I was willing to bet he had a decent facade. His glare was killer.

"What about you?"

The question startled me enough to still my hands on his chest. "What about me?"

"Why are *you* here?"

"Because you asked me to be."

"Cute, but that wasn't the real question."

"I know."

Dom let it go, perhaps realising the answer was obvious—I needed the money, and the fact that I'd managed to score a hook up as fine as him was pure fluke.

The notion that I could've easily been here with someone I *really* didn't want to touch me was almost enough to wilt the boner I'd been sporting since I'd walked into the room, but then Dom's hands finally closed around my hips and desire surged through me.

He slid his palms over my skin, gliding beneath my jeans and into my underwear. My pelvis jutted forward, and he squeezed my backside just enough to draw a gasp from me.

I wanted him to squeeze me harder; to stake a claim over my body, and the craving caught me off guard. I'd been fucked by men who'd mistakenly thought they really had owned me, and that their possessive dominance in the heat of the moment actually meant something, but this wasn't like that. I wanted Dom to take what he wanted from me because the sense that he *needed* to was making me dizzy, and I couldn't work out why it mattered so much.

Couldn't work out why *he* mattered so much.

Or why I was angsting over it when now, after I'd coaxed him into getting started, all he clearly wanted to do was get on with it.

Dom shoved my jeans down, sending my underwear with them until they were halfway down my thighs. My dick sprang free, and Dom gripped it before I registered the fresh air. He pumped slowly—torturously—and swiped his thumb over the tip. I gazed down as a bead of sticky moisture seeped out, there for barely a second before Dom gathered it with his thumb and brought it to my lips.

I stuck my tongue out and licked him clean, and then I sucked his thumb into my mouth and worked it like it was his thick cock.

Dom groaned. "Christ, you're fucking magic."

I hummed in response, but was cut off by Dom's other hand finding my dick again. He jacked me until my legs trembled, and then he pushed me down on the bed, ripping his thumb from my mouth, and yanked my jeans and boxers down my legs and over my feet.

Naked, I scooted back on the bed and splayed myself for him, my legs wide, my chest heaving, staring at him over my throbbing dick. He'd said he wanted to suck me off, but the gleam in his eye said he wanted far more than that. Dom wanted to fuck me, and every fibre of my being screamed at me to let him. "You're not naked."

In answer, Dom crawled onto the bed and positioned himself between my splayed legs. "Not yet."

His mouth on my cock cut off any retort I may have made.

"Fuck!" I threw my head back, arching from the bed, my hands scrabbling for purchase on the pristine white sheets. "Jesus, Dom."

He ignored me, and sucked harder, opening wider than he had last time, like he'd spent the last week thinking about it and building up the confidence to let me slide down his throat while I moaned and writhed beneath him.

I can't take this. Over and over, his head bobbed up and down, his tongue riding my shaft as I chased the sensation, the friction, the white-hot pleasure of oblivion, even though the thought of blowing my load so fast was fucking sickening. My hands found their way to his hair, and I tangled my fingers in his dark, silky locks, my whole torso rearing up from the bed as I bent my legs and dug my heels into the mattress. "Fuck, Dom. Don't let me come yet."

His gaze snapped up to me. We locked eyes and orgasm rushed me, but a split second before release, he heard my plea, and eased off.

The blood in my ears faded to a dull roar. Panting, I fell slack and sagged on the bed. "Shit, I should be paying you."

Dom said nothing, and it took me a moment to notice he'd stood and was shedding the rest of his clothes.

Jesus Christ. His lower body was as breathtaking as the rest of him. I already knew his dick was perfection, but his thighs called to me. I wanted to dig my fingers into them while I rimmed him, working him up into the kind of frenzy that was only attractive in a man who held themselves like he did in every other moment.

I took myself in hand, like jacking my dick could fucking ground me; 'cause that's the kind of idiot Dom was apparently turning me into. "What now?"

He shrugged. "You choose."

I patted the bed next to me. "Come here so I can touch you while I decide."

He hesitated, as though lying on a bed with me was a hard limit.

I sat up and grabbed his hand. "Please?"

"This isn't how I expected it to be."

"Me either." I gently tugged him down so he was forced to use his other arm to brace himself on the bed. "But roll with it, yeah? What's the worst that can happen?"

Dark eyes flashed at me. "You have no idea."

"So? Either enlighten me, or lie down. I'm cool with both."

Sweating, my heart pounding, I was anything but cool, but Dom didn't seem to notice as he gave in and stretched out beside me like the mattress was made of nails. I wondered if he'd ever been to bed with someone before—like *really* been to bed, instead of making each other come, and then going their separate ways. If he'd ever felt the closeness of someone spooning against his strong back, whispering in his ear, and nuzzling his neck as he fell asleep.

I rolled onto my side and faced him, throwing a leg over him before he could get too far away. His dick was a fucking steel rod. Hard. Thick. Distracting. The emo in me scattered, blown apart by the sight of him so turned on, so ready for something he couldn't seem to articulate. "Do I get to blow you now?"

"If you want."

I reached out and grazed a finger down Dom's chest. "I do want. I've been thinking about sucking your cock all week."

Dom gave another delicious shiver. "Why?"

"Why do you think?"

"I don't think anything."

"Are you trying to decide if I've been thinking about you all week because I like your cock or because I want your money?"

"Maybe."

A humourless chuckle bubbled out of me. I didn't have an exact answer to my question either, and I wasn't entirely sure which one he'd prefer. Which one would keep him on the bed, his expression halfway to something that might've been open, instead of the closed-off look he seemed so determined to hold on to. "Does it matter?"

Dom caught my wrist and pushed my arm lower. "Not right now."

I gladly took the hint and closed my hand around his dick. It pulsed against my palm, hot and heavy, and I pictured myself bending over for him, pushing back on him as he screwed me from behind—no, from the front—I wanted to see his face.

Just like now. My mouth watered for the taste of him, but I couldn't bring myself to look away just yet.

I jacked him with one hand while the other played with his taut nipples. He squirmed as I pinched it a little too hard. "Fuck."

"You like that."

It wasn't a question, but he let his eyes fall closed and nodded anyway. "Do it again."

"Say please."

"Please."

His voice was low and gravelly, but the desperation lacing the single syllable went straight to my dick. I twisted his nipple again, gasping as he jerked and moaned, and my hips drove forward of their own volition, digging my cock into his ripped abdomen.

I humped his stomach while I worked him with my hand. I didn't mean to, but I couldn't fucking stop. And he didn't seem to even notice, which relieved and irritated me in equal measure.

But I didn't think on it too long. Couldn't, because his ragged groans sucked me into a vortex I didn't want to escape. I'd had hot encounters before, with men and women, but something—everything—about this was different. The sounds he made, the wet puffs of air he breathed against my cheek. Even the way his toes flexed set me on fire.

I pushed him onto his back and nudged his legs open, spitting on his dick with a long, slow dribble of saliva. In my head, I straddled him and impaled myself on his cock, but my soul craved harder the ecstasy I'd seen in him last time. The blissful agony clenching his whole body as I'd fingered him with his dick in my mouth. "Tell me to stop."

His eyes flew open, though the lids were hooded. "Why?"

"Because I need to know what you want."

"You know what I want."

And I did. I crawled between his legs and took him in my mouth, kissing up and down his length, taking my time, enjoying the frustrated gasps my feather-light lips earned me. His balls were hot and heavy in my mouth as I tongued and suckled them. He gasped again, spreading his legs wider, and I saw my moment.

I punctuated my finger pressing inside him by swallowing his cock down my throat. The double-edged sensation drew another strangled cry from him, and fluid wept from his dick, letting me know that we wouldn't be playing this game long.

Which was just as well. I ground myself against the mattress as I sucked him, but the friction wasn't anywhere near enough. I wanted his tongue inside me as I made him come, but I sensed he wasn't ready for a sixty-nine yet, and settled for latching onto his growing pleasure, absorbing his rising peak as though it was my own.

He was so wound up. Skin flushed, muscles jumping. His thighs quivered like he was connected to the mains, but somehow it still caught me off guard when he choked out a warning. "*Lucky.*"

Or maybe it was the way he said my name...the way he growled it through clenched teeth as he shot hot come down my throat. Either way, him falling apart tipped me over the edge. I swallowed every drop of him, and then reclaimed my finger and scrambled to my knees, my hand blurring over my dick as I chased a release I was pretty fucking sure I'd die without.

Heat pooled in my groin, spread through my belly, and then out into every nerve. My vision whited-out, and I came hard, spilling all over Dom's chest without stopping to ask if he was down with that shit.

"Fuck, I'm sorry." I lurched forward, sticky hand flailing to somehow wipe him clean, but he caught me before I fell on him.

"Easy. It's fine."

Panic over, I collapsed in a heap beside him, my chest burning as my lungs fought to catch up. Beside me, he panted too, but when I looked at him, he was far more dignified about it than me, even with bloodshot eyes, flushed skin, and come splattered on his chest. "Wow."

Dom graced me with an almost smile. "What?"

"I thought last time was a fluke, but you make me come so hard."

"I didn't make you come. It was your hand."

"Uh-huh. And watching you bust had nothing to do with it." I closed my eyes and let my body sink into the bed. It was way bigger than Jamila's, softer too. I pondered if Dom had booked the room for the night—and if I had time to take a nap.

The bed shifted and I opened my eyes to see Dom wiping down and reaching for his clothes, dashing my hopes of a second round. "Going somewhere?"

He flicked me a flat glance, the faint good humour from a second ago all but gone. "Home. It's late."

It was barely ten o'clock. Our entire encounter had taken less than an hour. "Have you got an early start?"

"What?"

"For work...or something. What do you do, anyway?"

"What do you care?"

I sat up on my elbows, sensing the shift in Dom's mood with every item of clothing he pulled on. "I guess I don't."

He said nothing, just yanked his T-shirt on and turned away to stamp into his pristine Nikes.

I suddenly felt grubbier than ever, despite raiding Jamila's Lush stash. Taking my cue from Dom's stony silence, I rolled off the bed, and retrieved my clothes from the floor. I threw them on and slunk across the room to my boots.

Dom still wasn't looking at me. His cap was back on his head, jammed down low, like he could block me out. Ghost me. *Fuck that.* He might've paid me to blow him and stick my finger inside him, but that didn't give him the right to treat me like crap. He didn't want a conversation? Fine. I'd say goodbye without words.

I stepped into my boots and bent to tie them. In my peripheral vision, I saw him move, and when I looked up, he was by the door, his hand gripping the handle, knuckles white. I traced the tendon up his arms to his stiff shoulders and set jaw, and my irritation with him faded a touch. Dom was the nothing man—the man who didn't think anything and had nothing to say—but I didn't believe him. Whatever was going on behind his sealed-off gaze was making him feel like shit, and he'd paid me not to make him feel worse.

My bag was by his feet. I picked it up and slung it over my shoulder, and then I stepped to him and stretched up to kiss his cheek. My lips brushed skin that smelled of expensive cologne and clean sweat. I expected him to ignore me, or back away, but when he turned his head, his eyes were hungry again—*alive*, like I perhaps hadn't seen them before.

Something inside me shifted. It was infinitesimal, but drove me forward, backing him against the closed door. I kissed him again, on the lips this time, and he responded with the hunger I'd seen in his dark gaze, but he wasn't rough. Didn't crush us together or plunder my mouth with his tongue. His kiss was soft and sweet, his hands on my shoulders gentle and light, and even though I was the one who'd started it I was so fucking bewildered.

This wasn't how this was supposed to go down. Wanting to see Dom again had fucked with my head all week, but I'd still expected to blow him and leave. That I'd objected to him silently suggesting I do just that didn't make any sense.

And nor did the way his kiss was making me feel. I was prepared for the heat that sluiced through me when we were fooling around, but this? The slow-spinning top of warmth spreading through my chest? The tingling and pulsating of every nerve?

Nah.

But I didn't stop kissing him back. My bag slipped to the floor, and my body moulded itself to him, his wider torso the perfect resting place for my scrawny frame. His muscles fit around my sticky-out bones and I could've leaned against him, lost in his soft lips, forever.

The buzz of a phone brought me back to reality—*my* phone. I ignored it, but the persistent vibration shattered the magic.

Dom broke away. "You'd better get that."

I couldn't think of a single reason why, but I reached for my phone anyway.

Jamila's face flashed up, reminding me that I'd never let her know I was safe. Guilt surged through me, replacing the crazed desire that had led me to pretty much rugby tackle Dom to the door.

I cancelled the call and tapped out a quick message.

Lucky: *srry. all fine. leaving soon*

Jamila: *You'd fucking better be okay.*

Jamila: *I saved you some chicken and rice.*

The perfect contradiction in her emotions made me smile, despite the age-old guilt at having a friend who was so fucking good to me.

"Girlfriend?"

"Huh?" I glanced up at Dom to find his hand on the door handle again. "Oh, no...she's my, uh, flatmate. She saved me some dinner."

"That's nice. It's late, though. Didn't you eat before you came out?"

What do you care? But the spiky retort died on my lips as I realised Dom was opening the door to show me out. That he wasn't leaving with me. "Are you staying here tonight?"

"No."

"Right." It came together in my head with painful clarity. "You just don't want to walk out with me?"

"Walk out where? We're not going to the same place."

With his designer clothes and immaculate shoes next to my deadbeat scrubs, he'd never said a truer word. The high from his kiss evaporated and I forced a nonchalant shrug as I slipped into a nondescript corridor that led to nowhere. "Fair enough. Take care, *Dom*. See you around."

SIX

Dom

I wish he hadn't kissed me. Until then, I'd been able to persuade myself the current between us had been entirely in my imagination—that I'd obsessed over him because he'd made me fly so high after a four-month drought, but the moment his lips had grazed mine, a blast had gone off somewhere inside me, sizzling my synapses, and robbing me of coherent thought.

I'd kissed him back like a starving man.

Like a man who'd never had another man's lips on his.

Three weeks on, and I still wasn't over it. My lips still burned and tasted of him, and despite stalking away from me with a scowl marring his delicate face, his smile still haunted my dreams.

At least, the dreams where I saw his face instead of his cock, 'cause *those* kind of dreams were haunting me too, night *and* day when my thoughts got away from me.

Fuck's sake. I stopped at a red light and glared down at my tightening jeans as flashbacks of our last encounter took up residence in my apparently sex-crazed brain. I'd managed to resist contacting Lucky again, or even looking at Grindr, but every part of me he'd touched *throbbed*, and I craved him so badly I totally zoned out, imagining what we would do next time round.

A car horn blared behind me. I jumped and threw my car into drive, considering flipping a bird to the angry twat in the gaudy white Range Rover before I remembered that I was the one driving a wanky Lexus.

And it didn't take long for my thoughts to return to Lucky. He'd seemed different when we'd met at the hotel—less spiky—though his poise when it came to getting off was as enticing as ever. I'd always been kind of frigid. For years, I'd blamed it on people expecting me to like girls, but even with blokes I was fucking lost. The only guy I'd nearly had a relationship with—if you counted screwing him more than once—reckoned it was because I was too messed up by repressing my sexuality to let myself really feel anything, but I'd called him a hippy prick for that shit and sacked him off. The dude had been a yoga teacher, for fuck's sake. What did he know about being the only queer on a top-flight football team? And I'd never kissed him.

Disquiet coursed through my veins as my thoughts did their best to return to Lucky, to his silky hair, and mile-long legs. His creamy skin and slender bones. But even recalling his glorious naked form couldn't ease the shame lacing my blood. My daddy would turn in his grave if he knew, and the scandal would kill my ma if it reached her in the tiny Portuguese village she'd returned to a few years ago. Cruel? Backwards? Yeah. But it was what it was, and no amount of driving my flash car around London while sporting a Lucky-fuelled boner would change anything.

I shifted in my seat, cursing myself for letting the clawing obsession get a foothold in my soul again. For months at a time, I was able to forget it, convince myself I didn't have a sexuality at all, but then the voice in my head would grow louder, more insistent, and the desperation to feel whole, if only for a lust-driven moment, would eat away at me until I found myself trawling Grindr or Scruff for a profile I could pay to keep my sordid secrets.

No one I'd found had affected me the way Lucky had. Every other bloke had scratched the itch and disappeared from my consciousness, but Lucky? Damn. He'd put his lips on mine and ripped a whole new crater in my affection-starved soul. *You sad fuck. Twenty-six years old and never been kissed.* And now I knew what I'd been missing, I wanted more.

My phone rang in my gym bag. For a heart-stopping moment, I wondered if Lucky had somehow heard my thoughts, but then I remembered he didn't have my number, and the only people who did were my employers and Isha.

I pressed the button on the steering wheel to take the call. "Yeah?"

Isha laughed. "I swear I could phone you up with a billion-quid deal and you'd still sound like your dog just died."

"I don't have a dog."

"Maybe you need one."

"Why?"

"To stop you dying alone."

"You think my make-believe dog is going to outlive me?"

"Yeah, man. Your billy-no-mates-itis is definitely terminal."

I let out a long-suffering sigh. "Is that why you called? To heckle me on my bachelor status?"

"Kind of." Isha's tone sobered. "Where are you?"

"Tottenham. My car needs a service. Why?"

"I wanted to give you a heads up on the papers before you got to the ground for training this morning."

My heart stopped. Vision blacked out. "What?"

"You made the gossip pages of the *Daily Mail.*"

With shaking hands, I turned off the busy Tottenham street and pulled into a dead-end loading bay. "Why?"

"Because they seem to think you're shagging some Victoria's Secret model."

Relief and horror warred in my churning stomach. I slapped a hand over my mouth like I could push the dry heave back down.

Counted to ten and sucked in a silent, shuddery gasp. "Why the fuck would they think that?"

"Does it matter? Maybe the club threw them a bone to cover someone else's mess. Point is, this girl is pretty hot stuff, so there's gonna be reporters hounding you for a couple of days before they get a new sniff."

"Brilliant."

"Aw, c'mon, Dom. It's not that bad. She's a nice girl by all accounts, and you're a good guy. It won't do either of you any harm."

Easy for him to say. Isha lived in the shadows of other people's chaos, taking care of everyone else, folding dirty laundry that would never stick to him and ruin him by wrecking a career in the only thing he'd ever been good at. Pressing my fists into my eyes, I growled a goodbye, and hung up on him. I wanted to go home. To hide away in my apartment and stick my head in the top-of-the-range gas oven.

The faint scar on my wrist, a legacy of a time long ago when thoughts like that had overwhelmed me, tingled. Burned. Singed me from the inside out. I hadn't even come close to killing myself back then—too young and naive to do the right kind of damage—but things were different now, even if underneath it all I was the same terrified teenage boy.

I leaned into the passenger footwell and retrieved my phone from my bag. My thumb flew over the screen as I erased my Grindr account without checking for new messages and deleted the app from the phone. My habitual monthly clear out usually granted me a brief solace, like I'd closed a rusty trapdoor on my sexuality, albeit until the next time, but as I backed out of the loading bay and rejoined the Tottenham traffic, the relief in my chest was hollow.

No Grindr meant no Lucky, and there was nothing comforting about that.

Lucky

"No offence, mate. But you don't look like mechanics are your thing."

"Why's that?"

The old boy had the good grace to look awkward and offer nothing in return. I sensed a window and pushed on with my pitch. "Listen, I might not be a gym rat covered in bad tats, but I know car engines, okay? I grew up playing in my grandpa's garage, and I prefer the black on my nails to come from dirty oil."

The man's gaze dropped to my hands, clearly checking for a fucking manicure, and I wondered for the thousandth time why I was putting myself through this. Why I was traipsing around east London's auto shops, begging for an apprenticeship I could complete with my eyes closed, all the while making excuses for how I carried myself in my own goddamn skin.

Because you need money, remember? And food, and a place to sleep.

And to stop blowing Dom for cash, but I let that thought fade to nothing. I'd spent a couple of days hiding out in Jamila's room, angsting over my enigmatic benefactor, and I was done with it now. Done with him. Had to be. Because for three weeks he'd ignored my messages and ghosted himself from Grindr, so regardless of the fact that I couldn't get him out of my head, hooking up with him wasn't a viable plan.

Not that I wanted it to be.

Or did I?

Dom's overpayment had set me on a hopeful path, fed me, and left me enough to slip some into Jamila's mum's purse when she wasn't looking, but beyond that, I had become dangerously obsessed with him, scrutinising his Grindr movements—or lack of them—for hours when I should've been pounding the pavements, looking for work.

It wasn't healthy.

Then again, healthy wasn't a word I tended to live by. The fresh needle mark in my arm was evidence of that, as was the lingering high that had carried me this far, despite being awake for two days straight.

Reflexively, I tugged on my sleeves, checking my arms were still covered. If I scored some work I'd have to cover it with a plaster, or scratch it open to disguise its telltale shape, and shame rippled through me as I pictured myself huddled up behind the kebab shop, slamming just enough bubble to get through the night. I wasn't proud of it, but I couldn't bring myself to regret it either.

Such a fucking white-trash cliché—

"So," the garage owner said. "If you can do that for me by the end of the day, I might consider taking you on. What do you say?"

"Hmm?"

The old boy stared at me, and then shook his head slightly and pointed beyond me to a shiny gangster SUV. "I said if you finish off that service for me, and valet the interior, then I'll take you a little more seriously."

Jesus. Trust me to zone out on the most constructive conversation I'd had in months.

I nodded my head like the Churchill dog on meth. "I can do that. When do you close for the day?"

"Five o'clock," the man said. "But I'll give you until half past because the owner won't be here until six. Don't fuck up."

It was the story of my life, but I liked a challenge when I had the tools to face one, and the swish garage was a petrol-head's dream.

I scrounged some overalls and got to work, losing myself in the rhythm of giving an engine a bit of TLC. Under the bonnet, I felt as at home as I did with a fat dick in my mouth, and the smell of fuel and oil was enough to give me a semi.

It had been a long time since I'd serviced a car, though, and I'd never done a Lexus.

A friendly mechanic took pity on me and brought me a manual. With the instructions in front of me, and any tool I needed within arm's reach, I began to fly, and distantly pondered why I bothered to get buzzed on drone when I could be doing this shit.

When the service was done, I moved onto valeting the interior. Cleaning out an already immaculate car seemed kinda pointless, but I did it anyway, and it wasn't long before the mindless activity gave my restless thoughts licence to drift.

And as had become my new normal, they immediately settled on Dom. For a moment, I almost convinced myself I could smell him and his expensive scent. It was so intense I felt sick, but that could've been the drone comedown—the teeth-itching hangover I was still waiting to hit me full force. Or maybe it was the upholstery shampoo. Why did they make that shit reek like burning rubber?

I got the Lexus done with a minute to spare on my extended deadline. The garage owner—Jim, apparently—came over to inspect my work, bushy eyebrows raised, stretching his face into an expression of surprise so transparent I nearly laughed the fuck out loud.

He walked around the car, peering at my work, and running through the service check sheet, even sniffing the seats to check I'd shampooed them. "This ain't half bad. These nuts need tightening another couple of notches, but that's a fault with the car, not you."

Damnit. I still felt like kicking myself, especially as I'd sensed sceptical eyes on me as I'd hefted the heavy alloy wheels around. "I can tighten them now?"

Jim nodded. "Go on then."

I tightened the back wheel while Jim disappeared into the depths of the back office and I wondered if that was my cue to get lost. I knew I'd done a fair job considering I'd never touched a Lexus in my life, but was it good enough for a garage like this?

Who the fuck knew.

I was folding my branded overalls when Jim came back with an A4 envelope.

"This is our apprentice pack," he said. "There's usually a bunch of interviews and red tape, but I run this place the old-fashioned way. Take this home with you and have a read through the materials. The pay is shit, but I'll raise it to a living wage if you stick it out a couple of months."

"Wow. You serious?"

"As a bank raid. Question is, are you?"

"I—"

Jim silenced me with a wave of his hand. "Don't answer me now. Take a couple of days, and if you're up for it, come back on Monday morning and we'll draw up a proper contract. You got an NI number?"

It was the one thing I did have. I nodded. "Yeah."

"Good lad. Now piss off so I can get this beast back to its owner and go home for my tea."

I left him to it and slipped out of the garage. My brain was slowing down as the lingering drone high from the night before wore off, but the rush of scoring work carried me all the way to a bench outside an Ethiopian restaurant before I had to sit down.

Oil-smeared hands trembling, I pulled out my phone to text Jamila and ask if I could use her address as my own. She was pretty good at intercepting the postman, and her mum didn't pay much attention to random mail anyway.

But texting proved beyond me as my comedown kicked in with a vengeance. I dropped my phone into my lap and put my head in my hands, willing away the shuddering depression that was fast leaking into my limbs. In a couple of hours, I'd be curled up in a ball, hopefully in Jamila's bed, while I styled it out like the muppet I was, but the thought of walking back to Dalston made me want to puke.

Maybe I would puke. The thought of that made me want to die too, but then I remembered Jim's garage and the flash of hope kept me upright.

I sat up and took a heaving gulp of fresh air. Around the bench, the busy Tottenham streets went on without me, faceless people rushing by, getting on with lives that had no place for a quivering queer washed up on a skanky bench. I watched them come and go through scratchy eyes as my muscles began to ache with a combination of an afternoon of hard graft and chemical fatigue, and it took me a while to notice someone had sat down beside me.

The hand on my arm scared the crap out of me, but the oddly familiar heat of it kept me from jumping out of my skin.

I turned my head, expecting a tactile weirdo or a not-so-friendly copper wanting to search my pockets or some shit. "What the fuck?"

Dom stared back at me.

SEVEN

Dom

Lucky squinted at me, holding his hand up to block the light from a nearby streetlamp, his eyes bloodshot and drooping. "Dom?"

"It's me," I replied cautiously, resisting the urge to take a furtive glance around. "Are you okay?"

More staring. Lucky blinked like he couldn't quite believe I was real, and his shielding hand drifted closer to me, as though he needed to touch me to be sure.

Lacking what little common sense I'd been born with, I wanted to let him do it—to let his grubby fingers graze my face before I took his hand in mine. But I couldn't do it. "*Lucky?* Are you okay?"

Life finally filtered into his dazed features and he seemed to shake himself slightly. "Shit. Fuck. Yeah, sorry...I was half-asleep."

"Out here?" I chanced a pointed glance at the drizzle misting down from the dark sky. "Mate, it's freezing."

"I know."

Something was off. I didn't know much about Lucky except how his dick felt in my mouth, but I knew something was wrong more than I knew the rain dampening my face was wet. *Fuck it.* I took his hand and hid our entwined fingers under my jacket. "Listen, I was on my way home, but I was thinking of grabbing a drink. Wanna come?"

"A drink?"

"Yes."

"With you?"

"Yes."

"Just you?"

"*Yes.* Just me. There's a pub across the road we could go to."

Lucky's gaze flickered beyond me, and then back to himself, giving his ripped jeans and tatty boots a once over before his gaze settled on me. "What kind of pub? Ain't some fancy wine bar, is it?"

"Nah. It's a proper boozer."

Lucky nodded slowly. "Okay."

He stood and picked up the bag he'd brought with him to the Shoreditch hotel. The sight of it gifted me a jolt of desire, but as hot as Lucky was in any light, fucking around with him was the last thing on my mind.

I steered him into the boozer and sat him in a quiet corner while I went to the bar, which was thankfully staffed by the kind of students who were unlikely to recognise me. Despite the gossip-column inches I'd gained today, I wasn't the kind of player who graced people's bedroom walls, or popular merchandise, and I was more grateful right now to be a faceless defender than I'd ever been.

Clutching two bottles of beer and a Pepsi, I returned to Lucky. He had his head on the table, his face drawn and pale.

I slid him the Pepsi. "Drink that. I can get you some food if you're hungry?"

Lucky blanched. "No, thanks. This is good."

He sipped the Pepsi while I watched him, taking in his sunken cheeks and tired eyes. I wanted to ask him again what was wrong, but pressing him didn't feel right.

I settled for a weird, weighted silence while the sugar in the Pepsi brought a faint flush of colour back into his cheeks, but he didn't seem to notice, and instead fixated on his own hands, which I belatedly noticed were trembling.

Even if I'd been out and proud, the friendly Tottenham boozer wasn't the kind of place where I could take his hands and squeeze them until he felt safe enough to confide in me. I nudged his knee under the table and tried for a smile.

Lucky just stared.

"Are you sure you don't want something to eat?" I asked.

He shook his head. "I'm good."

"You don't look it."

"I'm tired."

"Why? Long day?"

"Yeah. I scored some work, and I didn't get much sleep last night."

"What kind of work do you do...um, I mean besides...?"

For fuck's sake.

Lucky narrowed his eyes. "Why should I tell you that when you looked at me like I was some kind of freak when I asked you the same question?"

The sudden fire in him startled me. "I didn't look at you like that."

"Yes, you did. Then you let me kiss you, before you ghosted off Grindr and never spoke to me again."

No one was close enough to hear us, but anxiety clawed at me anyway, and the urge to run was so strong my palms began to sweat. *Keep your voice down.* But I didn't say it. Couldn't, when Lucky was glaring at me with a hurt in his eyes I didn't understand. "I'm sorry."

It was barely a whisper and Lucky's glower remained. "Don't be sorry. You don't owe me nothing; just don't get up in my face about my life when you don't give a shit, okay? It ain't fucking necessary."

His words stung, but I understood. We'd hooked up twice—we were hardly BFFs.

But still. I needed him to be okay.

I took a deep breath and tried again. "I'm sorry I was a dick to you last time we saw each other. I'm—uh—not good at being nice, especially in situations like that. My ma thinks I'm emotionally stunted."

"Does she know you're gay?"

"Shut the fuck up."

Lucky raised an eyebrow. "Gotcha. Closeted. Let me guess, wife and kids at home while you score paid hook ups online?"

Agitation twisted in my gut again, and this time, I couldn't contain the compulsion to glance around. There was still no one paying us any attention, but I leaned forward anyway, and nudged my cap a notch lower. "You've nailed it. I'm a closet fucking fag, okay? But I ain't got no wife and kids, so don't paint me with that shit. I'm not out 'cause I *can't* be, but that doesn't make me a scumbag."

The irony that I was the kind of scumbag that picked up men on Grindr then dumped them like trash wasn't lost on me, but the tired anger in Lucky faded a touch as he finished his Pepsi and reached for the beer. "You should've told me."

"Why?"

"Because then I'd have known."

It was apparently the only answer he was prepared to give, and I'd run out of nerve to continue this conversation. My leg bounced up and down, and I needed to get the fuck out of here before I lost my mind altogether. Only the overwhelming need to make sure Lucky was okay kept me in my seat. "Listen," I said. "I'm sorry I ditched Grindr, but I can't have that shit going on all the time. I've got no one at home, but my life would fucking implode if I got outed or if someone found out I was using Grindr to pay—"

"Pay what? Whores?"

"No...*men*, though it wouldn't be much worse if you were a hooker. It's still not right."

Lucky pushed his half-full beer bottle away. "It didn't feel wrong to me. I chose to be there with you both times, I took your money with no shame. That hasn't changed."

"It's not about you, mate. You could be anyone and I'd still be a fucking mess."

"You're not a mess, Dom. Look at me."

"I am." I couldn't look away.

"Then you should know what a real disaster is."

There was no humour in the cynical smile twisting his cracked lips. My heart ached for him, for both of us, and a rush of madness had me reaching across the table for his battered phone. "What's your passcode?"

"My name."

I spelled out "lucky" on his keypad and typed my number in. Then, before I could change my mind, I thrust the phone back at him. "That's my number. Don't save it under my name, okay? But call me anytime you need something. If I don't answer, I'll get back to you as soon as I can."

"Why are you giving me your number?"

I shook my head and stood, turning away from him even as every instinct screamed at me to rip his phone back and erase every digit I'd just punched in. "I have no idea, but don't make me regret it."

Lucky

I rolled over in the bed, selfishly spreading myself across the space I had no right to claim as my own, but with Jamila and her mum gone for a week, I had their flat to myself.

Not that I was enjoying it much. Drone comedowns were brutal at the best of times, but slamming that shit made it worse. Like the higher you flew, the harder you fell.

I opened my eyes and the room span. Shadows danced where there should've been light, and my heart pounded a sickening beat. *Fuck's sake. Not again.*

Screwing my eyes shut, I swallowed convulsively, but there was no fighting it. The churning nausea gained momentum, roaring up my throat, and I heaved myself out of bed just in time to upchuck for the millionth time that day.

When I was done, I cut my losses and stayed on the frigid bathroom floor. My muscles hurt too much to handle another dash down the hallway.

For a while, I dozed, absorbing the cold from the tiles into my aching bones, and let my imagination take me somewhere else—back to Jamila's bed, or even the bed I'd oh-so-briefly shared with Dom... the pristine king-size that had been as spotlessly white as his fresh Nikes. I'd wanted to sleep with him—in more ways than one. *Bet he's not a cuddler, though.* But even as I thought it, an instinct I couldn't quite decipher rebuked me, as though my soul knew something about Dom my brain didn't.

Or maybe it was the drone playing tricks on me. I'd slammed it to keep me awake when Jamila's mum had been home for the night and the cold outside was too much to bear with a straight head, but I'd regretted it the moment it had hit my veins. The euphoria from my very first time was a distant memory. These days it just kept me conscious, with paranoia and flashing spots in my vision thrown in for good measure.

Fuck my life.

I must've passed out on the bathroom floor, because it was getting dark when I opened my eyes again, and colder than ever. Shivering, I sat up and rubbed my arms, trying to force some heat back into my circulation. My stomach growled, reminding me I hadn't eaten since...fuck. I didn't even know.

In Jamila's kitchen, I helped myself to a bowl of Crunchy Nut, thankful her mum kept the cupboards stocked with long-life milk. I made tea too—proper tea, rose coloured, and loaded with sugar—and then I retreated to Jamila's bed to read through the envelope Jim had given me. Somehow, it had survived the chaos of an epic comedown unscathed.

Squinting, I read through the contract and handbook, but beyond the weekly wage figures and the actual work and training expected of me, I didn't take it in—I didn't care about health and safety, or codes of conduct, I just wanted to work.

I dropped the paperwork on the bed and closed my eyes. The room had stopped spinning, but I still felt like I could puke again if I moved around too much. So I stayed where I was, meditating like a junkie hippie, and prayed I'd be on point by the time Monday morning rolled around.

It was Sunday evening by the time I allowed thoughts of Dom back in. All weekend, I'd fought the obsession, and the scraping sensation in my brain had proved an effective distraction, but the fog was clearing now, leaving Dom's blazing eyes in its wake—his heated stare as he'd punched his number into my phone. His gentle hands as he'd wrapped his fingers around mine under his coat.

I made myself presentable for the following morning, washed my clothes, and tucked my hair into a tight knot. Then I curled up on the couch with more cereal and my phone. Grindr was dead to me if Dom wasn't on it, but his username gave me something to save his digits under.

Then I stared at my message screen for an hour, tapping and erasing messages like some kind of maniac. 'Cause, *fuck*. What the hell was I supposed to say? Thanks for buying me a drink when all I wanted was to suck your dick one last time, but I was too fucked up to say so?

Right. I still knew jack about Dom, but unless he majored in chemsex behind closed doors, I was willing to bet he didn't dig getting high. And the chemsex theory was flawed too. I'd spent enough time with him to guess that losing control when he was naked enough to be vulnerable wasn't his bag. He wasn't like me.

He was vulnerable, though. I'd seen it in him, and it hurt my savage little heart. I'd never hidden who I was, and it had cost me relationships with people who were supposed to love me whatever, but I couldn't imagine living my life as someone else. What did that *do* to a man?

I wasn't going to find out if I didn't contact Dom, but none of my messages felt right, and as night closed in on me, I let my mind wander too far as I considered why. I huddled up on the couch and pictured us together—in Simone's flat, the hotel room, and then in the dodgy Tottenham boozer, when I'd slumped on the table like a hobo and shown him a glimpse of who I really was.

But what had he shown me? All I knew about him was what made him come, and that he was so fucking *not out* that the thought of someone overhearing our conversation had terrified him.

I didn't want him to be frightened, not for me. If I knew anything, it was that I wasn't worth the damn trouble.

EIGHT

Lucky

I held out until the third day of my apprenticeship at the posh garage. By then, Jamila and her mum had reclaimed their flat and I was hiding out in a public library, killing time before I tried to find somewhere safe to bed down for the night.

Lucky: *hey*

Perignon55: *who dis?*

Lucky: *who do u think*

Perignon55: *don't play with me*

Lucky: *k.*

Perignon55: *Lucky?*

Lucky: *yeah*

Perignon55: *u ok?*

Lucky: *yeah*

Perignon55: *good*

Perignon55: *what u doing?*

Lucky: *not much. u?*

Perignon55: *finishing work then gym*

Lucky: *i've never been in a gym*

Perignon55: *u ain't missing much*

Lucky: *i'm missing u getting sweaty*

Dom didn't reply for a while, and I fidgeted in my seat while I pretended to read a crime novel. I'd gone round in circles wrestling over whether to contact him, but ultimately, the fire in my gut for him had won out. Did he feel the same? Or had he given me his number to check I wasn't dead?

Logic told me it would've been easier for him to take *my* number if he'd just wanted to check up on me, but then I remembered the state I'd been in, and wanted to die that he'd seen so clearly that I had been too fucked up to recite my own phone number.

Perignon55: *u hungry?*

I blinked. Seriously? *That's* what he wanted to ask me?

Lucky: *a bit. y?*

Perignon55: *i'll be done in a bit. u wanna eat?*

Lucky: *eat what?*

Perignon55: *food*

So he really wasn't talking about his cock then. I chewed on my lip and tapped out a reply that quickly led to arranging to meet him in Dalston, close to the flat where we'd first met. And then he was gone, leaving me to stare at the screen and wonder if I'd been dropped into another world.

But I didn't have time to ponder it long. I'd washed up at work, taking advantage of the shitty shower in the staffroom, but I still needed to put myself back together after a day hunched over a Range Rover. Tame my hair and find some clothes he hadn't seen me in before. Jesus. How was this my life?

An hour later, I leaned against the wall of a closed cafe, drumming my fingers on my thigh as I resisted the urge to smoke. I didn't know what direction Dom would be coming from, if he'd be driving or on foot, and keeping watch for him, tracking every face that could be his, was enough to give me a headache.

"Lucky?"

I jerked left. Somehow, he'd managed to sneak up on me, and was lurking in the shadows with his usual designer cap pulled low on his face. "We can go to a hotel if you want?" I blurted.

Dom met my gaze with a flat stare. "This isn't like that."

"I meant so you don't have to hide."

He nodded, and warmth crept into his unreadable expression. "Maybe next time."

My heart jumped. "Next time?"

Dom said nothing. Just glanced both ways up the street and pointed to a hole in the wall place I'd never been in. "My mate reckons that place is quiet."

It looked like walking salmonella, but I shrugged. Anywhere with Dom was a fucking gift.

We slipped into the Turkish place and claimed two seats at the back, half-hidden by a chintzy curtain. Dom relaxed a little as a waiter took a drink order without looking at us, but tension rippled through me as I asked for tap water. I had a fiver in my pocket I'd found on the floor at work, and a tenner I'd taken from my stash under Jamila's bed, but it wasn't nearly enough to buy us both dinner.

Dom kicked me under the table. "Are you freaking out about money?"

"What makes you say that?"

"I'm rich, Lucky—I can't deny it—but it hasn't always been like this. I know what it's like to have nothing."

"Uh-huh."

Dom cocked his head sideways. "You don't believe me?"

"How can I believe what you say when I don't know anything about you?"

Dom shrugged and trailed the tip of his right index finger around the rim of his glass. He seemed uncomfortable, but that was kind of his baseline, and despite craving his weird brand of company so badly, I wasn't in the mood to go easy on him. After all, he was here because he wanted to be, right? Unless he'd figured that two paid hook ups was enough and I was ready to start doing him for free.

I swallowed thickly. Even though I was totally at peace with trading sex for cash on Grindr, there was a part of me that wished it hadn't been with Dom. That our odd nearly friendship wasn't clouded by suspicion and doubt. Shadowed by question marks over each other's motives...because as my mind played devil's advocate, it occurred to me that he might've been doing the exact same thing.

My fingers twitched as I fought the urge to close them around his wrist. I didn't get him, but I didn't understand myself too well right now either. Did that mean something?

Fucked if I know.

I pulled a menu closer for something to do, and the prices turned out to be more affordable than I'd feared. If I got something for a couple of quid, I might be able to buy Dom something decent after all. "Do you know what any of this shit is?"

"Hmm?" Dom blinked. "What?"

I tapped the menu. "The food."

Dom glanced down at his menu, frowning in a way that somehow eased the lines of dismay from his gorgeous face. "I've had Turkish stuff before. There's a place in Islington the team—uh, *we*, sometimes go after work."

I ignored the slip—and how it made me feel—and leaned across the table. "You're right about me flipping my lid over money, but only because I wanted to buy you dinner. What's this one? If it's cheap and nice, I'll have it."

"You don't have to buy me dinner, Lucky."

I pointed at the two-quid dish again. "What is it?"

Rolling his eyes, Dom turned his gaze back to the menu. "It's a flatbread, with chicken and spinach. I reckon you can eat more than that, though. How about we get a bunch of them and split the bill? That okay with you?"

I loved him for not waving his wealth in my face. By his own admission, he was rich, but perhaps he was richer still in the things that mattered.

Or maybe I was delirious with hunger. I couldn't remember the last time I'd eaten something that wasn't cereal, or a stolen banana.

"It's fine by me," I said. "I don't eat much anyway."

"Why not?"

Dom's gaze was genuinely curious, so I shrugged and flexed my lanky arms. "There ain't much of me to feed."

"The size of you doesn't mean anything. I mean, you're slim, but you look pretty strong, and you need fuel for that shit."

"You think I look strong?"

Dom nodded. "Yes. Even if I hadn't seen you—uh—before, I can tell by the way you carry yourself, the way you move. You don't have to be a tank to be hench."

"Hench?" I nearly spat water across the table. "I can hand-on-heart promise you that no one has ever called me that."

"So?"

"So..." I searched for a coherent sentence. "Most people think I'm a girl 'cause I'm skinny and I rock the long hair."

Dom snorted. "I've known plenty of women stronger than me."

"I didn't say *I* thought being weak equated with being female."

"Good, because I like your hair."

"Why?"

But I didn't get an answer because Dom got up to order our food at the service counter, and when he came back, the moment had passed.

He'd also brought olives and bread with him. I picked out three green ones and shoved them into my mouth, offering him the leftover weird purple ones.

"You don't like the black ones?"

I pulled a face. "Nah. They taste like arse."

"That right?"

"Well, not good arse, obviously, but they're still rank."

Dom popped one in his mouth, his dark eyes gleaming with a challenge I couldn't quite decipher. So I stuffed myself with bread until his leg nudged mine under the table.

"I want to ask you if you're feeling better than last time I saw you, but I'm wondering if you might tell me to do one."

I relinquished the bread I was clutching like a starving man and pictured myself as he'd last seen me, slumped over a table, and sweating for all the wrong reasons. Shame washed over me, but it didn't last—didn't stand a chance in the face of Dom's suddenly gentle frown. "I didn't feel well last time we saw each other."

"But you're all right now?"

I nodded. No one looking at my life was ever gonna say I was doing all right, but the desire to spill my guts to Dom was non-existent. "How about you? You told me some stuff that day that I don't think you meant to. How are you doing with that? Or is that why we're here? So you can check I'm not going to out you?"

"Are you going to out me?"

"Who the fuck to? I don't know anyone who knows you."

For a brief moment, a ghost of a smile changed Dom's whole face. "Can I take that as a no?"

"If you like."

"I do like, but it's not why I wanted to meet you."

"You wanna hook up again?"

"That's not why either—I told you that outside."

He had, but I was saved from admitting I'd hoped for something different by the arrival of our food. True to his word, Dom had ordered three variations of the cheap-as-chips flatbread. Chicken and spinach, lamb and spiced onions, and some kind of vegetable shit I didn't recognise.

I pushed that one towards Dom.

He laughed. "Picky eater?"

"No...I just don't eat unidentified orange stuff."

"Fair enough." Dom claimed the vegetables and pushed the chicken and spinach plate my way.

There was far more to the cheap dish than I'd anticipated, but I dug in, and didn't look at Dom again until I'd hoovered up three bulging rolls of stuffed flatbread.

His amusement was clear. "Thought you said you don't eat much?"

I reached across the table to sample the lamb flatbread. "I don't—doesn't mean I can't."

"Why would you—" Dom stopped and shook his head slightly. "Never mind. It's not my business. Eat as much you like, okay? We can always get more."

Sweet, but once my initial crazed hunger had worn off, I quickly found myself full. I polished off the chicken plate and admitted defeat, sitting back in my seat while Dom ate his supper with considerably more dignity.

He caught me watching him. "Do you want a beer or something?"

A beer sounded awesome, but I was doing my best to stay clear-headed for work, and I'd restricted myself to smoking weed to take the edge off the lingering yuckiness from my drone binge. "Nah. I'm good. What do you want to do after this?"

Dom wiped his hands on a paper napkin. "I hadn't really thought about it. To be honest, I wasn't sure we'd both show up."

"Why would I not show up?"

Silence, then it clicked in my shambolic brain: Dom hadn't been sure if he was enough to entice me on his own...if it really had been all about the money. *It* being the mind-bending chemistry we shared whenever we touched, from a brush of knees under the table, to fuck-hot blowjobs...and to the soul-searching kiss I couldn't keep out of my thoughts. *He doesn't know if it's real.*

Fuck this.

I pulled my crumpled money from my pocket and tossed it on the table. "Come with me."

"What?"

"Let's *go*."

Dom didn't strike me as a man who put up with being bossed around, but he rose with me from the table anyway, and dropped a twenty on top of my money. His hand hovered, like he wanted to give me some change, but I pre-empted that shit by shoving my chair back and booting it out of the restaurant.

He followed me—I hadn't left him much choice—but kept his distance once we were outside, and my hasty plan suddenly grew gaping holes. "Look," I said. "We can go to that flat and I can blow you again, or we can do something else—whatever you want—I just—"

Suddenly, he was right in front of me...close enough for me to pull him even further into my personal space if I hadn't been categorically certain he'd evade my touch. "Just what?"

I shrugged, shoving my hands into my pockets. "I don't want to leave you."

"Why?"

"Because I don't think you've got what you came for."

"I don't know what I came for."

His tone was flat, but conflict raged in his liquid eyes, and I believed him. He wanted me in some capacity, but he didn't know what. Did he want to fuck me? Probably, but it wasn't enough. And whatever I'd given him tonight wasn't enough either.

Dom

Lucky's face fell like life was draining out of him. Alarmed, I stepped closer, and gripped his arms. "What's the matter?"

He laughed, bitter, and devoid of any humour. "What's the matter with *you*? You don't know why you came, and yet you're still here? What the fuck?"

I had no answer for him that made any sense. I'd given him my number because I'd been genuinely worried about him. Answered his message because he'd sparked a light in me I couldn't ignore. And now he was right here in front of me, up in my face on a Dalston pavement, I had no idea what to do with him. *So take him back to that flat, screw him, and forget all about him.* But the cold-hearted devil on my shoulder couldn't feel what I was feeling—the lightness in my heart that warred with fear and so very nearly won...or the current thrumming where my fingers were wrapped, vice-like, around his slender wrists.

Whatever happened next, I would never forget Lucky.

"I—" My grip tightened of its own volition. "I don't know what to do."

Lucky stared at me. "Do you know what you want?"

"Yes."

"Is it something we can do here in the street? Or do we need to find cover?"

I couldn't find the words to tell him that *everything* we did had to be behind closed doors.

Shaking my head, I let go of his wrists. "I need to go."

"No."

"I have to." I stepped back.

Lucky grabbed my arm. "*No*."

I had nothing.

For a long moment, he glowered at me, and then he let go and jerked his head up the road. "I'm going to the flat to see if it's empty. Follow me if you want, or piss off back to your castle. I don't care anymore."

That he'd cared in the first place was news to me, then I remembered his kiss and tracked his retreating back until it disappeared around the corner, waiting only a millisecond before I followed him.

I walked ten paces behind him with no idea if he knew I was there or not. He didn't look back, and I didn't call out, even when he stuck a fat spliff in his mouth and lit it with no apparent care as to who smelled the herbal smoke drifting in his wake. *Damn it, Lucky.* Every rule I'd ever lived by screamed at me to turn around and chip back to my car, boot it out of the all-night car park, and block his number from ever contacting me again. Burning him ran the risk of him fucking me right back if he ever found out who I was, but I was screwed in that respect anyway. I'd come too far to turn back unscathed. Whether I liked it or not, Lucky had left his mark on me.

The grotty building appeared in front of me. Head down, I

hurried to the exterior door and slipped inside, trailing the echoing footsteps up the stairs to the front door I remembered from the very first time.

It was ajar. I pushed inside and shut it behind me, cloaking myself in darkness, my heart thumping like a fucking horror film. "Lucky?"

He appeared in the bedroom doorway. "I'm here."

"Is anyone else?"

"No...but I don't know for how long."

I stepped up to the doorway, unsure of my actions until I closed the distance between us, and took Lucky in my arms, kissing him.

He let out a surprised gasp, but I swallowed it down, crushing our lips together as I backed him into the cracked wood of the doorframe.

It creaked, as though it might split, and the sound echoed the crack in my soul as everything I'd denied myself my whole fucking life poured out of me and into the kiss I was forcing on Lucky until he responded.

And when he did respond, it caught me off guard.

His hands hit my chest and he shoved me. I thought at first he was trying to get me off him, but then he lunged at me, throwing me against the other side of the doorframe, and kissed me like I should've been kissing him all along.

I let my head collide with the wood, relishing the sting against my scalp as it zipped through me and joined the cacophony of sensations battling for dominance. My hands found their way to Lucky, sliding under his coat. One came to rest on his protruding ribs; the other cupped his elegant neck. I moaned into his mouth and tentatively let my tongue loose.

It slipped past Lucky's dry lips and found liquid velvet. I groaned again and any control I may've had was instantly gone. Whatever he wanted, or needed from me, was his.

I was his.

Too soon, he pulled back, panting, eyes watering with the need to breathe. "Fuck," he said. "I knew you needed that, but I didn't think you'd do it."

I hadn't thought I'd do it either, but, fuck, I couldn't undo it now. "I'm sorry."

"Don't be sorry," Lucky growled. "Just promise me you didn't do it because you felt sorry for me, or because of some fucked-up Grindr kink."

"Grindr?" Since I'd deleted the app from my phone, I hadn't given it a second thought—hadn't had time when my thoughts had been so consumed with Lucky. "What's that got to do with anything?"

Lucky glared hard before his expression softened. "Sorry. I'm messed up, okay? My life's a pile of shit, and having someone like you kiss me just because you want to doesn't make any fucking sense."

"Someone like me?"

Lucky said nothing. Just knocked his head on my shoulder then took another step back. "We should go. I don't know how long my friend will be gone and I need to fix her lock before we leave."

"Fix her—?"

But I stopped myself before I became a robot who just asked bonehead questions, and trailed Lucky as he left the bedroom doorway and went to the front door. I couldn't see anything wrong with the lock, but he did something with a wire that made it click, and motioned for me to get the fuck out.

Outside, reality hit me like a black cloud, and Lucky didn't seem surprised when I made tracks to leave. His grin was almost a sneer. "Take care, *Dom*. Call me next time you need a top up."

He was gone before I could answer.

NINE

Dom

"Call me next time you need a top up."

I replayed Lucky's departing words for the thousandth time, but a week had passed since that night, and I still had no idea what he'd meant.

That wasn't unusual when it came to Lucky, but it bothered me almost as much as the kiss my lips refused to forget. My days became predictable: wake up, think about Lucky. Get up, think about Lucky. Training and preparing for a big game gave me some respite, but then it would be time to go to bed *and dream about Lucky*.

I was obsessed, even more so than before. I fucking *ached* for him. *So why don't you call him? Take him out again? Or stay in—*

"Oi, cockhead!"

A ball smashed into my ribs, knocking me off balance. I turned to rip into whoever had hoofed it my way, but found myself face-to-face with Micah Roberts, the only player—Maldano aside—I regularly came across who didn't make me want to sit on a spiked dildo more than talk to them.

He was still a bit of a dick, though, so I punched his arm hard enough to really fucking hurt.

"Hey!" He rubbed his bicep. "No need for that, mate."

"Right. What do you want? I thought your club wasn't getting in till later?"

"I drove in. Wanted to get here early in case Isha was around."

"What do you want with Isha? Something up with you and that helmet from GMC Management?"

Micah rolled his eyes. "Jesus. Is there anyone you don't hate?"

A dozen Lucky puns danced through my mind, but I ignored them and took a seat on a nearby bench, tipping some foul performance drink down my throat. "I hate everyone with good reason—you're all arseholes. Now tell me what you want with my agent."

Micah swiped a bottle from the basket and pulled the same face as me as he sampled the contents. "Man, you'd think with all this dosh floating around they'd manage to make this shit taste right."

I cocked an eyebrow. Micah wasn't usually evasive, but I didn't see him often enough to know what was going on in his life, and I didn't keep up with industry gossip. "Seriously, man...what the fuck? You looking to switch up, or what?"

"I'm looking for a favour, actually." Micah dropped down beside me. "I heard Isha had a mole at one of the rags and I need to get a story killed."

"What story?"

"It don't matter what, I just need it gone."

The already sickly sports drink turned to acid in my belly. "What makes you think Isha can help you with that?"

Micah didn't look at me, apparently engrossed with de-labelling his bottle. "Everyone knows it," he said. "It's why you only ever get hook-up stories with supermodels while the rest of us get lumped in with the reality show nut jobs."

"Isha doesn't plant those stories."

"Of course he does...unless they're true, which I don't believe for a fucking second. You don't go out—you barely socialise with your own team. How the hell are you winding up at all these showbiz parties without anyone who actually knows you ever seeing you there?"

He had a point, but not one I wanted to concede, especially while my mind raced through every inch of tabloid space I'd ever found myself occupying. How on earth would Isha have that much clout? How would anyone?

I ran out of time to brood on it. Micah disappeared without gifting any more information, and I drifted back to the dressing room to get ready for the evening game. My brain switched to autopilot, like it always did on match days. Even Lucky left my mind, though the dull ache in my chest remained.

Isha found me in the dressing room after the match. "Good game, mate."

I nodded curtly. "Micah Roberts find you?"

"What?"

"He was looking for you this afternoon." I kicked my boots off, sending clumps of mud flying across the already filthy floor—immediately post-match was the only time top-flight football bore any resemblance to Sunday mornings at the local park. "Said he needed an in with your mole at the rags."

I started to get up.

Isha's hand on my shoulder forced me back down. "Dom."

My heart sank. To an outsider, we probably looked like we were having a friendly chat, but Isha's reaction had given him away in one syllable. No denial, horror, or amusement. Just my name uttered in a tone that let me know he needed me to shut the fuck up. "How long?"

"What?"

"How *long*?"

"Dom—"

"Piss off." I squirmed free of his grasp and stormed away to shower, hoping he'd be gone when I got back.

No such luck, but I'd lingered long enough under the hot spray for the dressing room to be deserted.

"Come for a drink," Isha said. "Please, Dom. I can explain."

I ignored him and stuffed my personal kit into my bag. His explanations meant nothing to me. He was my *friend* and he'd lied to me for fuck knew how long. Lied to everyone *about* me. There was nothing he could say to make that right, and I was damn good at shutting people out who'd screwed me over. In this world, there were many.

"Dom."

"Stop saying my name." I slung my bag over my shoulder. "Do me a favour and pass me on to an agent who won't fuck me, yeah?"

Isha laughed. Anyone else, I'd have chinned them and walked away, but something in that dark chuckle was off enough for me to turn back and look at him.

"What's so funny?"

Isha shrugged, shaking his head slightly. "Nothing's funny, mate. I just think it's ironic that you're worried about *me* fucking *you*, when all this time I've been busting my arse trying to stop the opposite."

"What?"

Isha's gaze levelled out. "Come on, Dom. If you know as much as I think you do, then you must know why I went to such lengths to control the press narrative, especially with you."

My blood ran cold. "The fuck are you talking about?"

"Nothing that you want to talk about here, am I right?"

I opened my mouth, but nothing came out.

Lucky

"Are you pissed off that I won't fuck you?"

Jamila rolled over and looked at me, her gaze amused. "Of course not. Though I don't get why you won't. You're frustrated, and I'm lonely while Meg's deployed. She doesn't mind us screwing around, and your mystery man doesn't even know you're alive."

I scowled at her. "He knows I'm alive."

"Yeah? So why hasn't he called, huh? Why are you taking up space in *my* bed instead of his?"

There were many reasons why I slept with Jamila, and I loved her so fucking much, but hooking up with her while we were both bored and hard up was starting to mess with my head. I imagined myself glancing down while she was blowing me and seeing Dom's face. In an instant, I'd be somewhere else entirely. Her soft skin would become his stubbled jaw, and I'd shoot in her mouth with his name on my lips.

I wasn't arrogant enough to believe that Jamila hadn't done the same when I'd got her off in the past. Didn't stroke my hair and see Meg, but that didn't make it right. Or healthy. And Jesus, I didn't need any more bad habits.

Sighing, I reached for Jamila. "Don't make this shitty, babe. You deserve better than this."

Jamila pulled me into a tight hug, and then settled down to sleep. "We both do, Lucky."

She was out like a light, and I watched her for a while, jealous of her ability to fall asleep so easily. I'd grown so used to watching my back at night that it was too hard, even with her, to switch off. The only time I slept well was when I was truly alone *and* somewhere safe, and the two rarely coincided.

Tick tock tick tock.

That damn fucking clock.

Smirking at my deadbeat poetry, I rolled over and retrieved my phone from the bedside table. It was still on silent from when I'd been at work, so I hadn't heard the message come through.

Perignon55: *u there?*

My heart skipped a beat. The message had been sent three hours ago, and it was the early hours of the morning now. *Fuck's sake.* I'd been waiting on Dom all damn week, and now I'd missed him because I was messing around with someone else. *Twat.*

Too twitchy to even think about sleep now, I slid carefully out of Jamila's bed, and retrieved my dwindling bag of weed from under her bed. Outside, I turned my back on the biting wind, and rolled a spindly jazz fag. I lit up and blew smoke to the moon, and then went back to staring at Dom's message. What the fuck did I say to that? *No, I wasn't, but I'm here now.* Like it meant something. For all I knew, he'd been after nothing more than a quick shag—*but he's not like that, remember?*

I did remember. I remembered him kissing the hell out of me, *and* the dejection in him when I'd called time on being with the only man who'd ever touched me like I mattered.

Damn. How was this even my life?

Lucky: *i'm here*

I was convinced he wouldn't respond, that he'd be tucked up in bed in his mansion or whatever, but my phone flashed almost immediately.

Perignon55: *i need you*

That was a new one. I swallowed thickly and took a deep enough drag on my joint to make me cough.

Lucky: *why?*

Perignon55: *just do*

Lucky: *yeah, but why me?*

Perignon55: *never mind x*

Was he drunk? He'd never punctuated a text with a kiss before, and the sensation that something wasn't right needled me. I finished my smoke, but I didn't go back inside. My thumb hovered over the call button. Would he even answer? What the fuck would I say?

Screw it. I called. Rustling came down the line, and then Dom's gravelly voice, scratchy, and hoarse.

"'Lo?"

"You sound like I woke you up, but I know that's not true unless you were texting me in your sleep."

"Hmm. Maybe I was."

"I don't believe you."

"So?"

"So...you said you needed me, and here I am."

Silence. Anyone else and I might've hung up, but I'd been around Dom enough to picture him frowning and measuring his words as he gauged how much he could trust me.

So I waited, lighting a plain old cigarette for something to do.

"Something happened today."

I exhaled. "Something good?"

"No."

"Okay. How bad was it?"

"I don't know."

"You gonna give me more than that?"

"I don't know."

I sucked back another drag. "Fair enough. How about I guess and you let me know if I'm on the right track?"

Dom snorted.

I took it as my cue to continue. "Did someone die?"

"No."

"Did you lose your job?"

"I wish."

"Really?"

"Some days, then I wouldn't be so fucking scared."

Bingo. So it was his job that kept him closeted. "Something happened at work?"

"Yeah. Someone I thought I trusted knows too much...knows about me."

"He's going to fuck you over?"

Dom sighed. "I don't know. He says not, but he's been lying to me for years, so I don't know what to believe."

"How well do you know him?"

"Not well enough, apparently."

"Why did he lie to you?"

"He reckons to protect me, but it doesn't work like that in my, uh, industry. It's all about the money, man, and being queer is a quick-fire way to losing it all."

"Is the money that important to you?"

"Not in itself, but I don't know anything else. If I didn't do what I do, I'd have nothing."

I could relate to that, even if the realities we were talking about were worlds apart. "What's going to happen next?"

"Dunno. Probably nothing, but I can't handle any more looking over my shoulder, you know? It's fucking killing me as it is, and this guy? Shit, I thought he was the one dude I could almost be myself with."

"You can't be yourself with him now you know he knows?"

"Nah. He's a liar, man. Whatever he says, it was himself he was trying to protect. If it got out about me, he'd be screwed too. My livelihood is his—as in, his depends on mine."

Dom had lost me, but his bleak tone was tearing me in two. I wanted to touch him, comfort him, and kiss it all away until I found that rare smile he was still hiding from me. I *wanted* to help, but I couldn't see how. What was I gonna do? Take out a hit on the guy who'd discovered Dom's secret? Right, 'cause even without the melodrama playing out in my overactive imagination, the reality was that if one bloke could find out, so could another. Secrets never stayed secret forever.

"Anyway," Dom said after a protracted silence. "Sorry I bothered you with it. I just—I just can't lay it on no one else. There *is* no one else."

I closed my eyes. *There doesn't need to be.* "Can I see you?"

TEN

Dom

Another hotel meet was peak stupidity, but I booked it anyway. Gave Lucky a false name to check in with, and paid online with a prepaid credit card. I couldn't gather my thoughts enough to know why I was doing it, just thanked god I had a rest day scheduled today, and didn't have to wait until evening to skulk up the road to Shoreditch.

That afternoon, Isha called while I was driving. I ignored him, but a message flashed up while I was at a red light.

Isha: *Dom, I'm sorry. Call me.*

He was the only fucker I knew who used proper punctuation in texts. It used to amuse me. Now it made my skin crawl as I recalled the bitter end of our conversation the day before:

"Dom, I planted those stories for your own sake...for appearances."

"Why the fuck would you do that?"

"I think we both know why."

He'd known for years, though not until after he'd signed me, which was probably why he'd kept it to himself. All the bullshit stories in the rags. The alpha male endorsement deals. Even manipulating my sale to London's roughest top-flight club had been part of his game of painting me as a moody hetero bachelor.

"Come on, Dom. I saw the way you used to look at me, back in the day. That on top of the fact you've never picked up a girl in your life, how on earth wouldn't I work it out?"

Prick. I'd managed to leave him in the car park without punching his lights out, but beyond losing myself in Lucky, I still had no idea what I was going to do next. Dumping Isha as my agent was logical, but stupid at the same time. He held my darkest secret in his hands. Fuck him, and he'd fuck me, even if he'd denied over and over that he wanted to hurt me.

"Dom, I've known you since you were a teenager. Don't you think I'd have done something with this before now if I wanted to?"

My hands clenched around the steering wheel. I wished there wasn't part of me that wanted to believe him.

The hotel I'd met Lucky at before loomed into view, and a lick of anxiety tainted the thrill buzzing through me. Perhaps I should've chosen somewhere else, but this place was stripped back and basic, no restaurants, gym, or bars inside. Just a self-service check-in desk and a fish tank in reception. And it wasn't far for Lucky to come. I still knew next to nothing about him, but it had become obvious that money was an issue for him. If I could make his life easier, I would.

Yeah, 'cause a few hours in a shit hotel with you is just goals, right?

I exhaled loudly and drove into an extortionate underground car park—the only kind in London my wank-mobile wouldn't get jacked from. Parked up, I threw a bomber jacket over my hoodie and got out; pulling my hood up when I reached the street, thankful it was cold enough for my mash-man look to blend in.

My phone rang again as I approached the hotel. I cancelled the call without looking at the screen and turned the phone off. The temptation to dump it was strong, but responsibility won out. Coach Fernando always checked in on rest days. If I didn't respond to his habitual evening email when I eventually rejoined the real world, I'd have a million more fucked-up questions to deal with—hassle and bullshit that left my mind the moment I found myself outside the room Lucky should've checked into an hour ago.

I raised my hand to knock, but the door flew open before my knuckles hit wood, and Lucky dragged me inside, knocking my hood back. "What the fuck?"

He gifted me an impish grin and hung the DND sign on the handle before shutting the door. "I got a bit overexcited 'cause you don't have your hat on for the first time ever. Also, I figured you wouldn't want to hang around the corridor too long."

He was right about that. I leaned back on the door, counting my thumping heartbeats. It was only the fifth time we'd seen each other, but I'd missed him and the strange reality he brought to my messed-up world. He barely knew me, but he knew so much more than anyone else.

Except Isha—

But I cancelled that shit too. For however long I had Lucky to myself, there was nothing else.

"You look wrecked," Lucky said.

I focussed on him, falling down those sharp blue eyes. "That's nice."

"I'm not saying it to be a dick." He somehow got up in my personal space without touching me. "I just mean you look like the last few days have fucked you."

"They have." I couldn't deny it.

"Wanna talk about it?"

I shrugged. We'd talked about it already, and without giving Lucky as much ammo on me as Isha had, there wasn't much else to say, which was sad, because now Isha was off my Christmas card list, besides Maldano, who I rarely saw outside work now he had a million kids, Lucky was pretty much my only almost friend.

Lucky hummed, a low sound deep in his throat, and took my hands. He led me to the bed and sat me down on the edge. "I think you need to lose these creps."

"Creps? Since when do you speak gang slang?"

"I've been in Tottenham all morning. The bus stop is right outside the high school. I'm well up on it now."

"You weren't before?"

"Nah, I'm from Brighton."

"How did you end up in London?"

He glanced up at me. "Why do you want to know that?"

"Because I'm interested?"

"That right? You don't seem too sure." Lucky eased my trainers off my feet and set them aside like they were made of glass. "And why should I tell you my life story when I know nothing about you except that you're a closeted queer?"

"Are you shaming me for that?"

"Of course not. I'm stating a fact."

Lucky nudged his way between my legs. He placed his hands on my jean-clad thighs and brought his face level with mine.

I wanted to kiss him, but I didn't—I didn't move at all, just stared at him like an idiot. "There's more to me than being in the closet."

"I know."

"Do you?"

"Yes. The details are missing, but I know who you are."

I couldn't see how that could possibly be true, but I didn't challenge him. Being close to him again was like a drug, and I greedily drank him in. I swear down, I felt his pulse through his cool palms on my legs.

He leaned forward, and for a moment I thought he might kiss me, but his lips stopped an inch away from mine. "What do you want?"

I swallowed noisily. "Want?"

"Yeah. From me. Right here. Right now. What do you *want*, Dom?"

I want it all. But I couldn't say it. I closed my eyes and inhaled shakily. "I don't know."

His reaction went unseen by me, but his hands warmed with every inch they slid up my legs until they reached my hips. They hit my chest as he pushed me onto my back, and he straddled me.

I opened my eyes to find him leaning over me, his expression as confused as I felt. "You're such a fucking mystery, and I don't even care. I'll do whatever you want, even if you want to pay me to fuck, and never see me again."

"Is that what *you* want?"

"No."

"I can give you money if you need—"

"Fuck off, Dom."

He didn't move, but his steely gaze was absolute: he didn't want my money.

I reached for him, grasping his slender shoulders first, squeezing gently, and moving higher to cup his face. His jaw was as smooth as mine was rough, and his hair was falling out of his messy bun, the strands damp and twisted. "Did you get caught in the rain?"

"Nah. I had a bath when I got here. Hope that's okay."

"It ain't my bath, mate."

Lucky bit his lip. "I know, but you invited me here, so..."

"So, nothing. It's just a room, Lucky. Do whatever you like with it."

"Don't say that. I'll be naked and swinging from the light fittings before you know it. This is the biggest bedroom I've ever seen."

I glanced around the cramped hotel room. "Seriously?"

"Yeah. My childhood bedroom was built for a hamster, and I haven't really had one of my own since then."

"You share a bedroom at the moment?"

"Kind of. I kip in with my mate when her old dear's at work." His gaze flickered away from me. "*Anyway*. Point is this place is a world away from mine."

"Enjoy it then."

"How long have we got?"

I'd paid for the whole night, but I had training in the morning, so I'd have to be gone in time to be in my own bed by midnight. And even then I'd be tired. But none of that was Lucky's problem, so I shrugged and left it at that. "Are you hungry?"

"You always ask me that."

"'Cause I always want to know."

Lucky slithered off me with enchanting grace and went to the window. "This view is shit."

I rolled onto my stomach so I could see through the net curtains he was holding open. "You don't like hipster coffee shops and McDonald's?"

"I don't like coffee, but I'd kill for a box of dirty nuggets right now."

"You eat that shit?"

"Course I do. It's cheap and delicious."

"It's crap."

Lucky spun around. "So? Bet you'd eat it if I put it in front of you."

I was willing to bet I'd eat anything Lucky asked me to, but I hadn't eaten McDonald's or its skanky cousins in years. "If I said I might, would you let me buy you dinner?"

"It's three o'clock, but yeah...I reckon that would be a fair deal."

There was no way I was risking showing my face in a high street McDonald's, and I didn't fancy letting Lucky out of my sight for the ten minutes it would take him to shoot out by himself to get it, even if I could technically see him out of the window. But this was London, the city that delivered just about anything, and it didn't take Lucky long to download an app onto his phone and order enough crap to give us both heart attacks.

The smile on his face was worth the filthy stench when it arrived.

He danced back to the bed with a stuffed paper bag. "I got you the meatiest option—it's some limited edition thing I saw on the telly."

I accepted a damp cardboard box and warily peeked inside. The contents looked disgusting and smelled even worse, but I knew the moment I took a bite I wouldn't be able to stop.

The parallel was tragic, not that I was comparing Lucky to a burger that had likely never seen any part of a cow I'd want to eat.

We ate the food, and as I'd feared, it was fucking delicious, even the nuggets that were basically chicken-flavoured doughnuts.

I sat back on the bed while Lucky licked grease off his fingers and stuffed the rubbish into the tiny waste bin, and I admired his back. He'd long abandoned his tatty coat on the floor, and he was wearing the vest he'd worn the first time I'd seen him, the one that gave me a good view of his torso. I tried not to stare, but he caught me anyway.

"I'll take it off if you lose your T-shirt too."

It sounded a fair deal, but I couldn't decipher what it meant. Last time, I'd wanted nothing more than to know he was okay, but then he'd kissed me, and my pure intentions had evaporated like they'd never been there at all.

I didn't know how I felt right now, beyond being desperate to see his milky-white skin.

Lacking any brighter ideas, I took my T-shirt off. Lucky shed his too and eyeballed my jeans. "Is it weird that I want to get into bed with you?"

"Define weird."

"I'd rather not. There's some things we're better off not knowing."

"Ain't that the truth." I unbuckled my belt and undid my jeans. "But to answer your question, I don't think you're weird at all."

"That's not quite what I asked."

I stood and pulled one leg out of my jeans, as though standing in front of him half-naked was fucking normal, as though *any* of this was. "Yeah, but I'm going to get in the bed anyway, and I'd really like it if you did too."

We left our underwear on and slid under the duvet. My cock stirred immediately, but I forced myself not to check out Lucky's package and rolled onto my stomach, watching him as he fiddled around with the stack of pillows.

"Who needs six pillows?" he wondered aloud. "Surely it would bend you in half to sleep on them?"

"I think they're just for show. I have a bunch of them on my bed that I chuck on the floor every night. Somehow they always find their way back."

"Neat freak, are ya?"

"Nah. I have a housekeeper."

"Oh." Lucky turned away from me to reach for the TV remote, but I didn't have to see his face to know his expression would be carefully blank, like he didn't want me to know how alien my lifestyle was to him.

He rolled back with a bland smile. "You wanna watch a film, or something?"

"You know I'm not an arsehole, don't you?"

"Why are you asking me that?"

"Because I get the feeling it's something that bothers you."

"That you're an arsehole?"

"No, that I'm not wanting for money."

"It's not my business."

"Trust me, I wish it wasn't mine right now. I'd give it all up to be free of this shit."

"So why don't you?"

I brushed a stray lock of crazy hair back from his face and the light touch grounded me a little. "Because I don't know who I'd be without it."

"Someone happier, maybe?"

"Are *you* happy?"

"No."

His blunt response caught me off guard, but I believed it. Lucky had an old soul, man, the soul of a kid who'd been through the mill and come out a bruised, cynical survivor.

I let my thumb trail his cheek again, rubbing briefly over the shadows beneath his eyes. "I wish you were."

"Why?"

"Stop asking me that."

"Because you don't know the answer?"

It wasn't that. I knew the answer was because I cared more about him than people who'd been in my life for decades.

Lucky closed his hand around my wrist. "Don't do that."

"Do what?"

"Shut down. I don't care who you are to the rest of the world, Dom. You don't have to be that person with me."

"I don't know how to be anyone else."

"Not true." Lucky released my wrist and shifted onto his back, stealing his face out of my reach. "I might be really fucking wrong about this, but I don't think you're getting naked with anyone else right now—and I don't think you have for a while."

"Even when I have, it hasn't been like this."

"I know."

"How do you know?"

"Because it seems too fascinating for you, and I know it's not *me* that's so interesting."

"That so? Well maybe it's your turn to be wrong."

Lucky didn't answer. He flicked the TV on and ran through the channels until he came to an old western I vaguely remembered my father falling asleep to on Sunday afternoons. "This okay?"

"Uh...yeah."

Lucky dropped the remote. For a moment he looked like he would simply lie on his back and watch the TV, ignoring me completely, but then he sighed and reached for me. "Come here."

"Where?"

"*Here*, numbnuts."

I still didn't know what he meant, so I let him arrange me until I was where he apparently wanted me, curled into his side with my head in his lap.

It was so comfortable, his hands so soothing as they rubbed the back of my neck, that I wanted to cry.

ELEVEN

Lucky

I knew Dom would be beautiful when he slept, but I never imagined he'd trust me enough to let me see it.

Warm, and stuffed full of dirty McDonald's, I settled back against the marshmallowy pillows, and made the most of him. I rubbed his neck, and grazed my fingertips over his rough jaw, and then I wove my fingers into his dark hair, and bent to smell it, breathing in his clean, spicy scent. Damn. It wasn't enough that he looked like a walking cologne advert, he smelled like one too.

When it became clear he wasn't stirring anytime soon, I moved my attention further down his body, stretching so I could reach as far as his ribs.

He flinched. Perturbed, I lifted the duvet to see why, and caught sight of a mark I hadn't noticed when he'd undressed, a ragged, mottled bruise that made him look like he'd been run over by a motorbike. *Huh.* Maybe that was the job he was so desperate to conceal from me—GP rider. They made a shit ton of money, right?

Like I cared about the cash. Dom reckoned he'd give his wealth up in a heartbeat, and the more time I spent with him, the more I believed him. I ghosted my fingers over the bruise again, and then brushed my lips over his temple. *I got you.*

At some point, I fell asleep too. It was dark when I woke up, and Dom was awake, staring at me like I was some kind of mutant. "What?"

"Nothing."

"Liar. Are you twisting your melon because we slept together?"

"Um...no?"

I snorted, but my amusement was fast tempered by the realisation that I'd somehow wrapped myself around him like a limpet, and my dick was hard as fuck.

Brilliant.

I started to disentangle myself, but Dom stopped me.

"Don't go."

His cock pressed against mine, hot and hard.

Heat rippled through me. I hadn't come here for this, but I couldn't pull away from it either. I wanted Dom as much as I had the moment I'd laid eyes on him. I *wanted* to kiss him.

So I did, over and over until I sucked a deep, throaty groan from him. He pulled the elastic from my hair with one hand, and ripped my underwear down my legs with the other, freeing my aching dick. I braced myself for his tight, hot grip, like I could prepare myself, but my imagination had nothing on reality.

Dom squeezed my cock, pumping and twisting just how I liked it, but oh-so-fucking slowly I wanted to scream. I tore my lips from his and threw my head back. "Faster."

"No."

"Please."

"Not yet."

I groaned, though it came out more of a whimper, and fumbled with the waistband of his designer boxers. His cock sprang free, rigid and weeping, and my mouth watered, but I wasn't ready to give up on his slow torture just yet.

He brought our lips back together and we kissed a sensuous

dance as he worked my dick and ground his own against my thigh, undulating a gentle rhythm that left me panting like a horny dog.

"You're so fucking cruel," I murmured between kisses.

He smirked against my lips. "Masochist."

"Yeah." I thrust my hips up, chasing his vice-like grip. A shot of pleasure burst in my belly and I dropped my head to his shoulder. "Don't stop."

Dom obeyed me for a while, but just when I thought I could come from his hand alone, he eased off, and pushed me onto my back. He shoved the duvet away and kneeled between my legs, hooking his arms under my knees, and lifting my pelvis from the mattress. Caution kept me from begging him to fuck me, but I was unprepared for the sensation of his tongue sweeping over my hole.

"*Fuck!*"

If he hadn't had absolute control over my body, I'd have jack-knifed from the bed. I gazed down at him, stunned. His eyes widened, like he hadn't expected me to react so strongly either.

I sucked in much-needed air. "Do that again."

He licked me again, softly at first, but then with more purpose as I turned into a shuddering, moaning mess beneath him. His tongue drove steadily into my hole, and his delicious grip returned to my cock.

"Jesus." My head fell back and I grabbed the bed frame to tie me down to the world. "That's so fucking good."

Dom hummed against me. The vibration sluiced through me and the first stirrings of a shattering orgasm bloomed in my belly. He replaced his tongue with his finger, and then added another, and when he found my sweet spot, I was fucking done.

I cried out loud enough to wake the devil and came like a freight train. "Oh god...fuck yeah."

It seemed like it would never end, and when Dom had milked the last drop out of me, he eased his fingers free, and scrambled to his knees. His hand was a blur as it flew over his dick, and then he came too, growling out dirty words that sent more shivers through my still-trembling limbs.

He fell forward, catching himself on one hand, his strong arm easily holding him up. "Fuck me."

"If you say it again, I just might."

I expected tension to ripple through him, to steal the glow seeping out of him, but his grin was uncharacteristically easy.

"One day, maybe."

"For real?"

He shrugged. "Who knows?"

Not me, but I wanted to. He got up to pad to the bathroom, and I mourned the loss of his pulsing skin sliding against mine, of his warm hands holding me down, but when he came back with a damp towel that meant I didn't have to get up, I just about fell in love with him.

He slid back into bed, more at ease than he had been any other time we'd splashed jizz all over the place.

I wiped myself clean...ish, and then surgically attached myself to his side.

He laughed. "I'm not going anywhere."

"Damn fucking straight, though it might be my turn to pass out on you. I think you've ruined me."

"Did I hurt you?"

"God, no. I'm just not used to coming so hard."

Dom propped himself up on one elbow, a tiny frown creasing his forehead. "How do you usually come?"

"Is that what you really want to know, or are you asking me if I'm fucking anyone else?"

"Both."

"Well, I usually come pretty good...but it's not the same as what you do to me. I can't explain it, but it's like you flip a switch no one else knows how to find."

He nodded slowly. "Makes sense. I've never—uh—I've never been so hot for anyone in my life. It's fucking insane."

"True that." I forced myself to sit up a bit and mirrored his pose. "Do you really want me to answer the second part of your question?"

"Yes. I think. I don't know. I suppose it's none of my business."

"It's not, but you want to know, and I don't mind telling you, so it doesn't matter."

Dom chewed on his bottom lip and waved his free hand for me to continue, while I searched for the words to explain my messed-up co-dependent relationship with Jamila.

"I sleep with my best friend sometimes. We try not to fuck, but it happens when we're both lonely. I keep trying to stop, but I can't seem to help it when she's the only one who gives a shit about me—which makes *me* a piece of shit, right?"

Dom's hand twitched like he wanted to touch me, but he didn't. "How does she feel about it?"

"The same as me. She has a girlfriend, but she's away in Afghanistan. Meg won't be back for a while, so my mate's hard up and lonely, and Meg doesn't mind her fucking around with me because she knows it doesn't mean anything."

"Everything means something, Lucky."

"All right then. She knows it's friendship and nothing more, happy? I'm not in love with Jamila, and she's not in love with me."

"But you do love each other?"

"I suppose. She's an awesome friend to me, but I don't know what I contribute right now. I'm kind of a mess."

"So am I."

"You don't have a Jamila in your life?"

Dom snorted. "Hardly. My job is basically my life, and I hate ninety per cent of the people in my industry, so I'm a grumpy loner."

"There's nothing wrong with being alone if you like it that way."

"Uh-huh."

"So...are you? Alone, I mean. I know the profile you used to meet me on Grindr is gone, unless you've blocked me, but—"

Dom laid a gentle hand over my mouth. "I'm not doing anything with anyone. Before you, I hadn't hooked up in months, and before that, it was even longer. In case you hadn't noticed, I'm not very good at this."

"At what? Spending time with people, or making them come?"

Dom reddened adorably. "I don't know."

"What did you do with the last person you hooked up with?"

"Paid them to blow me."

"And before that?"

"The same."

"You didn't fuck them?"

"No." Dom drew a pattern on my forearm. "I haven't fucked anyone in years...since I—uh—worked—up north, and even then it was sticking my dick in a glory hole. I've never fucked anyone I care about."

"You've never had a boyfriend?"

"Nope."

"Girlfriend?"

"Nah. I don't swing both ways."

"You don't know what you're missing."

"That's true of lots of things, mate."

The sadness in his low voice broke my heart enough to let him be, but there was one last thing I wanted to know. "Have you ever bottomed?"

I expected him to flush some more and shake his head. The heated glint in his gaze surprised me.

"Not for a long time, but yeah, I have...and I loved it."

Dom

My car smelled like Lucky. It was fucking impossible, but I swore his scent was wafting out of the heat vents.

You're fucking insane.

Yup. I was starting to believe it.

I pulled into the player's car park and fished my phone out of my bag.

Perignon55: *morning*

Lucky: *sure is x*

Perignon55: *u good?*

Lucky: *u tell me*

Perignon55: *brat*

Lucky: ;)

I grinned and turned my phone off, locking it in my glovebox, as had become my habit since Lucky and I had started texting regularly. At first, I'd deleted his messages seconds after reading them, but I couldn't bear it now. It had been ten days since I'd last seen him, and I was missing him hard. He was my damn Patronus; I was sure of that shit too.

Training passed in a haze of drills and cardio work, and when the team was done, I moved to the onsite gym to blow off some steam—another habit that added to my rep as a bad ass defender.

The place was deserted, but I left my headphones off, and kept my guard up. Isha had snuck up on me a few times this week, and I wasn't in the mood to evade him.

Half an hour into my favourite resistance circuit, footsteps sounded behind me. I glanced at the mirror, fully prepared to smash someone's face with a kettlebell, but it wasn't Isha or anyone else I could sack off. It was Coach Fernando.

"Come and see me when you're done."

He walked away without another word, leaving me the option of working out until he'd gone home, or cutting my routine short so I didn't have time to angst myself into a motherfucking stroke.

Had Isha ratted on me?

The possibility wasn't as alarming as it might've been a couple of weeks ago. Somewhere along the line of my newfound Lucky obsession, and my dwindling passion for the beautiful game, my apathy for the rest of the world was growing impossibly stronger.

Not quite strong enough for me to style out Fernando, though.

I called it quits in the gym, showered, and approached his office with dread lacing every step. His door was open, and he wasn't alone. His assistant coaches were in there too.

Fuck.

I still had time to run, but even as I thought about it, Fernando glanced up and caught me loitering.

"Come in, Dom."

I edged into the office and took a seat in the circle. "What's up? Something going on?"

"We're talking with Madrid about a potential player swap. You've opted out of international duty, correct?"

I nodded. I had the option of playing for England or Portugal, thanks to my father, but I wasn't first choice for either team, and making myself available for campaigns I rarely contributed to was a pain in my arse. And...I hated flying, but no one knew that about me either.

"How would you feel about heading up to Manchester for some European training? I'd need you back for match days and pregame training, but you're so well drilled I think I can spare you a couple of days a week."

"A couple?"

"Three," Fernando said. "It would mean cutting your rest time, but I think you can handle it more than anyone else."

"That's why you're sending me? Because I won't pussy out?"

"No, apart from the fact that you have no woman and kids who need you here, I'm sending you because you're the most intuitive defender in the Premiership, and I believe you'll get more out of training with the Spanish than anyone else, which is important if we make Europe this year."

Like I gave a fuck, but I nodded again like the puppet I was, and agreed to spend three days a week two-hundred miles further away from Lucky than I could bear to be.

Once more in the back: *you're fucking insane.*

TWELVE

Lucky

"Oi, mate. It's kick-out time."

I glanced up irritably from the coursework I'd been trying to complete in a rowdy pub. "Already?"

The barman jerked his head at the clock. "See for yourself."

I didn't bother looking. When I'd had nothing and no one to look forward to, days had stretched into weeks, and then I'd check the time and see only minutes had passed. These days the hours flew by. All I knew for certain was that it had been twelve long nights since I'd last seen Dom, and the craving for another hit of him was just about killing me. That I'd managed not to substitute it with anything more than weed and cheap vodka was a fucking miracle.

I tucked my work carefully into my bag and left the pub on my way to nowhere. Jamila's mum had the flu, so I was sleeping out for the third time that week. It was a mild night—thank god—but it would still be a while before the streets were quiet enough to bed down on.

Habit took me to the Dalston end of Kingsland Road, and I shuffled into Tottenham an hour or so later. An alley caught my eye, but someone was getting blown at the end, and the nicer doorways were all taken.

I claimed a space outside a betting shop, far enough from the pubs so I wouldn't get pissed on, but close enough to the taxi rank that I wouldn't get murdered without someone noticing. It was still dodgy as fuck, but short of trying to get myself locked in at work, I was fresh out of options.

My bag was my pillow, and Jamila had loaned me her warmest blanket. With scavenged cardboard beneath me, it wasn't so bad. I dug my phone out of my pocket and messaged Dom on WhatsApp, even though I'd learned by now that he went to bed early when he wasn't with me.

Lucky: *goodnite xx*

There was no reply, and I was about to tuck my phone out of sight when it vibrated with an alert I hadn't seen since my last jobseeker's allowance payment yonks ago. It was from my bank: money had been deposited in my bank account.

Damn. For a long moment, I feared it was some kind of hack, or that I was tripping my nuts off from the tiny spliff I'd rolled to get me to sleep, but fuck me if the notification wasn't real.

Head spinning, I swiped it and opened my banking app, guessing at security details until they somehow worked. My bank account filled the screen and my balance was a figure that sent me right back to assuming I was hallucinating. *Jesus.* Six-hundred quid, my apprentice wages for three weeks of solid work. Fuck all for most people, but for me it was everything. Food, credit for my phone, and combined with the money—*Dom's* money—I had stashed beneath Jamila's bed, I had enough for a month's rent at the halfway house...the hellhole I'd sworn never to go back to before I'd spent night after night shivering behind a skip.

I couldn't decide how I felt about it. Relief warred with horror and settled in a kind of flat place that made me want a hit of bubble even more than being homeless did. I rolled another spliff and took a swig from my vodka bottle. It would be nice to sleep in a bed without burdening Jamila, have a place to store my stuff when I could afford a shit-hot padlock, but the hostel up the road was fucking terrifying. Fights, robberies, mashed-up idiots setting fire to things and nearly burning the place down. Was it worth it for somewhere to store my three pairs of jeans and two T-shirts?

Probably not.

I'd changed my mind by morning. It had rained overnight, soaking me to the skin, and even a scalding hot shower at work couldn't seem to warm my bones.

And Dom hadn't replied to my goodnight message either, so by the time my co-workers started filtering in for the day, I was in a shit mood.

Someone brought me tea. I ignored them and the person who came after to tell me the boss wanted to see me. It was only when Jim himself came to find me that I looked up from the SUV I was working on.

"I asked Tony to come and find you."

"He found me."

Jim eyed me like a man who knew he had to bollock someone but couldn't decide who. Tony was a bit of a twat, liked to tug on my hair and call me Lucy, so I considered fucking him over, but my old nan had been obsessed with karma and I'd never forgotten her favourite gin-laced mantra: "*The axe forgets, but the tree remembers.*"

"Sorry." I straightened up and wiped my hands on my overalls. "I wanted to get these screens installed before lunch."

"Lad, I ain't got no complaints about your work rate."

"No?"

Jim smiled in his gentle way—I'd learned early on that he was a mild-mannered man, never shouted, and rarely swore. "You taking the mick? If I had five of you instead of ten of those plonkers out there I'd be a millionaire."

"Looks like you do all right."

"I get by, but that's not what I wanted to talk to you about."

"Okay." Wariness laced my tone before I caught myself. Jim had been good to me, but he had that look about him—that earnest frown my teachers used to get when I came to school with bad haircuts and handprints on my face.

"It's all right, kid. You ain't getting sacked."

I sniggered nervously and followed Jim through the garage, keeping my head down, though I'd been around long enough by now that the other mechanics had stopped openly wondering if I was Jim's idea of an off-season April Fool.

In his office, he sat me down and plied me with more tea. I accepted his packet of ginger nuts and eyed him over the rim of my chipped mug. He was *definitely* about to parent me.

"So..." he began, looking everywhere but at me. "I was checking the CCTV this morning and noticed you've been here at the crack of dawn every day since you started."

"I like to be early."

"Two hours early?"

"There's always stuff to do."

"True, but you ain't clocking on till eight, so anything you do before then is unpaid."

"I know."

Jim scrubbed a grubby hand over his balding head. "Listen, son. I get Gill in that time to open up, do whatever claptrap she does on the computers, and take deliveries. There's no need for you to be here too, especially looking like you ain't slept in a week. She reckons you're a right fright when you rock up with the sun."

"Look all right by the time you get here, don't I?"

"I don't pay much attention, truth be told."

"So what are we talking about exactly?"

Jim sighed. "We just talking, I suppose. You're a bit older than most apprentices we've taken in the last few years, but we still have a duty of care towards you. Are you sure there's nothing *you* want to talk to *me* about?"

"Like what?"

"Anything. We've got a link going with The Prince's Trust and whatnot. I'm sure there's something they can do if you need help with anything."

"I don't." I finished my tea and stood. "But thanks for checking in. Can I go now?"

Jim waved me away, and I considered the conversation over, but when I went to my locker that night, a bag of clean towels was attached to the lock.

It was worse than I remembered, and it had only been four months since I'd last been in this shithole. *Don't be so fucking dramatic.* But damn, it was hard. Thanks to my apprenticeship, I was eligible for—and could afford—a room at the halfway house, but the whole place still scared the shit out of me, and I pretty much wanted to die instead of trudge up the steps to the entrance.

A support worker showed me to my room. "There's a canteen downstairs where you can get breakfast and dinner, and an employment centre open Monday to Friday."

"I'm all right, thanks, mate. I've got a job."

"It's still a useful place to go if you have some free time."

I ignored him and wandered to the single window in the small, cell-like room. It had a red frame and seemed out of place in the otherwise grey room. The view was shit too...there wasn't even a McDonald's.

As if on cue, my phone buzzed in my pocket, and it was torture to wait until the support worker—*Mike*—finally let me be.

When he was gone, I put the chain on the door behind him, and sat on my unmade bed, blocking out the stained mattress and squeaky frame.

Perignon55: *what are u up to?*

Lucky: *moving house*

It was kind of true.

Lucky: *u?*

Perignon55: *driving home*

Lucky: *from where?*

Perignon55: *manchester*

Lucky: *why have u been there? work?*

Perignon55: *yeah. crazy few weeks.*

I wondered if he'd ever send me a message longer than five words.

Lucky: *when can I see you?*

It was the first time I'd asked him directly, and I waited on his response as I pined for the weed I'd stashed behind a Biffa bin back in Dalston. Despite the fuckton of drugs already floating around the hostel, I hadn't had the balls to bring it with me. Getting kicked out would be end game, which meant I'd have to find a new way of getting to sleep from now on.

Perignon55: *tomorrow?*

My heart jumped.

Lucky: *serious?*

Perignon55: *as a heart attack*

Perignon55: *if ure free?*

Of course I was fucking free. I'd been waiting on this for two weeks.

THIRTEEN

Dom

"You brought pizza?"

Lucky lowered the stack of boxes so I could finally see his face. "Yeah. Figured it was my turn to provide, and we don't want to go out, right?"

"Right." I loved that he laid that on both of us. "You know you really are gonna give me a heart attack with all this junk food, though, don't you? I haven't eaten shit like this in years."

Lucky rolled his eyes. "You're obsessed with heart attacks. Get some new lines. Besides, you're clearly some kind of gym rat, unless you were born with those killer abs, so I don't think you need to worry."

"Gym rat?"

"Yeah." Lucky stopped waving his precious pizza at me, set them on the desk, and came close enough that I could almost touch him. "You have an amazing body. Don't act like that's news."

My body was a machine that didn't belong to me. I worked it hard so it stood a fighting chance of supporting the bones and cartilage that got clattered by rival players twice a week. If it looked good, it wasn't by design, but I didn't know how to say so without sounding like a privileged prick. "What kind of pizza did you get?"

"Meat feast. And a spicy one. Ooh, and chicken strips."

"More nuggets?"

"For real."

I was too pleased to see him to complain. I was fucking starving too. My only rest day of the week had turned into a mad rush to get my shit in order. Truth be told, I didn't have time to hang out in a hotel room with Lucky, but I was fresh out of fucks.

"Dom?" Lucky clicked his fingers in front of my face. "You in there?"

I blinked. "Sorry. Miles away."

"Nah. You're right here. And so am I."

Sometimes I lay awake at night wondering if these sporadic encounters meant as much to Lucky as they did to me. Sometimes I even thought I knew the answer, but when his gaze was as heated as it was now, I didn't have a fucking clue. *Does he look at everyone like that?*

I had no right, but I really hoped he didn't.

Lucky gave up on rousing me and took the pizza boxes to the bed where he'd already laid out a towel. "I used the bath again. This room's gotta bigger one."

"That's nice."

"You being sarky?"

"No."

Lucky narrowed his eyes. "You'd better not be."

"Or what?"

"Dunno yet."

There was something refreshing about his puerile humour. I took my jacket off and followed him to the bed, hesitating only a moment before claiming the space next to him.

He knocked my shoulder with his and held up a slice of pizza. Orange grease dripped from the spicy meat onto his fingers. I wanted to suck them clean, but settled for accepting the slice, and taking a huge bite.

And revelling in his answering smile. If me eating filthy junk food made him happy, I'd do it all day long.

The realisation jolted me.

Perhaps visibly, as Lucky seemed to feel it too. "What's the matter?"

"Nothing."

"Sure about that? You look like someone just came at you with a cattle prod."

He was so frighteningly on the money, I laughed.

That seemed to shock him too. "Man, you're weird."

"Sorry."

"Don't be."

We demolished the first pizza in silence, though I ate slower than Lucky to make sure he had enough. When the box was empty, I put it on the floor and brought him his precious chicken strips.

He groaned. "Is it wrong that I still really want to eat them?"

"It's wrong you ever wanted to eat them, but don't let that stop you."

He didn't, and there was something oddly satisfying about watching him eat. Maybe it was his obvious enjoyment or the relief on his face when he was done—as though he could finally relax now he had a full belly.

I didn't dwell on why that might be. Lucky's issues were his own unless he chose to share them. "What do you want to do now?"

"You mean you didn't come all the way here just for the pizza?"

"If I had I'd be long gone."

Lucky rubbed his hands together and sniffed them. "I kind of want another bath so I don't smell like the morning after a pub crawl."

"Have one then."

"Come with me?"

"Um. Okay."

Lucky ran a bath hotter and deeper than I usually had time for, unless it was a hydrotherapy pool and any relaxation vibes were cancelled out by the presence of a bazillion physiotherapists.

He stepped into it and held out his hand, even though I was still stubbornly dressed and observing him like a stalker from the doorway. "What's the matter? Too clean already?"

The things going through my mind were far from clean, but, as ever, I was struggling with the conflicting compulsions being with Lucky brought. Being naked with him was fucking heaven, but the intimacy that seemed to come naturally to him choked me.

I took a tentative step forward.

"Shoes, Dom," Lucky teased. "At least get your feet wet."

"Is that a metaphor?"

"Wouldn't know, mate. I ain't much of a literate."

"That doesn't make any sense."

Lucky's gaze sharpened evilly. "So?"

I sighed. "So...I like things to make sense."

"Then your life must be shit."

He was more right than he knew, but watching him enjoy the water with almost childlike happiness torpedoed my indulgent self-pity.

I toed my shoes off and nudged them into the corner. Then I stripped and folded my clothes on the counter.

Lucky sniggered.

"What?"

"I knew you were a neat freak."

"You know nothing."

He rolled his eyes. "Don't quote *Game of Thrones* at me unless you're prepared to be as freaky in the sack."

Blushing around Lucky had grown less frequent as I'd got used to his sharp tongue and filthy sense of humour, but I blushed now, and he saw it.

His expression softened. "Come here."

As if I could refuse. As if I wanted to. I stepped to the bath and dipped a foot in. "Wow. That's hot."

"Yeah. I don't like it when the water gets cold fast. It's like a limp dick then."

"Jesus Christ. Do you ever stop?"

"Not on purpose."

I shook my head and got in the bath. Lucky moved to the tap end and stretched his legs out to tangle with mine. Our knees touched, and with the heat of the water consuming the madness raging in my renegade brain, it was pretty damn perfect.

"See?" He smirked like he'd read my mind. "Just what you needed, eh?"

"It's not the bath I needed, mate."

"If you say so."

I did, but saying it twice seemed a waste of our limited time together. "Come closer."

Lucky edged down the bath, and then spun around so he was between my legs. I fought every dirty thought that ran through my mind, but my dick sprang to life anyway, nudging Lucky in the back as he leaned on me.

He ignored it and closed his eyes. "You're so comfortable I could fall asleep right here."

"Don't let me stop you." Lucky always looked like he needed a good night's sleep. "I'll wake you up before it gets cold."

Lucky's lips twitched with a humourless smile, but he said nothing.

I trickled hot water on his chest and played with his hair for a while, until my hands began to wander.

His chest was smooth and bone-white. His ribs were a little too visible for my liking, but his stomach was a perfect slender plain leading to a dark dusting of hair. I followed the trail to his half-hard cock, and grazed it with my fingers.

Lucky shivered and pushed back on my dick. "Don't get rowdy in here. It'll make a mess."

His tone was light, teasing, but a second shudder spurred me on. I ghosted my fingers over him again and gave him a gentle squeeze before I relented and went back to drawing wet patterns on his chest. "So..."

"So what?"

"What have you been up to since I last saw you?"

"Working. I got somewhere to live too."

"You're not staying with your friend anymore?" The friend he occasionally fucked...*Stop it.* I had no claim on him, and no right to ask for one. "That's great that you've got your own place."

Lucky snorted. "It's a room. A shit one. But it's mine at the moment, and that's all that matters for now."

"How's work going?"

"It's hard. I thought I knew most of the basics, but it's a difference kind of place to what I'm used to. Newer, better stuff to work on."

"But you like a challenge, right?"

"Do you think I'd be here if I didn't?"

I had no answer to that, and Lucky seemed to know it. He lifted himself off me with a sigh and turned over, straddling my waist. His knees dug into my hips, but I didn't mind. The pain was worth it to see his dick sliding along mine.

"Your turn," he said. "How are things going with that bloke you thought might out you?"

"They're not. He's disappeared on me."

"How do you feel about that?"

"Nervous."

It was true. Isha had gone from calling me every hour to vanishing off the face of the earth. No one could get hold of him. Maybe he'd sold his story and didn't need the money from his clients anymore. *Right, 'cause you're important enough to make him millions?*

Of course I wasn't. The tabloids would have a field day with my sexuality, and I'd seen enough of what had happened to the very few top-flight players who'd come out to know it would go on and on and on until my life was pretty much ruined, but I wasn't arrogant enough to believe that I was worth what Isha would need to give up his job.

But still. His absence terrified me. Unless finding out that he knew about me had been a never-ending bad dream.

Lucky rubbed my forearms underwater. A soft wave sloshed up my torso. "Sorry."

"What for?"

"I get the feeling you come here to forget, then I ask you a bunch of questions and send you right back there."

"I came here to see *you*."

"Yeah?"

"Yeah." I punctuated the statement with a kiss, and it was like fully opening a dripping tap. My lips met his, my tongue slid into his willing mouth, and temporarily the world—my world—was a perfect place.

Lucky moaned softly, and ground down on me, sending more water rushing over the edge of the bath.

I caught his wrists and broke the kiss. "Let's get out before we drown ourselves, eh?"

He didn't protest as I stood carefully, bringing him with me, and stepped out of the bath. I set him down long enough to dry most of the water from his skin, and then threw him over my shoulder.

Lucky's laugh did insane things to me. For a young man so hardened by a life I knew nothing about, he was different when he laughed. Free. I tossed him onto the bed and his grin was a mile wide as I pounced on him.

"What do you want, Dom? You want to fuck me?"

I did, so badly I'd dreamed about it a thousand times over, but something held me back. "Not yet," I whispered.

If he was disappointed, I couldn't tell. He merely smirked and turned the tables on me so absolutely that coherent thought was gone.

He flipped us over, straddling my chest so his dick pressed insistently against my mouth while he swallowed me down.

The double-edged pleasure was insane. I loved sucking Lucky's cock, and combined with his wicked mouth on mine, I didn't stand a chance.

I came first, fucking up into his mouth, and shooting with a cry that was muffled by his dick in my mouth.

Then I redoubled my efforts on him.

He groaned. "Shit, Dom. You're gonna make me scream, man."

A residual bolt of heat rocketed through me, and I squeezed his balls as hard as I dared. *Scream, Lucky. Scream for me.*

He started to come. Frantic, ragged moans tore out of him, and he spilled into my mouth, his body rigid until it was over and he sprawled limply on the rumpled hotel sheets.

Grinning, I sat up and gripped under his shoulders, tugging him up the bed until he was where I wanted him: draped over me, head on my chest while I played with his hair.

He was quiet for a long while. I thought he might've fallen asleep, and was dozing off myself when his barely audible sigh cut through the sated silence. "What are we doing, Dom?"

"Hmm?"

Lucky sat up slightly and fixed me with a stare that made me squirm. "What are we *doing*?"

"Why are you asking me that?"

"Because you're treating me like a long-lost lover."

I begged to differ. "We're friends, aren't we?"

"Friends?"

"Yeah."

He rolled his eyes. "If that's true, then you're the worst friend I've ever had."

"Thanks."

"Don't do that."

"What?"

"Hide behind one word answers like a cheating husband. I'm just asking where your head's at. This ain't no inquisition."

I wanted to reach for him, to pull him back into my arms and lose myself once more in all that was him, but I couldn't, because he was right. Somewhere along this weird path, we'd crossed the line from hook up to—to what?

Jesus. I had no idea.

Lucky's scowl deepened. "Okay. Let me ask you one more thing. If things were different, for both of us, would you want to keep seeing me? I know it's messed up because you're you, and I'm me, and we don't really know each other, but I, uh, I like you, Dom."

My heart stilled as I imagined how things might progress if we carried on, how junk food, hot baths, and making each other explode could become normal. Maybe we'd fuck until that was normal too. My pulse quickened, and my sated cock stirred again—but then reality kicked in and I saw Lucky splashed across the tabloids as he left the hotel, with me skulking out behind him, my career overshadowed by the scandal, and my entire world falling to bits as the paparazzi hounded me into an early grave.

Lucky sat up properly before I could make sense of any of it, his damp hair falling into his face. "Actually, don't answer that. I can live without the awkwardness of you rejecting me."

"Whoa." I caught his arm. "I wasn't going to reject you."

He snorted. "It's all right, Dom. You don't have to pretend there's some magical way you and me could make something out of this. I know what I am to you."

"Do you?"

"Course I do. I'm your outlet, right? For your dirty homo secret? You come here so I can make you come, and then you go back to your real life—back to being a dude bro hetero for everyone else's benefit... except yours, 'cause I could be anyone and you'd still be fucking miserable."

I reeled back from his abrupt onslaught. "What the fuck are you talking about?"

Lucky slid off the bed and started gathering his clothes. "I'm talking about the fact that the way you live is going to kill you if you're not careful. You don't have to want me, Dom—it's not about me—but if nothing changes for you, you're always going to want something—or someone—you can't have."

"Do you think I don't know that?"

It came out sharper than I'd intended, and my growl seemed to wind up Lucky more. He yanked his jeans up his legs and pulled his T-shirt over his head. "How would I know what you know? It's not like we tell each other anything we don't have to, is it? Which would be fine if we were just fucking, but we don't even do that."

Was he for real? He was pissed off because I *hadn't* rolled him over and fucked him like a piece of meat? "Do you want me to fuck you? Would that make this better?"

"It would make it easier."

"How?"

"Because that's all it would be." Lucky stamped into his boots and jerked his shoulders into his weathered coat. "You can't have it both ways, Dom. You can't be stroking my hair, gazing at me, and making me feel like something, then dropping me when it gets real for *you*. Use me, or fucking lose me, yeah? 'Cause I'm not up for the bullshit in-between."

He started towards the door. My brain finally caught up with his intention to walk out on me and I scrambled to my feet. "Lucky—"

"Don't." He evaded me. "It's okay. I get it. Whoever you are, you can't change your world for someone like me, but don't think I'm gonna play make-believe with you either. I can do that shit by myself with a ten-bag of fucking bubble."

I literally had no idea what he was saying to me, and he was gone before I even halfway caught up. The door slammed as I reached it—just as well as I was still naked—and I laid my palms on it, my head dropping with my heart. I didn't understand Lucky, or how I felt about him, but somewhere along the line I'd fucked up, and I needed to fix it fast.

My clothes were in the bathroom. I retrieved them and threw them on, and it was only when I went back to the empty room that I realised Lucky had left his phone behind.

FOURTEEN

Dom

I kicked the door of my borrowed bedroom shut and leaned against it, eyes closed, head bowed, fighting the urge to punch myself in the face. Manchester was the worst city on earth for no other reason than it was the last place I wanted to be. Two days here felt like twenty, and I still had a lifetime to go before I could go home.

Sighing, I pushed off the door and ventured further into the room I'd been assigned at the Manchester club's visitor accommodation. There was so much luxury I wanted to puke, but I settled to stripping down to my boxers and throwing myself on the bed, taking my two most precious things with me.

I set the phones on a pillow, one sleek and up to date, the other cracked and antiquated in iPhone years, but both equally valuable to me. I'd kept Lucky's fully charged since he'd run out on me four days ago, mine too, but neither had buzzed with any contact from him.

You should've left it in the room so he could retrieve it without you taking it hostage.

And for once, the devil on my shoulder was right. I'd kept Lucky's phone for my own sake, praying that he'd care enough about it to face me to get it back, but I'd heard nothing, and selfish anxiety was starting to lose space to genuine concern. *No one* had called Lucky's phone, and the idea that there was nobody in his life to worry about him scared me to death. He was fine—of course he was—but what if he wasn't? How would I ever know?

That's right, bring it back to you.

Groaning, I closed my eyes, praying for the sleep I so desperately needed to give me a break, but nothing happened. Agitation clawed at my fatigued muscles, and panic built in my chest until I was sweating. I was such a fucking idiot. All I'd had to do was be honest—to tell Lucky I could promise him nothing but furtive evenings holed up in a crappy hotel, clipped text messages, and cryptic phone calls. Nothing but secrets and silence. But instead I'd let him leave believing it was *his* fault. That we had no future because I didn't want one with him, and now I had no way of fixing it, even if all the apologies in the world could make things right.

Frustration boiled over. I rolled off the bed and stumbled onto the balcony, gasping in frigid winter air until my chest ached, but I barely felt the cold as I leaned on the rail. Numbness warred with a new pain in my heart and I fucking hated myself.

The years-old scar on my wrist throbbed. I glanced, half-expecting to see it bulging out of my skin, but I couldn't see it in the dark. Perhaps that wasn't real either.

A knock at the door broke through my haze. I turned slowly and stared back into the room. *Did I imagine that shit?* The state I was in, I could believe it, but then the knocking came again, louder, and more insistent.

Dazed, I hurried inside and grabbed some joggers from my open bag, yanking them over my junk in time to open my door to Micah—who'd been sent from his own club—and a player from Madrid we'd been training with.

"Get dressed, dude," Micah said. "We're going out."

"Out?"

"Yeah. Management want us to hit a few bars, show some face. Figured yours would too."

By management, he meant our commercial teams, not our clubs, and he was probably right, but I'd never cared about that bullshit, and everyone knew it—Micah especially after our conversation a few weeks ago. "Whatever. You kids have fun."

I started to close the door, but Micah blocked it with his foot. "Come on, mate. Don't be a drag. We're gonna get food first. You gotta eat, right?"

Food was the last thing on my mind, but I'd skipped dinner, and left to my own devices, wouldn't bother to rectify that—a dangerous game where pro sport was concerned. *Fuck it.* "Give me five minutes."

I'd made a shit ton of mistakes recently, but letting myself be talked into hanging around Manchester city centre was right up there. Getting food turned out to be tiny plates of crap at a VIP bar, and if I hadn't been so wound up, I'd have been bored out of my tiny mind.

As it was, I was veering between a panic attack and punching the next person who tried to touch my arse.

"Man, you really do hate the whole world."

I spared Micah a flat glance. "Fuck off."

"I will when the booze runs out." Micah topped up his glass from the three-hundred quid a bottle champagne—Dom Pérignon, obviously, 'cause life was a fucking box of chocolates right now—and sat back in his seat. "You need to chill and get laid. I'd be all over that shit if any girl could see past you to notice me."

"Are you taking the piss?" The bar was teeming with wannabe WAGs and plenty of them had come by Micah's personal space in the last few hours. "Take your fucking pick."

"Says you."

"Yeah, says me. Fuck the taxi driver for all I care if it gets you out of my face."

Micah gave me a strange look, but it was fleeting and gone before I could even begin to figure it out.

It didn't help that I was drunker than I'd been in a good while, something I'd pay for tomorrow when I was training with some of the best players in Europe.

I turned away from Micah and surveyed the bar. The place was tacky as hell in a super expensive way. With its deep purple furnishings and black accents, it was everything newly rich people thought they wanted, and everything I hated. My skin crawled with the need to escape, but it was too kicking for me to bail now—I'd have to wait until someone more recognisable than me made for the door, and then slip out behind them. *Fuck's sake—*

A girl dropped into my lap, older than the last few who'd tried their luck, but still not far out of her teens.

"You look sad," she whispered.

"Yeah?" I replied in the bored tone I'd perfected over the years. "Maybe I am."

"Maybe you're lonely too, but I can help you out with that."

"Doubt it."

"Why?" She flicked her hair back, and despite everything about her being the last thing I'd ever want, I realised she was beautiful: auburn hair, huge eyes, legs that went on for miles. She wasn't dressed quite like the other women I'd seen tonight either. Her full breasts were covered, and the only real skin in my eye line was her long, elegant neck. I wished with everything I had that I wanted to fuck her.

I put my hands on her hips, twisting her slightly so we were face-to-face. "I'm gay, darling, so unless you've got a dick in your handbag or some shit, there ain't nothing you can do for me."

Wide eyes got wider. She stared at me, and I stared at her, even as the bar carried on hyping around us. For a moment, my world narrowed to this perfect stranger I'd just split myself open to, but then her shock melted into amusement, and she started to laugh. I laughed too, though more through hysteria than humour—there was nothing funny about my life right now.

The woman swiped my glass, tipped its contents down her throat, and she turned back to me with a wry smile. "You had me going for a minute, but if you're that desperate to get rid of me, I can take a hint."

"I'm not desperate to get rid of you," I said honestly. "Just not in the market for whatever you're looking for."

"Seriously? A footballer not looking for an easy lay?"

"Nothing about this is easy, love. If it was, you wouldn't still be circling the pack this late in the day."

"Arsehole." But the woman's smile remained, like she'd been around this block as many times as me, and I kind of liked her.

I turned in my seat with the woman still on my lap and nudged Micah. "Dude, this is...?"

"Rhia," the woman supplied, extending her hand. "I'm a real good pal of your friend here, and it's a pleasure to meet you."

Micah was like a pig in shit—though his canary grin seemed to have a slightly hysterical edge to it. I waited for Rhia to ditch me for him, but she stopped as she began to slide off my lap, turned back, and planted her lips on mine in a long sensuous kiss that had no destination. "Thank you," she murmured. "He looks cute enough to have some respect. Look after yourself, Dominic."

She was my second kiss. Horror filled me as I compared it to my first, and I fleetingly wondered how she knew my name, before I remembered that *everyone* knew my name in a club like this. And though it had been that way for as long as I'd been old enough to drink, I suddenly couldn't bear it.

The bar blurred out as I lurched to my feet and stumbled towards the exit. The place was guarded by a pack of thirsty paparazzi, but I couldn't bring myself to care. I pushed past anyone who got in my way, ignored the voices that called my name, and shoved my way to the big glass doors that stood between me and some desperately needed air.

A group of people I vaguely recognised were on their way out too. I trailed them past the doormen and jogged down the steps. A big dude was right in front of me, and I thought I'd got away with it, but he stepped aside at the last moment, exposing me to an explosion of camera flashes.

Wankers. I shielded my face and sacrificed the fresh air I craved by jumping in the nearest executive car. I garbled out the team accommodation address, and shut the partition between me and the driver.

Safe behind blacked-out windows, I hunched up on the seat and buried my face in my knees, covering my head with my arms. *Fuck this. Fuck this. Fuck this.* I wanted to go home. Nah, I wanted to go back to the hotel room with Lucky and rewind to those precious few hours before I'd fucked it up by letting the monster my career had become control every moment of my damn life.

I wanted Lucky.

Needed him.

Craved him.

The drive back to the team house took fifteen minutes. By then, the booze I'd drunk had started to wear off, leaving me still entrenched in self-pity, but with a headache for company.

I slipped up to my room and locked the door behind me, thankful for the discreet driver who'd barely looked at me as I'd stumbled out of his car. He'd probably thought I was wasted, and he was right, but it wasn't champagne or chemicals screwing my synapses. It was everything else.

My legs gave way and I slid to the floor, landing in a heap by the bathroom door. A shower to wash away the grime of tonight called my name, but I couldn't make myself move. A low, animalistic groan pierced the air. It took a few anguished heartbeats to realise it had come from me.

I felt like crawling into the bathroom and sticking my fingers down my throat, like I could retch all my problems away. Or finding a sharp to carve the pain out of my skin. But I didn't move. Couldn't.

Because without the rare peace I'd found with Lucky, this was who I was—a puddle of flesh and bone that meant nothing real to anyone, not even myself.

Misery was like a trance, but without the euphoria. I let it carry me for a while, half-asleep, but convinced I'd be awake for the rest of my life. Loud music echoed in my head, thumping in time with the migraine clinging to my skull, and I had no idea how much time had passed when I belatedly figured out that it was real.

Wincing, I sat up, and searched the dark room for the source. My blurred gaze was drawn to the pillow where I'd abandoned both my phone and Lucky's.

Lucky's was flashing, and vibrating in time with the obnoxious EDM track that was apparently his ringtone.

Fuck.

I scrambled to my feet and threw myself across the bed, snatching the phone and swiping at the screen and activating the speakerphone function. "Hello?"

"Hello," a female voice drawled suspiciously.

I frowned. "Who are you?"

"Nah, mate. Who the fuck are *you*?"

FIFTEEN

This was, without a doubt, the stupidest thing I'd ever done, and I'd made some pretty bonehead decisions lately, including leaving my security blanket slash baseball cap at home.

I parked my car behind a barber's, locked it, and then made my way to the fried chicken shop where I'd agreed to meet the woman who'd claimed to be Lucky's best friend.

Jamila was waiting for me outside, picking at a styrofoam tray of the worst chips I'd seen since I'd bought Lucky a McDonald's.

After an aborted phone call to identify each other, she narrowed her eyes at me in greeting. "I repeat," she said. "Who the fuck are you?"

That she didn't already know should've been a bonus, but the guilt that I'd never even told Lucky was too strong for me to feel any relief. "I'm a friend," I said. "I've brought Lucky's phone."

"Why do you have it?"

"Because he left it with me last time I saw him."

Jamila dumped her chips in a nearby bin and fished a cigarette box out of her coat pocket. She lit up and blew smoke in my face. "When was this?"

"Five days ago."

Something flickered in Jamila's eyes. "That was the last time I heard from him too."

Fear banded around my pinched heart. "Are you worried?"

"Should I be?"

I spread my hands. "I don't know. I don't—uh—know him that well."

"But you know him enough to drive your fancy car down Kingsland Road in the middle of the night to hand over his phone. What are you? Some kind of pimp?"

Fuck. In my hurry to get here, I'd been less careful than usual with my car, and I'd neglected to account for Jamila being as curious about me as I was about her.

She was the BFF Lucky sometimes slept with. Why it hadn't occurred to me from the moment I'd answered his phone, I had no idea.

I studied her as she glared at me, taking in her dark eyes, brown skin, and entrancing mane of onyx-coloured hair. She was the second beautiful woman to turn me round that week—where the fuck was my head at?

"I'm not a pimp," I managed eventually when the loaded silence began to suffocate me. "I'm just a friend. And if you're who I think you are, so are you."

"Who do you think I am?"

I rolled my eyes. "You're Lucky's BFF who he was sometimes living with until he got a new place. He told me he loves you, and you're the best friend he's ever had. Happy?"

Jamila was far from happy, but my knowledge of her relationship with Lucky softened her sharp edges. She took my arm and guided me away from the chicken shop and along the high street that apparently never slept. "I *am* worried about Lucky," she said. "He's been off grid for days. I went to his new place, but I couldn't get in, and I don't know where his job is."

"You don't?"

"No. He never told me. We spend most of our time together asleep."

I couldn't think of anything I'd rather do than curl up and go to sleep with Lucky. The prospect of meeting Jamila had kept me up most of the night, and the drive back from Manchester had just about killed me.

And now I was more worried about Lucky than ever. I retrieved his phone from my pocket and held it out. "You should probably take this. There's more chance of him turning up in your yard than mine."

"I bet."

"What?"

Jamila shrugged. "If you're the Grindr bloke then I know he doesn't know jack about you—where you live, where you work...your whole name."

"I don't know those things about him either."

"That's your choice. Lucky doesn't hide—he's been through too much to live like that."

I could believe it. Painful heat stung my eyes, and I turned away from Jamila. "I need to go."

"Uh-huh."

"Thanks for meeting me."

Jamila nodded. "Thanks for returning Lucky's phone. Hopefully he'll come by my place soon and I can give it back to him."

"I hope so."

"Do you?"

I spun around. "Yeah. I do. Then maybe I'll get the chance to tell him how fucking sorry I am. Take care, Jamila."

Lucky

Silence had become my best friend. Even with the blaring radio, the shouts of the other mechanics, and the relentless clang of metal on metal, I heard—and felt—nothing.

I was numb, and for once it wasn't chemically induced, though the craving for a sweet hit of something was getting harder to ignore.

Friday was the worst day of the week. The garage closed early—at five instead of seven—leaving me two days and three whole nights to amuse myself until work started again on Monday morning. I kept offering to cover shifts on Saturdays, but Jim wouldn't have it. Five days a week was enough, according to him, especially now he'd hired a new full-time mechanic, and I couldn't think of an argument that wouldn't get me sacked.

After work on the second Friday since I'd last seen Dom, I sloped out of the garage and made it as far as the first bench before deciding I couldn't face my room just yet. Weekends there were *bad*—worse than I remembered—and I usually tried to be drunk before I went home. And stoned.

Tonight, I felt like taking it further, but something inside me stubbornly held out—something that felt suspiciously like loyalty to a man I'd probably never see again, especially now I'd lost my phone.

I leaned forward on the bench and pressed my fists into my eyes. Losing my phone had gutted me until I'd remembered there was no one who'd be calling me anymore anyway—well, except Jamila, but I was going to drop by her place any day now. I just had to find the energy to drag my sorry arse back to Dalston.

Right. 'Cause Tottenham's on the fucking moon.

I snorted and screwed my knuckles harder into my eyes. I was losing my mind—I was sure of it—and all because I'd turned out to be the worst pro Grindr ever. Falling for my first—and last—paid hook up hadn't been in my carefully laid plans, and putting my heart through a blender hadn't either.

You daft twat. All you had to do was take his money and suck his cock. How the fuck had it come to this?

I had no idea. All I knew was I had a billion hours to kill before I could go back to work and staying right here on this bench was the best plan I could fathom.

"Lucky." Someone shook me. "*Lucky*. Come on, babe. You're not supposed to be tramping it anymore."

"Wha—?" I opened my eyes, pondering distantly why I hadn't jerked awake like I usually did when something on the street disturbed my sleep.

My vision cleared and focussed on the pissed-off face staring down at me. Huh. Perhaps I wasn't awake after all. Or maybe I was, and I'd simply forgotten trudging back to Dalston. "J?"

Jamila glared. "It's raining, Lucky, and you're sleeping outside like a vagrant, which had better not mean you've been kicked out of the halfway house again."

I straightened up, rubbing my drizzle-damp face. "I haven't."

"So...what are you doing conked out on a bench? You'd better not be using."

"I'm not using, you mad cow."

That earned me an arched brow, but we'd been mates long enough for her to let me wake up before she expected a sensible conversation out of me—'cause calling Jamila a mad cow was definitely *not* sensible.

I pulled myself together and lit the cigarette she stuck in my mouth. "Thanks."

"You're welcome," she said. "I've got something else for you too, but I want answers first."

"Is it your ma's peanut soup? Because I've been dreaming about that shit."

"Sure about that? You look like you haven't slept for weeks."

She knew me so well. I shrugged and wiped my scratchy eyes. "The centre is pretty rowdy...you know what it's like."

"But you've got your own room this time, surely that's not as bad?"

"That doesn't make it good."

Jamila sighed and flopped back on the bench. "I wish I could help you."

"You have helped me. I'd have spent a lot more nights on benches like this if it wasn't for you."

"You shouldn't be spending any nights outside. You have a job now...is there nowhere else you can go? An HMO, or something?"

"I might try for a multiple occupancy soon. I've heard they're just as bad as the hostels, though. At least, the ones I can afford are."

"There must be a room in a house somewhere that isn't a hell pit."

"You'd think." I blew out a lungful of smoke. "But it's not that bad, honest. Give me a few more months and I'll have saved more money. I've even started using my bank account again."

"Get you all grown up."

"Fuck off."

Jamila smirked, but her teeth dug nervously into her bottom lip as it belatedly occurred to me that she had tracked me down to a bench in the middle of Tottenham.

"How did you know I was here?"

It was her turn to shrug. "I didn't. I just remembered that you said your new job was at a posh garage in Tottenham. I've been wandering around all afternoon looking for it. I only spotted you by chance after I tried chatting up some hot guy at the Lexus place."

"That's Cash," I said tiredly. He's new and never speaks. Why were you looking for me?"

She speared me with an incredulous glare. "Are you taking the piss? You've been MIA for weeks, not answering your phone. I thought you were dead or something."

Guilt clawed at my conscience. Even after all this time, I often forget that she worried about me. "Sorry, sista. I lost my phone."

"I know."

It made sense that she did—that she'd joined the dots and concluded the obvious—but something in her face, in the features I knew so well, gave me pause. "What's that look for?"

"What look?"

"The one you get when you're about to try and set me up with one of your dickhead mates from work?"

"I don't do that...anymore. Is it my fault you hate relationships?"

"I don't hate relationships. Just your dickhead mates."

Jamila rolled her eyes, but her fidgeting remained, and after I'd stared her down a moment longer, she sighed. "Fine. Here you go."

She pulled her hand from her pocket and held a phone out to me —*my* phone, though without its cracked screen, I barely recognised it.

"What the fuck? Where did you get this? Please tell me you didn't reinstall that Find My iPhone app and stalk me?"

"As if, and I only did that when you were using really bad— because I was worried you'd die somewhere and no one would know."

"So how did you get it? I don't even know where I lost it."

"You left it in a hotel room."

"A hotel—" I stopped, my brain tripping over itself as I tried to make sense of what she was saying. "How do you know that? Did someone find it and call you, or something?"

"Not exactly. I called you, and someone answered."

"Who?"

Jamila bristled as my tone sharpened. "Well...I don't know who he is to *you*, but I'm pretty sure the sweet bloke who rocked up in Dalston last night and asked me to return this to you was Dominic Ramos."

White noise crackled in my head. Distantly, I knew she was talking about Dom, but his full name seemed familiar too, even though I'd never known it. "I don't understand."

Jamila lit another smoke. "Basically, I finally caved a couple of days ago and started calling your phone to see where the hell you were. Your Grindr sugar daddy answered it and brought it to me so I could give it back to you. I didn't place him until he was gone, but unless he's got an identical twin, you, my friend, have been banging a Premiership footballer."

I stared blankly, and it wasn't until she pulled out her own phone and googled Dom that what she was saying sunk in. Dom—Dominic Ramos—was the lead defender for the football team my father and brother had worshipped for as long as I'd been alive.

Fuck.

Fuck my life.

Jamila grilled me for details over kung-po chicken, but loyalty to Dom kept me quiet on everything except that I wasn't banging him, and he sure as shit wasn't my sugar daddy.

"He only paid me twice. After that, we sort of became friends, I guess."

"So you stopped hooking up?"

"Not exactly." I searched for a way to explain me and Dom that would make sense to anyone but us. "Other stuff happened, but it was natural, you know?"

"But you're not banging him."

"No."

Jamila stuck a plastic fork in a soggy ball of sweet-hot deep-fried chicken. "Good. Because otherwise I'd think he was ripping you off."

"I thought you said he was sweet?"

"He was...and he seemed pretty concerned about you, but that doesn't mean he wasn't just as worried that you'd pop up somewhere and out him. Man, I googled gay football players. I could only find three, none of them play anymore, and one of them committed suicide."

"Justin Fashanu." I knew about him, of course I did. How many times had I heard his name thrown around changing rooms and terraces as the worst kind of insult?

Too many.

"Fuck." I pushed my dinner away, despite it being the only non-cereal based food I'd had since I'd last seen Dom. "This is really bad for him. No wonder he was always so cagey. I pegged him as married at first, and then I thought he was maybe an actor or something."

"He's definitely hot enough," Jamila agreed. "And I reckon he's lucky he's a defender. If he was scoring goals every weekend he'd have no chance of ever walking down the street unrecognised."

"I didn't recognise him."

"That's because your old man messed you up so much you hide every time a game comes on the telly. And you walk around with your head in the clouds. You could've been shagging Liam Hemsworth and I doubt you'd have noticed."

"Who? And I *told* you, I'm not shagging him. It never got that far."

And now it never would.

The realisation hit me like a stone dropping through my body, breaking chips off my heart as it sank through my stomach and into my cold, wet feet. It didn't matter who Dom was—who I was—we'd already figured out that he didn't want me for anything more than an occasional bath-time blowjob, and I was too extra to maintain that shit.

And too hung up on a man who had everything in the world to lose. Dom's obvious fear when he'd talked about the so-called friend who'd figured him out now made sickening sense. I tipped my can of warm Lilt down my throat and swallowed noisily. My life was a bag of dicks, but at least it was my own. No one cared if I was queer as fuck—not anymore.

Jamila kicked me under the table. "What are you going to do?"

"What do you mean?"

"Are you going to call him?"

I shook my head. "What's the point? I'll only make things worse for him."

"That's his choice. Look, he didn't say much when I saw him, but he cares about you, Lucky, I could tell. And he said he was sorry, too."

"Sorry? What for?"

She shrugged. "I don't know, but whatever it was, I got the feeling he was pretty desperate to tell you in person."

Her words gave me a hope I didn't quite understand. I walked her back to Dalston, bought some credit for my phone, and then reluctantly meandered home.

Locked in my room, I brewed tea in the tiny fake kitchen, and took it to the single bed in the corner. Hard and lumpy, it was nothing like the squishy cloud in the hotel room, but it was better than a box behind a skip, so I couldn't complain.

I made a nest in the blankets and pillows the wardens had given me and typed Dom's name into Google. His face instantly filled the screen with stats and a vast playing history for several big-name clubs, including the one he was at now. Fuck, he'd even played for England, though he'd apparently retired from international duty.

That nugget took me to his personal information. He'd never revealed his age, but after a while, I'd pegged him as nearly thirty. I was surprised to learn he was only twenty-six, not because he looked old—fuck, no—but because he *felt* it...I'd seen it in his eyes. The rest of his info made sense: single, fierce, and half Portuguese. The football sites made him sound like a gladiator, the fan pages like some kind of god. It was only when I clicked on the tabloids and saw pictures of him in a club with a woman on his lap, holding her hips, her breasts pressed tight against him, *kissing* her, that I figured out how he'd kept his secret for so fucking long.

And the pictures were three days old.

SIXTEEN

Dom

The first clue I had that Lucky had his phone back was WhatsApp telling me he'd been online overnight.

My fingers flew over my phone screen.

Perignon55: *hi*

The message was delivered, which told me his phone was on, but remained unread for a full half hour before I was forced to abandon my staring and go to work.

At the club, I trained hard, and despite worrying that my recent diet of booze and bad food would fuck me up, it was obvious to me—and the coaching staff—that I was playing better than ever.

Fernando called me aside during set piece drills. "Manchester agrees with you."

"No, it doesn't."

"Problems?"

"I don't like being away from home."

"Tell me that when you've been stuck in a foreign country for the last seven years, boy." He slapped me on the back, and then dragged me to the dugout to go over his plans for the big game coming up, and to ask what I thought about him making a play to sign Micah when the next transfer window came around. "You've been working with him in Manchester, yes?"

I shrugged. "A bit, but you know what it's like when you get players from rival teams together. No one shows their teeth completely."

Fernando nodded. "I understand that, so I've been watching his games with the team. We like what we see, but there's some rumours we'd like to investigate before we take things further."

"Rumours?"

"Yes, about his personal life. I don't want him—or the team—distracted by goings on like that."

I had no idea what he was talking about, but that wasn't unusual when it came to player gossip. I didn't talk to many people, and I didn't read the papers or fuck around on social media. They didn't call me old man Dom for nothing, and I escaped the dugout, eager to get back to the only thing in my life that made sense—kicking seven bells out of a ball of stitched leather.

After training, I went home. My apartment was as cold and empty as it had always been, but Constance had stocked my fridge with custom-made meals from the team's nutritionist, so at least there was dinner.

I picked at the high-protein low-fat bowl of virtue while slumped on a stool at the breakfast bar. My body craved the salt, fat, and sugar Lucky had brought to my life, but the yearning ran far deeper than that, made worse when I checked my phone to find he'd been online, but had left my message unread.

There were a million reasons why he might not have opened my message, but the obvious one seemed most likely: he didn't want to.

Because he didn't want to talk.

Because he didn't want to talk to *me*.

It cut deep, but I forced myself to finish my dinner, take my third shower of the day, and call it a night.

Alone in my bed, I tossed and turned, alternating between hiding under the duvet with a pillow on my head, and throwing it all aside to face the night naked. It was a weird metaphor for my life in general, but I tried hiding from that too, in-between checking my phone every ten seconds.

It was the early hours when I admitted defeat and abandoned my bed, left my phone buried under a pillow, and decamped to the couch. The living room was a space I rarely used since I didn't watch TV and didn't like enough people to invite them over, so I remained antsy even when I did doze off.

I woke at dawn. The sun filtered through my heavy curtains and bothered me enough to drive me up and into the shower.

Scrubbed of whatever I'd dreamed about to make me sweat like a beast, I returned to my bedroom and dug my phone out from under my pillow. I expected a blank screen, but the single word text message lighting it up brought life back to my cold dead heart.

Lucky: *hi*

It was three days before I could escape to meet Lucky, and even then I wasn't convinced he'd show up. We'd never shared much via text anyway, but something had changed now, and I sensed a shift in him. The humour and banter was gone, and his demeanour—gauged from monosyllabic messages—seemed cold...business-like, almost. I tried not to fret over why, though. My angst levels were already sky high and the prospect of seeing him again, even if he lumped me one, was the only thing keeping me going.

On the night I was due to meet Lucky, I came out of training in Manchester to find Isha waiting by my car. Despite wanting to chin him for various reasons, I was actually relieved to see him, but his timing pissed me off enough for him to spread his hands in surrender the moment we locked eyes.

"Hear me out, Dom. I don't want a row."

I threw my bag in the back of my car. "Where've you been?"

"Away. I turned my phone off and took my kids to Disneyland."

"Nice."

"Yeah, it was, as it goes. Put some things in perspective."

I shot him a flat stare. "If you've come here to tell me all about it, you've picked the wrong day. I haven't got time for your bullshit right now."

Isha sighed. "You still think I've been protecting you all this time for my own gain, don't you?"

"I don't know what to think. And I really haven't got time to dissect it—I *told* you—I've got somewhere to be."

"So when can we talk? I don't want to inconvenience you, but there's some stuff you really should know before you shut me out."

"Who said I was shutting you out?"

Isha gave me a weary grin that in the past I'd have found attractive enough to look away. Now I just glowered at him, which earned me another heavy sigh. "Christ's sake, Dom. You haven't answered my calls in weeks, and now I find out Fernando has farmed you out to some fucked-up training franchise without adjusting your contract. Whatever's going on between us, you can't let it mess with business."

"It's all about business, Isha."

"No, it isn't. What I did, and why I did it, was personal. When we sit down and talk properly, I hope you'll see that."

He walked away before I found the words to respond.

I pulled my cap lower over my face and slipped into the hotel. Thankfully, the lobby was busy enough for an extra body to squeeze through without most people noticing, and I took the stairs to avoid unwelcome scrutiny in the lift.

Our room was on the twelfth floor this time, the highest I'd been since the team had played in a showcase tournament in Dubai. That weekend, with a bedroom window obscured by clouds, had been hell on earth—or on the fucking moon, depending on how you looked at it. The one time I'd braved a glance down I'd felt like I was falling off the edge of the world. *I fucking hate heights.*

I didn't repeat the mistake when I reached the right floor this time around. My irrational fear of heights seemed a million miles away, and finding room 1235 was the only thing on my mind.

It appeared in front of me, black and shiny. I knocked, and the door was pulled open before I'd reclaimed my hand. *Lucky.* Relief left me dizzy. I stumbled through the door, wrenched it from his hands, and kicked it shut behind me. My gaze found his and I nearly melted to the floor. "Hi."

"Hey." He didn't move. Just stared from his position a foot away from me, still wearing his coat and boots, eyes blank...*carefully* blank.

My heart lurched. Something had changed. "What is it?"

"What do you mean?"

"You're different."

"How so?"

As if I could explain it. As if I could explain *anything* that had happened in my life in the last few months.

As if I could ever explain *him.*

It was my turn to stare, but Lucky was more stoic than me. Or maybe he wasn't, and the emptiness in his gaze was real. Pain lanced my chest again. I brought my hand up to rub it away, like I could force it from my body and everything would be okay, but futileness hit me hard, and a low sound escaped me. *I can't keep doing this—*

"Fuck it." Lucky closed the distance between us and ripped my hand away from my chest. He claimed the other too, and then pinned my arms above my head with strength that belied his slender arms.

He kissed me fiercely, silencing another moan that had built in my throat as he'd stared me down. For a moment, I had no response, but then weeks of heartache and tension spilled out of me, and I threw myself at him with enough desperate force to tear my arms from his tight grip.

Lucky stumbled, but my hold on him was absolute—I'd die before I let him fall.

Before I let his lips leave mine.

I guided him to the bed and lowered us down, letting go of him only to help him push my coat over my shoulders while I kicked off my trainers.

His coat followed mine to the floor, and my hands were instantly beneath his trademark torn vest. Lucky gasped into my mouth and thrust his body up from the bed, arching against me, the bulge in his sinfully tight jeans scraping my own hard dick.

I went for the buttons keeping him prisoner and undid his jeans, yanking them over his hips and down his thighs, taking his underwear with them. His cock sprang free and I closed my fist around it, squeezing it, and rubbing my thumb over the already-sticky head.

"*Shit.*" Lucky broke our kiss, and his head hit the bed with a dull thud. "I'm so into you, Dom. You make me fucking insane."

I had more sympathy than ability to articulate it. My jeans were uncomfortably tight, and Lucky was apparently too distracted to help me out.

Still working his dick with my hand, I undid my belt with the other, and kicked my jeans away.

"My boots." Lucky squirmed beneath me. "Get my boots off."

Wrestling his grungy boots from his feet required two hands, but if it got him naked faster, I was happy to oblige.

I slid off him and into a crouch. His boots were perfectly worn and smelled of old leather. One day I wanted him on his back, wearing just them, but right now I wanted nothing but him.

His boots hit the floor, followed closely by his jeans, and by the time I returned to the bed, his vest was gone too.

I hooked my hands under his arms and dragged him further up the bed, and then I kissed him again, over and over, until only the need to breathe made me stop.

"What do you want?" Lucky whispered. "Anything. Just say it."

"I—"

Lucky took my face in his hands and unwrapped his legs from around my waist. "Fine. I'll say it. Fuck me, Dom. Please?"

Lucky

Dom's scramble for the condoms and lube I always had in my bag was almost funny, but when he came back to bed, the look on his face eclipsed the mirth bubbling in my chest.

Nerves replaced it. I was willing to bet I'd had more sex than him in the last few years, but this was *Dom*. Something—everything—about him was different.

Dom shed his underwear, sheathed himself, and lubed up like a pro—like he fucked people all the time, but even with the image of him and the hot red-haired woman carved into my brain, I knew he didn't. He was probably just really fucking good at it.

Anticipation took over my nerves. I licked my lips as Dom approached me, but he didn't go straight for me with his dick. Instead, he swooped down at the last moment and sucked my cock into his mouth, deep-throating me even better than he had that very first night.

His gargled, choking sounds shot straight through me, like I'd emptied a syringe of him into my favourite vein. My hands flew to his hair—which was longer now than when we'd met—and I fisted his soft locks, as though they could save me from the mind-blowing oblivion we were heading for. *Please god, don't ever stop.*

Dom pulled off my dick, leaving it wet and shiny. He crawled up and over me, and kissed me into another pleasure-hot trance before I could mourn the loss of his lips elsewhere. His cock pressed against me, lube mixing with the saliva dripping down my balls. I widened my legs, wrapping them once again around Dom's waist, and arched to meet him as his tongue drove into my mouth.

His kiss was almost enough to distract me from the stretching burn of him easing inside me. Almost, because when it came I wasn't as ready for it as the fire inside me made out.

"Fuck." I dug my fingers into his shoulder and screwed my eyes shut. "Wow."

Dom kissed my cheek far more sweetly than our current position demanded. "Shh. It's okay."

It was more than okay, but it still hurt like hell until my body adjusted to having his thick cock inside me.

Dom pushed my hair out of my face and coaxed me into opening my eyes. His gaze was less intense than I expected, and he grounded me with a gentle smile. He thrust his hips in a tiny, rocking motion, and rubbed his thumb over my cheek.

Pain gave way to pleasure. A shuddery groan escaped me and I bit down on my bottom lip. "Damn, that's so good."

"It is." Dom dropped his lips to my collarbone and sucked until it stung. Then he looked up at me again with a smirk. "Ready for more?"

"Fuck, yeah."

Notch by notch, Dom amped up the heat and took me apart. I'd come into this weird relationship we'd built with the upper hand—sexually, at least—but as Dom screwed me with increasing fervour, any advantage I'd had ebbed away with each drive of his powerful hips.

'Cause he didn't fuck me like I'd expected him to—tensely, and drawn back from the experience. Nah. He fucked me how I'd dreamed he would, hunched over me, my legs wrapped around him, as he thrust into me, our lips fused together.

Entwined so entirely, we were a mass of sweaty limbs and undulating hips. My gasps merged with his gravelly moans until we reached fever pitch and the sounds tearing from me were something I couldn't describe.

I clung to his neck. "Yeah. That's it. Right there."

Like he needed to be fucking told. Like he didn't know exactly where to find the tiny knot of nerves that made my eyes tear with pleasure.

I caught sight of us in the mirror above the desk—of Dom's tanned, muscular body clenching and tightening as he screwed me. Of my wild eyes as I clutched any part of him I could reach. I'd always loved getting fucked, but I'd never had anyone own me like he was right now. "You're gonna make me come."

Dom growled and fucked me harder, the jerk of his hips driving the bed against the wall in a thumping rhythm that upped the heat. He ravaged my mouth, his hand loosely at my throat, and then he sat up, unwrapped my legs from around him, and hooked them over his shoulders. The change in angle, combined with the pressure of his hard, unyielding abs rubbing my cock, tipped me over the edge.

"Fuck, I'm coming." Pleasure melted my synapses, sluicing through me as wet warmth spurted between us. It seemed to go on and on, and I shuddered with strangled gasps, my body locking down around Dom, taking him hostage in case he withdrew the source of the agonising ecstasy blowing me to bits.

His entrancing poise began to shatter too. Filthy words fell from his mouth as he slammed into me, and through the white haze clouding my brain I knew the moment he lost control.

His rhythm became erratic, his breath heavy in my ear. "*Lucky*."

"Yeah. Come, Dom. Fill me up."

His answering shout was deafening, his final thrust a brutal slam that drove another spurt of come from my dick, and then he slumped on top of me, his weight pinning me down, and his teeth digging into my neck.

The circuit was complete, and I was a fucking mess. I trembled beneath him until he came back into himself and shifted off me. "You okay?"

I nodded, then changed my mind and shook my head as the intentions I'd carried with me on the bus from Tottenham returned to the chaos he'd wreaked in my already convoluted mind. "God damn. You weren't supposed to be so good at that."

Dom hummed, and for long moments, there was no sound but my stuttering heart, and the blood slowly simmering in my ears.

Then he sat up and turned to me with a look that blew apart the resolution I'd fought so hard for. "Lucky?"

"Yeah?"

"I missed you."

SEVENTEEN

Lucky

I woke up alone, naked, my hair still damp with sweat. Coming to in an unfamiliar place wasn't a new experience, but the empty space next to me was fucking terrifying.

Heart pounding, I sat up, but Dom appeared from the bathroom before the panic seizing my senses took over. "Fuck. I thought you'd left me."

The words tumbled out before I could stop them, laced with an embarrassing dose of neediness.

Dom crossed the room in two strides and sat down beside me, pulling me close. "I'm still here."

For now. But I didn't say it. What was the point? I'd come here with every intention of telling him I couldn't see him anymore. Of kissing his cheek and leaving him to his own clusterfuck of a life. And yet somehow we'd ended up fucking, and now I was so far gone, so goddamn into him, he'd probably have to kick me out.

How is this even my life?

"I ran you a bath."

I blinked. "What?"

"A bath." Dom chewed on his bottom lip. "I know you like them —that you don't have one wherever you live—so..."

I leaned into him, noting his shower-damp skin. "Thank you. Just don't let me wallow too long. I can never seem to make myself get out before it gets cold, and that kind of defeats the object, you know?"

"If you say so, mate. You could top it up, though. It ain't like the hotel's gonna run out of hot water."

"Maybe I'm an eco-warrior." I tore myself away from his hypnotic touch and stood, wavering slightly until Dom caught me.

"What's up? Did I hurt you?"

I waited for equilibrium to return to me before I shook my head. "Nah. Just hungry, I think. Lunch was ages ago."

Yesterday, in fact, but I wasn't about to confess that my wages covered little more than my rent, Oyster card, phone top-ups, and a couple of boxes of Shreddies. Fuck that. Dom had his secrets, I had mine.

I let him guide me to the bathroom, though. His arm around my waist was magic, and the deep steamy bath he'd run for me? Yeah. I was pretty much in heaven, even when it became obvious he wasn't getting in the tub with me.

"I'm gonna get some food," he said. "Can't have you passing out on me. What do you want? Chicken?"

I sank into the hot water and shrugged. "There's not much I won't eat. Get whatever."

His chuckle sounded far away as I closed my eyes, but I didn't hear him leave the room, and when I opened my eyes a little while later, he was sat on the closed toilet, engrossed in his phone.

"You don't have to babysit me."

"I'm not." He spared me a fleeting glance. "I can go if you want some space, though?"

"That's not what I meant."

"What did you mean?"

"I don't actually know." I reached for the shampoo and set about washing the sex sweat out of my hair, though I missed it already.

"Maybe hunger really does make me crazy. What are we having for dinner?"

Finally, a smile. Dom leaned forward and held up his phone. "Italian. Figured you could use some carbs."

It was on the tip of my tongue to ask if professional athletes were allowed to eat such things, but I swallowed it down. The moment to reveal I knew who he was kept passing me by, and I couldn't seem to make myself chase it down. Besides, with the amount of crap he'd already eaten at my hands, what harm could a bit of pasta do?

The flimsy reasoning carried me through the rest of my bath, and back to bed when I'd banished my wet hair into a dude bun.

Dom tucked a stray lock behind my ear. "I love your hair."

"Yeah?"

"Yeah. When I was younger, I thought I had a thing for long hair because I was trying to feminise the blokes I fancied, like that would somehow make me straight enough to get by, but now I just fucking love it."

"You don't still try to be straight?"

"I don't think so." Dom withdrew his hand. "I told a lot of lies in the beginning...made up women and conquests, but I can't be bothered now. I say nothing and let other people talk for me. Apparently that's a thing now."

Bitterness laced his words, but with the image of him kissing that woman still fresh in my mind, I didn't push it. Logic told me it had been a publicity stunt—and one I understood—but I didn't want him to lie to *me*.

I did want to know more about him, though. About the man who existed beyond the superstar football player he was to the rest of the world. "Wha—"

A knock at the door made us both jump.

Dom recovered first. "Dinner. Um, could you—?"

"On it." I pulled on my jeans and swiped his T-shirt from the floor. Despite being abandoned almost the moment he'd arrived, somehow, it still felt warm—still felt like him, smelled like him—

"Lucky?"

"What?"

Dom pressed some cash into my hand. "The door."

Damn. I was so fucked.

I padded to the door, took the paper bag of food, paid, and shut the door without waiting for change. Drawn back to bed like a magnet to steel, I handed Dom the food. "Hope I didn't give them a massive tip by accident."

"Why? I'm sure they deserve it. It's pissing down out there."

"Is it?" I flicked a glance to the window and saw that it was indeed wanking it down, which seemed symbolic of the world we were hiding away from.

I got up and drew the curtains, adding an extra layer to our seclusion. Dom eyed me with obvious curiosity, but said nothing. Just handed me a container of broccoli-garlic pasta with a plastic fork sticking out of it. "This isn't spag bol." I sniffed it suspiciously.

Dom chuckled. "Nah, but it's got chicken in it somewhere, and lots of iron in the greens."

"What do I need iron for?"

"To stop you falling over when you get out of bed."

I let him have that one when I saw he'd ordered garlic bread, lasagne, and carbonara too. "We're never going to eat all this."

He shrugged. "So? Take it home, to work, whatever. I'm sure it won't get wasted."

The idea of having a hot tub of pasta for the next three days was too good to call him out for mothering me. And, I sort of liked it, in the oddest way. Warmth pooled in my groin, and it was only a different hunger that kept me from jumping him.

I ate myself into a carb coma, and swallowed every vegetable Dom put in front of me. When we were finally done, I flopped back, while he tidied away my care package and set it next to my bag.

"So you don't forget," he said without looking at me.

I threw a pillow at him.

Laughing, he came back to bed and slid under the covers with me. I flicked the TV on, but neither of us glanced at it as we lay on our sides, facing each other.

Dom returned to his apparent favourite hobby of tucking my hair behind my ears. When he'd run out of renegade locks, he absently stroked my face. His gentle touch was enough to send me back to sleep, but sensing our time together slipping away, I fought my heavy eyes. "How long have we got?"

"A little while. I can't stay over, but a late night won't kill me."

I imagined what it would be like to sleep all night in this bed with him, to wake up with his strong arms around me. And when the image came to me, I knew for sure that there was no way I could ever stop seeing him, even if we stayed like this forever—hidden under a blanket of half-truths and aborted sentences.

Dom cupped my cheek with his warm palm. "You seem miles away. You wanna sleep?"

I shook my head. "Nah. I wanna talk."

"What about?"

I hated the wariness that instantly marred his lovely face. "Nothing heavy. You choose."

"Me?"

"Yeah. Ask me something."

His hesitance made more sense to me than he'd ever know, but there was curiosity in his dark gaze too. Things *he* wanted to know about *me*. "Where are you from?"

"Brighton," I said. "You know that already."

"I asked you how you ended up in London and you told me to do one." Dom smiled faintly. "I'd still like to hear your answer, though... if you've changed your mind about telling me?"

"There's not much to tell." I scooted impossibly closer to him. "Me and Jamila grew up on the same street until she moved to Dalston. When I had some, uh, family issues, it made sense to follow her here 'cause I didn't have anyone else."

"What kind of family issues?"

"The stereotypical kind. My father is old school, you know? The kind of man who expects the women in his life to cook and clean, and the men to drink pints and play football." It took everything I had not to search Dom for a reaction. "I wasn't the son he wanted, and once I hit puberty, I lost interest in trying to be. One embarrassment too many and he kicked me out."

"How old were you?"

"Old enough."

"What about your mum?"

I sighed. "She tried to reason with him, but on the inside, I think she was relieved when I left. We don't talk anymore."

Dom's ever-wandering thumb passed over the scar splitting my left eyebrow. He didn't ask, but I got the feeling he knew who'd put it there. "I don't talk to my mum much either. I send her money, she takes it, and tells everyone in her village how rich I am. I'm okay with that if it keeps her off my back."

"Your dad?"

"Dead."

"I'm sorry."

"Don't be. He was an arsehole too."

Dom

We talked for hours—well, Lucky did. I listened, filled a few gaps, and lost myself entirely in the cocoon we'd constructed in our hotel bolthole. Bare skin and soft touches, gentle kisses and roaming hands—by the time I started to figure I'd have to leave soon, I knew there was no way I could.

"Stay," Lucky whispered.

I answered by rolling on top of him and pinning him to the mattress.

He let me overpower him, though I was, by now, under no illusion that he couldn't fight back if he wanted to. I'd explored him enough to discover the lean, sinewy muscle coiling around his slender bones, the tight grip in his hands, and the Rottweiler lurking behind his mischievous blue eyes.

For now, though, he was pliant beneath me, so I made the most of it. Of *him*. His skin was velvet to my lips and tongue. I sucked his nipples into my mouth, one by one, and revelled in his answering gasps. My body cried out to fuck him again, but I needed him to ask me, because despite sliding inside him only a few hours ago, it still felt too good to be true.

Perhaps sensing the perennial war in my soul, Lucky squirmed, and turned the tables before I could blink. Suddenly I was on my back with him on top of me, straddling me, grinding down on me to let me know exactly what I was missing while we both still wore underwear.

A damp spot was forming on his groin. Unable to resist, I pulled his briefs down and set his cock free. I gripped it tight and let him fuck my hand, imagining how it would feel if he was riding my dick too.

I'd never fucked like that—with someone on top of me. Never trusted anyone enough. Or wanted to even try.

I wanted Lucky to ride me.

Pulling him over me so I could kiss him, I drew his underwear further down his thighs until he took the hint and elegantly wriggled out of them. He relieved me of mine too, and then it was his turn to make a mad, naked dash for a condom.

Slicked up, he impaled himself on my sheathed cock so fucking slowly I wanted to scream, but the concentration on his face kept me quiet and still.

"Wow." He sat back on his heels and blew out a breath.

"You said that last time—I'm hoping that's a good thing."

Lucky let out a breathless chuckle. "It is. Consider me wowed."

I'd take that. Fucking Lucky had taken me by surprise, and I still wasn't all together sure how it had happened the first time around, but I couldn't deny that it had blown my mind. Before him, fucking had been mechanical—a means to an end that terrified me. But there was nothing frightening about the tidal wave of pleasure consuming me as Lucky took me inside his body. It was magical, and I couldn't fathom how I'd lived so long without it.

He started to move, undulating his hips in sensuous circles. It was too much, and not enough, all rolled into one, and the sound that tore out of my chest was more whimper than moan.

I slid my hands up his thighs and to his hips, gripping him hard. My fingers digging into him seemed to spur him on, and he fractionally upped his pace. "Damn, Lucky. You're gonna kill me."

Lucky gasped and fell forward, his wild hair obscuring his face. "Kill you? Try riding cock without coming in ten seconds flat then talk to me about death."

I laughed, but he cut me off by clenching around me, and something flipped inside me—a switch that made my blood run hotter, my heart beat faster, and my dick pulse a warning that I couldn't play Lucky's game for long.

My hips thrust up of their own volition, catching him off guard.

"Jesus." He arched his back, giving me a better angle to screw him from below. "Yeah. Like that, baby."

I couldn't remember anyone ever calling me baby, but the endearment, dripping so dirtily from Lucky's mouth, set me on fire. I tightened my grip on his hips and fucked him harder, losing myself to the criminal sensation of his wet heat, the smell of clean sweat, and the frantic noises he made as I slammed into him.

Pleasure snowballed in my veins, picking up pace. I groaned and brought one hand to the back of Lucky's head, weaving my fingers into his hair as I dragged him down. I found his lips in a frenzied kiss, and any control I'd ever possessed when it came to him was gone.

Skin slapped skin, and needing him and wanting him became the same thing. I buried my face in his neck and came, white-hot sparks of release rocketing through me. "Fuck, Lucky."

"*Dom.*"

The way he said my name—pleasure laced with the best kind of panic—tipped me over the edge. I thrust up one more time and spilled inside him, and then let him go so he could rear back and jack his cock.

Watching him fall apart, shout my name, and paint my chest with come, was just about the hottest thing I'd ever seen. I was fucking enchanted, and I couldn't look away. Couldn't stop myself seizing him when he was done, and crushing him against me in a suffocating embrace.

It was a while before I could bring myself to let him go, and by then, he was trembling.

I pushed his hair back. "Okay?"

He grinned dazedly and another violent shudder wracked him. "Yeah. You just get me, you know?"

If he felt anything like I did, then, yeah, I knew. "Do you want another bath?"

Lucky shook his head. "Nah. I wanna lie here with you."

I wasn't about to argue with that. Time was getting away from us. Soon, I'd have to leave him and go back to a bed that had never felt as welcoming as this one that thousands of people had likely slept in. But right now? I was all his.

We got cleaned up, and Lucky sprawled out on his stomach beside me, his leg hooked over mine while he drew patterns on my chest. Intimacy seemed to come naturally for us now, but the reality that it couldn't last hit home as I glanced at the clock on the TV. Tomorrow was a big day for training, and I should've already been asleep in my own bed, hydrated, my body loaded with perfectly balanced food.

Instead I was holed up with a man I could easily fall in love with if I was someone else entirely.

"So..." Lucky drawled lazily, but there was a question behind it.

I tensed, bracing myself, and he rubbed my chest. "Don't freak out, Dom. I just want to know who taught you to fuck like that if you've never had a relationship. You don't learn that shit in clubs or on Grindr."

Heat crept into my cheeks, and I was glad the room was dimly lit as I let my answer spill out of me, despite the urge to measure my words. "No one taught me anything. You're the only bloke I've ever—uh—been so intimate with. I never kissed anyone before you."

Lucky's hand stilled on my chest. "Seriously?"

"Yeah."

He sat up, hair tumbling over his shoulders. "Why me?"

"What?"

"Why did you let me kiss you when you never have anyone else? And don't tell me no one's ever wanted to."

I didn't want to talk about this, to think about the empty encounters that had led me to this moment, but the idea that Lucky didn't know how beautiful he was—how fucking mesmerising—made me feel sick.

Sighing, I leaned forward and pressed our foreheads together. "I let you kiss me because you made it all real."

EIGHTEEN

Dom

Match days had become the only time playing football made sense. The crowds and cameras had long ago become normal enough that I barely noticed them, but the desire to win was rooted so deep inside me that for ninety minutes perhaps I was the Dominic Ramos the whole world except Lucky perceived.

I was brutal—vicious, even. No one got by me and stayed on their feet. Studs scraped skin, and bones clashed. Men rolled off the pitch clutching their legs, but I played on.

Despite my efforts though, at half-time we were two-nil down.

Fernando wasn't impressed. He benched the captain and handed me the armband.

I was even less impressed. "Are you fucking serious?"

"Deadly." Fernando growled in Spanish and thrust the armband at me again. "And if anyone here wants to play in Europe next year, they'd better fucking join me."

Being capped had been the pinnacle of my career when it had first happened a few years ago, but it was a ball ache now. With glory came responsibility, blame, and a circus I didn't have enough fucks to put up with.

But, like so many other things in my life, I had little choice but to slide the armband over my elbow and get on with my job.

We left the tunnel for the second half. The whistle blew and the discontent of the home fans was obvious from the first kick. Despite a diet of late nights and junk, I was still playing better than ever, but the coherency of my team was something else. Or nothing at all, depending on how you looked at it.

When the ball went out of play, I jogged to the touchline to huddle with Fernando.

"Go wide and long," he instructed. "We don't have the pace in the middle to keep them out, but they're not watching you because they think you won't leave your line."

Ordinarily they'd be right. My primary job was to stop goals, not score them, but the growing fluidity of the game meant my role evolved with each match.

I swallowed a mouthful of a blue and sickly sports drink, and rejoined the game. A couple of set pieces didn't play out, but ten minutes into the second half, our strikers hit their mark. Six minutes later, we drew even, but a draw wasn't enough for us or our opponents.

The atmosphere in the stadium reached fever pitch. At three minutes till the whistle, the single mindedness that had carried me this far in the beautiful game took over. I sent the younger defenders deep into our own half, and pushed my wingman—Maldano—down the left side. "Go long," I shouted.

I dashed down the right-hand side of the pitch, chasing the ball, and nothing else. Playing out of position was risky, but so extreme and out of character for our defence line that no one would expect it.

Unchecked, I burst into the penalty box and caught Maldano's cross with my head. Half a dozen opposition players crashed into me, sending me sprawling to the grass, but they'd charged too late. The ball hit the back of the net, and my work for the day was done.

The dressing room was mental. At this stage in the season, every point counted. We stood no chance of topping the league, but qualifying for Europe was well within our reach. And it meant the world... to everyone, but me.

Maldano dragged me to the communal baths. The water was already cloudy with mud and dirty grass, which stopped the steamy encounter with a dozen nude men being as homoerotic as an outsider might think. Only Maldano had ever invaded my thoughts outside of the club, but it had been years, and regardless, a lifetime had passed since I'd last thought of anyone but Lucky.

Still, I made my escape as soon as I could, and grabbed a towel on my way to my locker. In the middle of the dressing room, the replay of the game was up on the big screen. Maldano stood in front of it, naked as the day he was born, arms folded across his chest, studying the aftermath of the last-minute goal.

"You're such a fucking ice king," he mused. "Smash a winner and you walk off like it was nothing."

"You think I should've whipped my shirt off and got myself some tasty grass burn for the weekend?"

"I don't think anything. You just confuse me, man."

Try being in my head for a day. I punched Maldano's arm and left him to it, retreating to my locker to get dressed and finally—*finally*—get the fuck out of there to check my phone. I was heading back to Manchester the following day, and if I couldn't see Lucky before I went, I was pretty sure I'd die.

I was ten metres from the player's exit when Isha ruined my day.

"Dom. We need to talk."

Sighing, I kept walking. "Crack on, mate. But make it quick."

"Why?"

"Why what?"

"Why the hurry? You haven't got anywhere or anyone to rush off to, right?"

His tone stopped me in my tracks. I spun around to face him. "What's it to you?"

"Everything while I'm still your agent."

I scowled. Despite being so pissed off with Isha I could hardly stand to look at him, I'd done nothing to replace him, and he knew it. He also knew me well enough to be fairly certain that I wouldn't. That I couldn't risk cutting him loose when he held all the fucking cards. "What do you *want*?"

"I told you already. To talk."

"Fine." I shouldered my way through the player exit and turned towards the car park. "You've got five minutes."

We sat in my car like gangsters, lurking in a car park, hiding behind blacked-out windows. "Get on with it," I said. "What have you got to say that I haven't already heard?"

Isha gazed out of the front window, apparently miles away, even though it was his doing that we were here. "Not much, really. There's just some things I want you to know before you write me off as the kind of agent we both hate."

"Manipulative bastards who are only out for themselves?"

"Exactly." He finally looked at me. "That's not who I am, Dom. You know that."

I stubbornly refused to meet his gaze, like I could discount the decade of evidence in his favour—years and years I'd spent genuinely believing he had my best interests at heart. Still believed, to a certain degree, whether I wanted to or not, because what had really changed?

Perspective began to seep into my month-long sulk. Logic returned, and I turned over what Isha had actually done in my convoluted mind:

He knew I was queer and he never said anything.

He fed the press bullshit stories about me and random women.

The second one left a bad taste in my mouth, but the first was more complex. Yeah, he'd known I was queer all along and never said anything to *me*, but he hadn't told anyone else either. *Why would he, though? You being queer could fuck him as much as you.*

I was so fucking confused. My hands clenched around the steering wheel, and I banged my head on the textured leather.

"Dom—"

I groaned. "Stop. I don't want to hear it."

"You have to."

"Why?"

"Because I know more than you think."

I raised my head and speared him with a glare that usually made him wince, but he met my gaze dead on, and my heart knew what he was about to say before he said the words.

But he said them anyway. "I know about the bloke at the hotel."

"Dom, slow down." Isha gripped his seat as I swerved through city traffic. "Where are we even going?"

I didn't answer, because I had no idea. I just knew I couldn't sit in that damn fucking car park while Isha spouted shit about Lucky—that I had to do something with my hands to keep me from throttling him.

We hit a jam at some temporary lights. I cursed and rolled my window down to suck in some fresh air. Then thought better of it and closed it.

Isha stared like I'd lost my mind.

Perhaps he was right.

"How do you know?" I demanded. "Tell me everything."

"Where do you want me to start?"

"I don't care. Just tell me how you seem to know more about my life than I do."

"I have a mole."

"A what?"

"A mole."

For a split second, I thought he meant Lucky, and my entire world tipped on the edge of apocalypse, but Isha was tapping his phone, and when he held the screen up, the first puzzle piece was laid. *The Gazette.* Jesus Christ. "That sick fuck gossip columnist is your mole in my life?"

"Not just yours. And it wasn't my choice. When he left the *Mirror*, he hired PIs to follow players he suspected might have something to hide. You were on his list."

"Why?"

Isha shrugged. "The obvious terminal bachelor bullshit, I guess. Perhaps we'll never know. The point is, he rumbled you years ago—years I've spent putting out fires where I can, which wasn't too hard considering you've never given him much fuel, but it's different now, Dom. You've met someone, and he knows about it."

"You've met someone..." Even now, it sounded like someone else's life.

Traffic finally began moving. I let the car roll forward as I tried to keep up with the bullshit carousel my sexuality had set me on. "How much does he know?"

"Just that you have someone and your favourite hotel to meet up. At least, that's all he's coughing to right now. He might have a file on your fella for all I know."

If such a file existed, then a gossip columnist at a scummy tabloid probably knew more about Lucky than I did. I swallowed thickly as bile rose in my throat. "This can't get out—for his sake, more than mine."

"I was hoping you'd say that."

"Yeah, 'cause protecting your fucking face is top of my list."

"That's not what I meant."

"What *did* you mean?" I snapped.

Isha sighed. "I'm trying to say that I'm glad you've found someone, Dom. Do you think I've enjoyed seeing you so lonely all these years? Knowing you had no one to be your true self with? You might be angry with me for keeping this from you, but you have to believe I did it out of love, man. You're a brother to me."

Brother or not, his sentiment was the final nail in whatever dreams I'd dared imagine since Lucky had slipped into my life. Because it didn't matter how I felt about him. How my body sang for him when we were together, or how my heart hurt for him when we were apart. I had to protect him from this—from *me*.

After tonight, I could never see him again.

NINETEEN

Lucky

"Sorry, mate." The warden shrugged awkwardly. "We're working on getting it fixed, but it might not be till morning. You got somewhere you can go?"

I sighed, turning away from my kicked-in door. "Do you think I'd live in this shithole if I did?"

There wasn't much else the warden could say. He offered to take my valuables to the staff area for safekeeping overnight, but I didn't have any. My cash stash had long since dried up, and my wages went straight into the bank to pay my rent.

Seven-fifty a month for a door with a foot-shaped hole in it.

Fuck my life.

I didn't leave straight away. It was chucking it down outside and with Jamila's mum home for the night, I didn't fancy pounding the streets in the rain. Of course, I could've stayed in my room, slept with one eye on my open door, but I didn't fancy it. On the street I could run.

A shudder ran through me as I huddled on my bed with a cuppa from my last teabag—the kind of shudder that usually freaked me out enough to seek out a chemical way to calm down, but I'd been so good lately. Hadn't even smoked a joint in the last few days. So I settled for patching into the centre's sketchy Wi-Fi and watching clips of Dom's latest game on YouTube, ignoring the fact that football was a trigger for some fucked-up anxiety I'd carried most of my life.

Perving over Dom on his own turf was a pretty solid distraction, though. Despite knowing he was desperately unhappy, I got kicks out of his tight football shirt, shorts, and muscular legs. And how he got rowdy on the pitch. He was a moody player—shouted a lot, pushed people over—which oddly suited him, though it contrasted with the artful way he fucked me.

Arousal flooded my veins as I recalled both times he'd been inside me the last time we'd seen each other. The first when he'd taken me by surprise with how *amazing* he was, how skilled, intuitive, and totally fucking deadly, and then the second when he'd let me climb all over him, and we'd both fooled ourselves for a while that I had the upper hand.

My cock thickened as I relived every moment, right up to when he'd confessed to kissing no man his whole life until me, but the prospect of wanking off with my door busted open cooled my blood, reminding me that I needed to get out of Dodge before dark.

With heavy legs, I left the centre and habitually meandered in the general direction of work. It was too late to sneak in for the night, but me and the new dude, Cash, had a thing going on. If I brought biscuits, he'd let me in by six, and not tell Jim.

I checked the time, then wished I hadn't.

The rain followed me all the way to Tottenham. There was a sheltered bin yard round the back of the garage, but it was lit up by security lights, so I settled in a doorway round the back of a greasy spoon that didn't open on Sundays. If I angled myself just right—squeezed flat against the door—only my feet got wet.

I could live with that.

Used to the rhythm of the street, sleep came easy; though it was nothing like the precious few hours I'd snatched in Dom's arms. And

I dreamed of him too—of him naked and rolling around that pristine white bed, of him kissing me, holding me, owning me.

Of him smiling.

He was on my mind the moment I woke up to clear skies, and apparently I'd been on his mind too.

Perignon55: *need to see u tonight*

That night I moaned savagely and clawed at the pillow that muffled my cries, arching my body to take Dom deeper. "Jesus, Dom. Harder."

He obliged, and his thick cock found my sweet spot as his hand pushed down on the back of my neck. I shoved a hand beneath me and squeezed my dick, but there was no need, 'cause I was already coming like a train.

"*Fuck.*" Dom's thrusts turned frantic, his hands roaming my body more urgently. He drove into me harder and faster, until he came with a ragged yell.

He collapsed on top of me, his chest slumped against my back, smothering me for a blissful moment before he rolled away, but I didn't move. Couldn't. He'd been on me the moment I'd entered the room in the strange new hotel on the other side of the city. Lying in wait, like the best kind of surprise. My back had hit the closed door, my bag slipping from my hand, and it was a blur after that—a haze of fierce kisses, stripped clothes, and tumbling to the bed—and now I was so fucking done, I didn't know which way was up.

"Lucky?"

Nope. Whatever he wanted that didn't involve staying right here, I wasn't interested.

"*Lucky.*"

I groaned and lifted my head a fraction. "What?"

Dom gazed back at me, his expression not matching what had just played out. Alarmed, I sat up slowly and scooted back against the headboard, wrapping my arms around my knees. "What's the matter?"

"Nothing."

"Right." I eyed Dom as he paced around, making a meal out of chucking the condom in the bin. The way his hands jittered and his eyes darted around, if I hadn't known better I'd have wondered if he was twitching for something. "You gonna come back to bed, or what?"

Or what seemed a more likely possibility the longer he stared at me like I'd grown horns, and then something seemed to visibly give way inside him and he staggered across the room.

He didn't say anything as we slid under the covers, just pulled me close, and hid his face in my hair. After a while, I wondered if he'd fallen asleep, but there was a jagged edge to his breathing that said otherwise.

I disentangled myself from him and leaned back so I could see him. His gaze was fixed somewhere behind me. I touched his face, cupped his strong jaw, and scratched the five-o'clock shadow peeking through his skin. He met my eyes and smiled slightly. I returned it and kissed his cheek, rubbing my face against his, nuzzling. "There you go," I whispered. "Relax, baby. I've got you."

He made a sound low in his throat, but didn't protest as I drew him into my arms and reversed our positions. I took advantage and ran my hands through his silky hair and over his corded shoulders. Damn, he was so fucking fine. How did my life lurch from ludicrous to glorious with such totality? *I couldn't make this shit up.*

Bit by bit, Dom relaxed against me, though the thrum of tension in him didn't entirely fade. I stroked his skin and rubbed his muscle, and chattered nonsense at him until my words found more purpose, and he finally looked at me with something more than sex-addled despair.

"What?" he said.

I repeated myself, but his incredulity remained.

"*You* played football?"

I chuckled and pulled the duvet higher; tucking it around him, like I could shield him with cotton and feathers from whatever was frightening him so much. "Playing is a bit strong, but I was on a local team for years. My dad was the manager." Dom's eyes flashed, but I ploughed on, even though talking about this shit was my idea of hell. "My brother played too, but he was a different son—a better one—I already told you what kind of man my dad is, right?"

"You mentioned him."

"Yeah, well. Let's just say me trying to play football pretty much tipped him over the edge, which was fucking ironic, 'cause he was the arsehole who forced me into it."

"What happened?"

"You mean the final straw that ruined our father–son bond?"

Dom shrugged. "I'm listening to whatever you want to tell me."

I'm listening too. Talk to me. "It was a friendly match with our sister team in Hove—which was the only reason I was playing, to be honest. He always benched me for games that mattered, and I was glad of it. Skinny and pale, I was a bit of a target, you know?"

"I can imagine."

Of course he could, but true to form, Dom gave nothing away. Just rubbed his cheek on my chest before looking up again, waiting for me to go on.

So I did. "My dad had a real thing about me embarrassing him, and I knew it, which seemed to make things worse. The harder I tried, the more I messed up, and I *really* messed up this game. Fell over, cried, even scored an own goal. He went ballistic at half-time, threw a boot at me—*his* boot, I think." Reflex had me running a finger along the scar splitting my eyebrow. "It hit me in the face."

"Bastard," Dom growled darkly. He batted my hand away and replaced it with his own. "How old were you?"

"Nine or ten, maybe? I can't remember." Lies. I remembered it all, down to what I'd had for dinner that night, alone in my room, blood dripping from my face and into the soup my mum had left outside my door. "Anyway, it was actually the last time he ever hit me, but he didn't need to after that. I was terrified of him, until—"

"Until what?"

I shrugged. "Until I wasn't. It was weird...I knew he could still really hurt me if he wanted to, but I just didn't care. I felt indestructible for a while."

"Then what happened?"

"I guess I went off the rails a bit. I came home off my nut one night when I was about fifteen and flipped. He wound me up, so I hit him. It was pretty dramatic, if you like soap operas—Old Bill everywhere, neighbours out on the street, and my brother trying to kill me. I ran away in the end."

"Did you ever go back?"

"No."

Dom nodded slowly, clearly absorbing the extended version of a story I'd halfway told him before. I bit my lip and waited, hoping, perhaps even expecting he would reciprocate.

But he didn't. He sat up and reached for his jeans. "I have to go."

"Go?"

"Yeah."

He stood and began dressing in jerky movements. I scrambled to the edge of the bed and reached for him, but he evaded. "Dom, look at me."

"No, I can't, Lucky. I can't—"

"Can't *what*?"

Dom bent to retrieve his damn fucking hat from the floor and jammed it on his head before he met my gaze with the dead eyes I'd long forgotten. "I can't be here."

"What do you mean?"

"What I said."

Dom stamped into his shoes and started for the door.

I lurched after him, tripping over the bed sheets, and caught his arm. "Dom, stop. Talk to me, please? Or don't—we can just fuck if you want...we don't have to talk—"

"It's not about that!" Dom shouted, wrenching his arm free. He glared at me for a heated moment, but then his expression shattered, and he shook his head. "Please. Let me go, okay? I can't explain, I just—"

"Just *what*?"

"Lucky, I…I can't see you anymore."

TWENTY

Dom

I'd broken bones, cracked my kneecap, and torn every ligament in my legs that I could spell, but nothing had ever hurt like leaving Lucky in that Edgeware Road hotel room.

The confusion clouding his lovely eyes haunted me—awake, asleep, always. I couldn't take a breath without thinking about him. I told myself over and over that I'd had no choice—that his life would be as fucked up as mine if the press got hold of his name—but the devil on my shoulder called me a coward. It was *Lucky* who'd had no choice.

The morning after I left him, I drove to Manchester. Isha came with me under the pretence of meeting with Micah, but I knew he wanted to talk to me—wanted *me* to talk to *him*. And lacking any better ideas, I did. We had no secrets anymore.

"How'd he take it?" he asked when I was done with my nausea-inducing recap.

I changed lanes on the motorway to avoid looking at Isha. "Dunno. I kinda left him hanging."

"Why?"

"Why do you think? It wasn't like I could give him a proper explanation, was it? If I could explain this shit to *anyone* I wouldn't be in this mess."

"How did you meet him, anyway?"

I shot Isha a dark look. "I'm not telling you that."

"Why not?"

"It's none of your damn business."

He shut up for a while. I focussed on the road, but the silence left me space to think—too much space—and my mind moved from the present to the past. "Can I ask you something?"

"Of course." Isha sat up a little and put his hand on the car door, like he was worried I was about to pull over and kick him out.

"How did you figure out I was queer? It can't have just been the bachelor thing. I don't tell you everything, so I could've had a bird for all you knew."

Isha snorted, but sobered when he looked at me. "Honestly?"

"You think I can handle more bullshit?"

"Okay, okay. If you must know, I found a porn mag in one of your academy bedrooms years ago. You weren't the type to play pranks on the other lads, so I knew it must be yours."

"What the fuck were you doing in my room?"

"Checking for drugs. It's not something I'd do now, but you were seventeen when I signed you, and ridiculously strong for how lanky you were. I kept a special eye on you for a while."

"You creepy fucking bastard."

"If you say so." Isha turned his gaze to the window. "At the time, like now, I was just trying to look after you. Most lads come up through the clubs with their dads, or uncles...you didn't have that."

"I didn't want it."

"Doesn't mean you didn't need it. Damn it, Dom, you shut everyone out."

Not everyone. But I didn't say it. What was the point? How I felt about Lucky was irrelevant now...right?

"You missed the exit."

I scowled at Isha. "You fucking drive then."

Hitting the training ground was a relief. For hours, I slammed balls back and forth, tackled players with far more prestige than me to the ground, and then I hit the gym, running inclines on the treadmill in a vain attempt to keep my mind occupied.

It was futile, though. Pounding treadmills was dull as rocks regardless of how much it burned my calves, and my thoughts returned to my disastrous private life anyway. And *fuck* if it wasn't a damn shit show. No one seemed to know about my early encounters with Lucky, but we'd been photographed leaving the same hotel twice—Lucky with wet hair—and in the pub when I'd found him half-asleep on a bench in Tottenham. I hadn't seen the pictures, but Isha had, and even though they proved nothing, they proved everything, because the stalker tabloid hack's assumptions were true. I couldn't explain without lying, and lying meant taking a risk with Lucky's identity. If the columnist didn't get what he wanted from me, there was nothing stopping him going after Lucky. Hounding him. Exposing him.

I couldn't put him through that. Couldn't see his face splashed across the red-top paper when it should've been mine alone.

"Covering this up is going to take money—a lot of it," Isha had said.

Shamefully, I'd agreed, and for the first time found myself thankful that Isha had spent years planting stories and burying suspicions to cover for me. My worst nightmare was old hat to him.

"What's to stop him holding the photos and extorting more and more money from me?"

"Nothing, in theory," Isha had said. *"But at this stage he's not even asking for money—we're offering it to keep him quiet, and if he takes it, he's as fucked as you."*

"And if he doesn't?"

"You're fucked anyway."

I got off the treadmill with shaky legs that had nothing to do with running on incline twelve for thirty minutes, and staggered to the deserted dressing rooms. Fear had been my constant companion for years, but until Lucky I'd always managed to keep it at a distant simmer. Now, it roiled in my ears every moment I wasn't on the pitch, and my nerves were frazzled wire, just one short circuit away from total meltdown.

"Dom?"

I jumped a fucking mile, and whirled around to find Micah behind me, lips turned up in a hesitant grin. "What?"

"Um...I was just gonna ask if you wanted to come out."

"Piss off, mate. I'm too old for that shit."

Micah rolled his eyes. "Not *out* out. I meant for dinner. I was gonna eat with Isha, but he's fucked off back to London."

"Why?"

"Dunno. He didn't say."

Paranoia tickled my sanity. Isha had other clients besides me, and a whole life outside the murky world of football, but the notion that something had happened to add to my mess made me dizzy.

I sat on the bench by my borrowed locker. *Fuck.* What if the PIs had found Lucky after all? Or if they'd been trailing him all along? What if someone was on Lucky's doorstep right now?

"What if he sells you out?" Isha had said. *"It's bullshit right now, but if they got him to corroborate, it'd be huge. Like, globally huge."*

I hadn't answered Isha at the time, had pushed the question aside without considering an answer, but I considered it now. It was easy to trust Lucky when we were together—sleeping, fucking, flicking fried food at each other—but away from the spell he cast on me whenever he was near, doubt oozed through my gut and surrounded my heart like creeping black vines. I knew shamefully little about Lucky, but I hadn't missed the fact that he'd been on his arse financially. That he needed whatever money a stranger might offer him to fuck over a bloke who'd hurt him.

Because I *had* hurt Lucky. He had eyes that didn't lie.

Micah sat beside me. "Don't punch me or anything, but are you okay?"

"What do you care?"

"Mates, ain't we?"

"Are we?"

Micah frowned. "Thought so. Wouldn't be asking you out for dinner if we weren't. Besides, Maldano is my cousin, so we're basically family."

I'd forgotten that. Distant memories of Maldano talking up his precocious young relative filtered back to me, and the fact that they were the only two bozos in football I actually liked suddenly made sense. "Sorry, dude. I'm tired."

"What the fuck are you doing rinsing the gym then? Haven't you got a big derby coming up?"

I hummed absently. The biggest domestic game of the season was right around the corner, and match days against our closest rival were always huge, but I hadn't paid much attention to the fixture calendar of late. Hadn't paid much attention to anything except my own selfish wants and needs.

Micah nudged me. "You coming for food, or what? There's a Mexican place round the corner. We could grab some fajitas and take them home."

Home. If only. But right now even heading back to London filled me with dread. Manchester was hardly the other side of the world, but with Isha gone, was it far away enough to pretend my life wasn't slowly falling to bits? That each day didn't make me hate myself a little bit more?

I sighed heavily and recalled how easy Micah's company had been last time we'd gone out. *Fuck it.* I nudged him back. "Let's go."

Lucky

"I can't believe this shit." I paced around Jamila's tiny bedroom, barefoot, and angry, kicking anything that got in my way.

"Calm down," she snapped. "If you break my stuff, I'll break you."

I spared her a glare, but wilted under hers. She was far fiercer than me, always had been.

"Sorry." I flopped down on the end of her bed. "I'm just pissed off. How does he get to carry on like nothing's happened when I want to claw my fucking eyes out every time I see his face?"

"Um...maybe because he can't see your face? And it's not his fault you're cyber-stalking him."

"I'm not stalking him."

"Right. Because you always read the Daily Fail." Jamila held up my phone, lit up with the open news app I couldn't seem to stop reading. "Besides, the article isn't even about him. He was just there."

"Yeah. *There*, having dinner with some hot black guy."

Jamila laughed. "Oh, you think that's what's going on, do you? That he's suddenly out of the closet and dating Micah Roberts? Get real, Lucky. He's a footballer—he's going to be seen with other footballers, and the bloke's gotta eat."

She was right, and I knew it, but irrational jealously burned in my gut anyway. *I* wanted to have dinner with Dom, huddled up in a big white bed, naked, telly on for background noise. Then I wanted him to fuck me, to *love* me, and the real world to piss right off.

A week had passed since he'd walked out on me and I thought of him constantly, letting my imagination take me far beyond the clutch of encounters our relationship actually comprised of. I pictured what life would be like if we were a normal couple: him without his closeted superstar status, and me with—well, anything would be a start. Not much changed from the eating and fucking we'd already done, but there was more of it, and it meant something. It meant *everything*. I'd spent the last few years convincing myself I didn't need anyone, that I didn't *want* anyone except Jamila in my life, because she was the only one who'd never let me down. But my outlook had changed when I'd met Dom. From that very first moment, he'd filled a void my heart had cried out for. And now he was gone that void was raw and open again.

I missed him so much.

"Have you heard from him at all?" Jamila asked gently. "Has he texted?"

"Course he hasn't. And I knew he wouldn't. You should've seen his face, J. It was so out of the blue, but so final, you know? He walked out of that room and he didn't look back."

I rubbed my chest, like I could cram the hurt back in.

Jamila shuffled down the bed to lie beside me. "I'm sorry, baby, but maybe it's for the best. I mean, what future did you have anyway? Even if this hadn't happened, it's not like he could ever be with you in the open, and perhaps he didn't even want to. He's lived his whole life in the closet...he doesn't know anything else."

"I never said I wanted him to *be* with me. I wasn't asking him for fucking marriage."

"So what did you ask him for?"

"Nothing."

"Uh-huh." Jamila took my hand. "And it was still too much for him."

I left Jamila's before she went to bed. She wanted me to stay, like I had done most nights since I'd last seen Dom, but I was done relying on her to patch me up when shit went wrong. Besides, avoiding my place didn't make it better. I had to go back eventually and too long between visits made the reality harder to bear.

As ever, Dom was on my mind as I walked home. Jamila had admitted to liking the Dom she'd met when he'd returned my phone, but the more I'd moped around her flat, the more that had faded. By the time I'd left, she seemed to be convinced he was a dickhead rich queer who'd fucked me for kicks.

I knew different. I had to, or the pain in my chest meant nothing, and I was the fucking fool. *And she doesn't know the full story, remember?* But I got the feeling I didn't either, and turning it over and over in my scattered brain was driving me crazy. *Please make it stop.*

Down the road from the halfway house was a bench I often sat on when I couldn't quite be bothered to go all the way home. I slumped onto it now and swiped at my phone screen until I found Grindr.

I hadn't looked at the app in ages. There'd been no need when Dom was just a text away, and I hadn't been in the market to hook up with anyone else.

Had he, though? A week ago I'd have sworn blind he wasn't, but the distance between us now was fucking with my head. The Dom I thought I knew was fading, leaving in his place the arsehole who'd left me naked and alone in a hotel room.

With shaking fingers, I opened the app and searched the grid for his profile—or any profile that could've been him. There were many possibles, the world was full of closeted blokes whose only escape was murky Grindrland, but none of them *felt* like Dom, and his original profile was still gone.

What if he's ghosted me and picked up someone else?

The notion taunted me, and my hand slid of its own volition into my coat pocket. I fingered the tiny plastic bag and then slowly drew it out, turning it over in my hands. The wrap of drone inside called to me, but I didn't need a hit of that right now—I needed to sleep, long and hard, and forget about everything, just for a few hours.

I opened the bag and dug out one of the Valium I'd scored on my way home from work. I hadn't intended to drop them until the weekend, but *fuck* I needed a break from my head, especially now I'd left Jamila. Sleeping alone had always been rough. The warmth of someone else grounded me, soothed me, and only drugs had ever been a fair substitute.

Screw it. I swallowed a pill and pocketed the bag. Then I went back to staring at my phone. I hadn't been on WhatsApp since I'd last seen Dom either, and I avoided it now, opening the regular message app instead so I'd never know if he'd consciously ignored me.

I tapped out a message.

Lucky: *i miss u*

Dom didn't reply.

TWENTY-ONE

Dom

Lucky: *i miss u*

My thumb hovered over the delete button, but in the thirty-six hours since Lucky had sent it, I hadn't managed to erase it. Keeping it was madness—newspapers hacked phones all the time—but reading it every ten minutes was the only thing keeping me sane. *Fuck, Lucky. I miss you too.*

"Are you even listening to me?"

I put my phone face down on the table and spared Isha a glance. He'd called a crisis meeting at my apartment to deal with the tabloid hack all up in my business, but with my thoughts dangerously obsessed with Lucky, I was finding it hard to focus. "Sorry, what?"

"I was saying that any payment you make will actually give you some insurance. If this ever comes out, he's guilty of blackmail, and you were just trying to protect yourself."

"But he never asked for money."

"No, but you can say he did, if anyone ever asks."

More lies. Bile rose in my throat and I found my gaze fixed on Constance as she bustled around my kitchen. Isha had wanted me to send her home, but I was fresh out of fucks. If she turned out to be the one who betrayed me then the whole world was screwed. "I need to think about it."

Isha shrugged and closed his laptop. "Fair enough. I can probably blag that you're caught up in training for the derby, but after that... damn. Look, I know it's awful, but you've got to move forward with this. Shut it down and move on."

"Move on with what? Being celibate until I retire and then spending the rest of my life dealing with this fucking circus anyway?"

I spoke to myself as much as Isha, but his eyebrows rose ridiculous amounts. "Dom, if there's another way you want to handle this, then I'm listening, but we can't ignore it, okay? We need to utilise what little control we have left."

We. I wanted to punch him in the face, even though none of this was his fault. Without him, I'd have no lead to the faceless dude who apparently wanted to ruin my life. No way to stop the avalanche barrelling down the mountain. But I still resented him for making this shit real. For bursting my Lucky bubble. It was hard to accept that it would've burst eventually on its own, because even without what was happening right now...I didn't even know his real name.

A bone-scraping sigh escaped me. "I don't have a better plan, but I'm not ready to pay someone not to fuck me over, either. Ask me tomorrow."

We'd opened our pre-match planning sessions to a bunch of injured military men once upon a time. They'd likened it to a special forces sit in, and I could believe it, though I didn't reckon the SAS paid eight quid for half-litre bottles of water.

Fernando went in hard, outlining his game plan in minute detail. In the past, I'd have taken notes, but I zoned out as he droned on, not thinking about anything in particular, just...lost.

Maldano kicked me under the table. "You okay?"

I answered his mouthed question with a listless nod. He didn't seem convinced, but I didn't care. We'd been trapped in the conference room for hours, and claustrophobia was starting to eat into my apathy.

"Dom."

I blinked. Fernando was staring right at me. "What?"

Fernando narrowed his eyes. "If you'd like to pay attention, I was pointing out that the norovirus outbreak has already left us five bodies down, and that's just players. It's in double figures if we count coaching staff. With that in mind, when we finish here, single guys you can go home and stay there until you come in tomorrow. Anyone with families, I want you to stay in the team hotel overnight—stay away from the bugs your kids bring home from school."

"What's the point in that if half the team already have it?"

Fernando intensified his glare. "The outbreak started in the local schools. We're just taking precautions."

I rolled my eyes. No player had kids at the local schools—they were all shipped out to poncy private academies, even the toddlers. Not that money could keep germs out, of course, any more than locking us all up. Still, at least I was one of the lucky—*ha*—ones who got to go home.

The meeting broke up, and I booked it to the exit. In my car, I left my phone turned off in the glove box. I hadn't replied to Lucky's message, and I knew him well enough to figure he wouldn't text again. Harassment wasn't his style, and I didn't deserve it anyway. Nor did I have the energy to deal with Isha's hourly reminders that I had other bullshit to deal with.

I drove home, glared at the out-of-service lifts, and hauled myself upstairs to my apartment. There'd been no physical training that day, but I felt like I'd gone ten rounds in the penalty box at Millwall.

In my kitchen, I discovered a covered dish of Nigerian pottage that Constance had left me, something she often did if she got wind of a big game approaching. It usually didn't touch the sides, but despite knowing my body needed fuel for the following day, I stuck it in the fridge without touching it. Food could wait. For now, I only had energy to brood.

I retreated to my bedroom and stripped my clothes. Then I flopped naked into bed and buried my head under the pillow. *Metaphor, much?* Probably, but I had a headache and the blackness suited my mood.

Despite my fatigue, though, I didn't sleep, and there was an itch in my bones I couldn't describe. A burn in my veins that kept me awake. After what seemed like hours of tossing and turning, I sat up, and turned my phone on.

Isha's messages flashed up on the screen. I hit delete without reading them, but my phone buzzed in my hand before I could toss it aside again, and my heart skipped a beat.

It wasn't Lucky...but it was the closest thing.

Unknown: *This is Jamila. Call me*

"You don't understand," Jamila snapped. "You don't know him like I do. He can't cope when things get hard, and he finds ways to get by—ways that get him in even more trouble."

The implication lacing her words wasn't lost on me, but I needed more than vague catastrophes. "Explain. I can't help you if you're not clear what the problem is."

Jamila's sigh rattled down the phone, conflict raging in every breath she'd taken since she'd admitted to lifting my number from Lucky's phone before she'd given it back to him. "I can't be the one to tell you these things, but I'm so worried about him. He's stopped going home, and that means he's out there somewhere on his own."

"Out *where?*"

"On the street. Dom, Lucky was homeless when he met you. He's only recently got a place, but it's horrible...dangerous, and he hates it. It doesn't take much to persuade him to take his chances outside instead."

Horror gut-punched me. Guilt merged with shock in a nauseating rush as pieces of an awful puzzle began to slot into place. Lucky's dishevelled appearance, marks on his arms I'd chosen to ignore. That he never went anywhere without his bag, and he was always, *always* hungry. "I-I thought he had a job."

"He does, but it's an apprenticeship that pays two hundred a week. Where's he supposed to live in this city for that?"

I had no idea. Ground staff at the club earned that in a day, and the players? Fucking hell. "When did you last see him?"

"A week ago. He was upset about you, but he told me he was going home. I let him be for a few days, but then I went by his work and he wasn't there either. They said he was on study leave or something for an assessment he has to take."

"So maybe he's studying."

"But *where*, Dom? The only places he feels safe are the garage and my place, and he hasn't been to either. He's turned the tracker off on his phone, and when I went by his place, the warden said he hadn't seen him in days."

"Have you called him?"

"Do you think I'm fucking stupid?" Jamila's voice rose. "Of course I called him, dozens of times, but he didn't answer, and he hasn't been online either. I'm worried his phone's been nicked—that he's been hurt, or—"

"I get it." It was my turn to snap as I faced up to what she was saying—that Lucky was more vulnerable than I'd ever imagined, and that he *needed* us, and he needed us now. "Listen, I'm going to call him now, okay? If I can't reach him, then I'll come and get you, and we'll look for him together."

"I don't know where to start," Jamila whispered, the fight in her gone.

"Neither do I, but we'll find him. I promise."

My promises meant nothing as Jamila and I circled the neighbourhoods she knew he'd slept out in before. When my eyes weren't scouring every shop doorway and alley they were trained on the temperature reading on my dashboard. It was dropping every ten minutes. "He's going to freeze if he's out here."

Jamila kept her gaze on the window, scanning the Tottenham pavements. "He's slept out in worse."

"That doesn't make it any warmer now."

"So buy him a fucking coat," she snarled.

"I–"

"Sorry, I shouldn't have said that."

"It's okay."

"No, it's really not. He wouldn't have let you do that even if you'd known how badly he needed one. He hates it when I buy him stuff. He even smuggles cash into my mum's purse when he stays with us—like she has any idea he's been there."

I turned down a side street, recalling what Lucky had told me about the blurred lines in his relationship with Jamila. I expected jealousy, but none came. How could it when it was clear she loved him so much? "I bought him dinner a few times; I could tell he didn't like it, though."

"Yeah. He only caves when he's hungry. I think he lives on cereal most of the time—fuck, stop the car."

I slammed my foot on the brake, jolting us both forward. "What is it?"

"There." Jamila pointed. "Come on."

I killed the engine and threw myself out of the car, trailing Jamila as she hurried down a dingy alley. At the bottom was a heap of cardboard boxes, and a tatty grey bag. *God, no. Please no.*

Jamila was two steps ahead of me, but I caught her easily and pushed past her. My trainers crunched on broken glass as I reached the boxes and crouched down, my breath misting the freezing air. I pushed the boxes away and brushed back a tangle of sandy-brown hair. "Lucky?"

TWENTY-TWO

Dom

"We'll take him to my place," I said. "Get in the car."

But Jamila was already backing away, shaking her head. "He doesn't want me."

"What?"

"He *doesn't*," she said. "If he thought I could help him he'd have come to me in the first place. Take him home, Dom. He needs you right now."

She ran off, disappearing into the night. I watched her go, but the urge to chase her down was drowned out by the slender figure passed out in the back of my car. I swallowed convulsively and opened the car door, slipping in beside Lucky, and trying not to recoil from his icy-cold skin. "Jesus, Lucky. What happened to you?"

A shiver was his only answer, and the pressing need to get him warm—*safe* and warm—overrode the mess of emotions surging through me.

I took my coat off and draped it over him, and then I clambered into the driver's seat and cranked up the heat. We were an hour from my Greenwich apartment—and taking him there was more risky than checking into an anonymous hotel—but Lucky was a mess. Getting caught at my place was bad enough, but stumbling around a hotel lobby with Lucky off his nut?

Fuck that shit.

I drove home, giving myself whiplash with the number of times I turned around to check he was still breathing. At my building, I parked in the underground car park, praying they'd fixed the lifts in the few hours I'd been gone, and for once being a rich prick in a rich-prick's apartment block paid off.

Lucky didn't weigh much, and I half-carried him inside, thankful the reason I'd chosen to live here was that the other residents were mainly foreign businessmen who wouldn't care if I slit someone's throat in the stairwell. In the lift, Lucky slumped against me, eyes closed, and I wondered if he was aware he was moving. That he was no longer in the cardboard shelter he'd built himself in a grimy Tottenham alleyway.

If he even cared. My horrified exchange with Jamila when we'd found him haunted me, and what could've happened if she hadn't called me? Fuck.

"Jesus, I think he's dead."

"Nah, he's just wasted," Jamila had said. *"He pops Valium when he's out here sometimes...when he's stopped caring what happens to him."*

I got Lucky into my apartment and double locked the door behind me while he slid to the floor. Lacking any brighter ideas, I left him there, and hurried to the bathroom. The walk-in shower would've been easier to manoeuvre him into, but my heart drove me to the freestanding bath I'd never used. I turned the taps on and threw in some scented salt that had come with the apartment.

Back in the hallway, Lucky was stirring. I crouched in front of him, my hands on his knees. "Lucky?"

He groaned, his head lolling so loosely he looked like a cartoon.

I tried again to rouse him. "Come on, mate. Wake up. I've got a bath ready for you."

Even with his eyes closed, confusion coloured his features. He shook his head and brought his knees to his chest, wrapping his arms around himself.

I touched his hand—still cold, despite an hour in the sauna I'd turned my car into. "Look at me."

"No."

The whispered word was muffled by his knees, but I heard it like he'd shouted it in my ear. Fear stampeded through my soul as I considered two possibilities: one, that he was so fucked up he needed medical help; and the other, that I'd hurt him so much he'd rather be on the street than anywhere near me.

A desperate sob built in my chest. I hadn't cried since my father's funeral in Rio Tinto a decade ago, and even then my tears hadn't hurt as much as they should've. But the pain in my heart now was something I couldn't describe. I dropped my head, resting it on his damp denim-clad knee. "Lucky, *please.*"

For a lifetime, he didn't respond. The silence was so loud I forced myself to look at him again, and slowly—so fucking slowly—he raised his head too. One eye slid open, and then two, and his woozy azure-blue gaze fixed on me. "Dom? Is it really you?"

Lucky

Hot water had always been my jam, but even with Dom pouring it over my shoulders, I couldn't get warm. I shivered, teeth chattering, until he cursed and hauled me out of the tub like a rag doll.

He carried me to a bed and dried me with a towel that smelled like him. "Where are we?"

"My place."

I tried to process that, but my brain was liquid Valium. My chin dropped to my chest, and it was only him manhandling me again that kept me conscious.

He moved me to the middle of the bed and propped me up

against a thousand pillows. "Stay there. I'm going to get you some food."

Panic overrode the chemical tranquillity pulling me under. "Don't go."

"The kitchen's ten feet away, Lucky. I'll be back."

He kissed my forehead, and then he was gone. I shuddered again and my sluggish gaze scanned the unfamiliar room. With the big bed, huge TV, and funky furniture, it was a larger, sleeker version of our bolthole hotel room—luxurious, but utterly meaningless without Dom in it.

I brought a hand to my bare chest, inhaled a shallow breath, and tried to join the scattered dots in my memory. If Dom wasn't the cruellest hallucination known to man, then somehow I'd found my way from my favourite bench in Tottenham to wherever he lived, all under the power of the extra Valium I'd known was a bonehead idea. That it might kill me if the cold didn't. I rubbed my arms, fighting the clouds I wasn't sure were born of apathy or drugs—

Drugs. Fuck. I scanned the room, but I was naked in Dom's bed with my clothes—and the contents of my pockets—who-the-hell-knew where. Dom didn't seem the type to go through my stuff, but if he did, chances were I'd find myself back on the street.

I swung my legs off the bed and planted my feet on the floor. My knees wobbled and I cursed my stupidity. Two Valium had always been enough to knock me out. *Why the fuck did you take three?*

"Need something?"

My head jolted up like a drunken giraffe. Dom was in the doorway, a mug in one hand, and my little bag of sin in the other. "Where did you find those?"

"On my bathroom floor." Dom ventured closer and sat on the edge of the bed. "They must've fallen out of your jeans when I picked them up to wash them."

"Don't wash my clothes. I'm not a fucking child."

"I know. I was just washing my own, so why the fuck not?"

"You don't wash your own clothes."

"Says who?"

"Says everything about this damn castle if it really is your house."

Dom set the mug down on the bedside table. "It's an apartment, actually, and yeah...I do live here, cleaning lady and all, but she doesn't do my washing. Now you gonna tell me what the fuck this shit is?"

"Why do you want to know?" I hated the slur in my voice.

I hated the guarded look in Dom's eyes even more.

"'Cause it's in my place," he said. "And I'd like to know what I'm about to flush down my toilet, unless you want to take it with you now and leave."

"Do you want me to go?"

"No."

"I..." I ran out of words—like, literally. My brain stopped working and everything was blank. I stared at Dom, he stared right back, and nothing happened. A buried-deep part of me wanted to snatch the bag and boot it out of Dom's swanky apartment, out of his life, like he'd apparently *wanted* more than a week ago, but the part of me that was cold to the bone and so fucking relieved to see him stayed put. "If I tell you what they are, will you throw them away?"

"Yes."

"It's drone and Valium."

"The fuck is drone?"

"Mephedrone."

Dom shook his head. "I have no idea what that is."

"That isn't a bad thing, but can you flush it...please? I can't look at it."

Dom got up and left the room. A toilet flushed and he came back with empty hands and an unreadable frown.

My heart sank. "Do you want me to go?"

"*No*, I already told you." He reclaimed his place on the edge of the bed and put his arm around me. "I do want to know why you had them, but more than that, I want you to be okay. I don't care about anything else right now."

I wanted to fall against him and absorb the affection he was offering. I wanted to find strength in my Valium-addled legs and walk out on him like he'd walked out on me.

I wanted the cup of tea he'd placed in front of me.

I wanted him to take his coat off.

"Lucky," Dom whispered. "Nothing matters to me more than you being safe and well. Just believe me, please?"

I woke with a jump, expecting the scratchy blanket of my rented room, and then, when it wasn't there, the chill of a frosty morning. Or a damp one. Basically, anything but the sweetly scented sheets, and the solid warm body curved around me from behind.

Out of habit, I panicked, and scrabbled to escape the strong arms wound around my waist. They let me go, and I pretty much fell out of the bed before Dom caught me.

"Fuck. Sorry. I forgot where I was."

"It's okay." Dom tugged me back to safety. "I wasn't sure if you'd remember."

"Remember what?"

"Anything. You were pretty out of it when we found you."

"We?"

"Jamila asked me to help her look for you."

Coherent thought returned to me in a rush of horrifying images. I had no idea how the fuck I'd wound up in a bedroom I was fairly sure was Dom's, but the idea of him and Jamila joining forces to scrape my sorry benzoed arse off the street was fucking horrific. "I'm sorry."

"What for? Putting her through hell or what you've done to yourself?"

I turned my head slowly to face him. "Are you seriously fucking judging me?"

"No. I'm trying to figure out how you got here."

"Literally? 'Cause if you work it out, I wouldn't mind knowing."

"I drove you here, Lucky. And this is my place, in case you've forgotten that too."

"I haven't...I remember you getting me out of the bath, making me tea, and feeding me some weird bean shit."

"Pottage," Dom supplied. "My housekeeper leaves it in my fridge from time to time. Reckons it has magical powers, and I pretty much believe her now. I thought you were dead when we found you—your lips were blue."

I cringed. "Stop. I'm sorry, okay? Please don't tell me anything else about it, though. I can't—I can't handle knowing you saw me like that."

"Why?"

"Because it was never part of whatever game we were playing. You don't know me, Dom. And I don't want you to."

Dom shifted away from me, and I mourned his warmth pressed against me, but the distance seemed far more real than the embrace I'd woken up in.

A heavy sigh escaped me. "I should go."

"Go where? It's five o'clock in the morning."

"So?"

"So..." Dom rolled onto his back and stared at the ceiling. "You're right—I don't know you—but I know you don't have a safe place to go at night, so I'm asking you to stay here...at least till it's light."

"Why?"

Dom blew out a frustrated sigh of his own. "Is that what we're doing now? Questioning every statement until we can't make anything right?"

"Does it matter? You were the one who bailed, and I was messed up long before I met you anyway. That isn't gonna change when I leave." My heart told me I was being unfair to him. That I had no idea what had driven him to call time on our...arrangement, but I was angry, dammit—embarrassed—and I was always the dickhead who came out swinging. "I really should go."

I started to climb out of bed before I remembered I was bollock-naked. "Where are my clothes?"

"In the wash. You can have some of mine if you're that desperate to leave."

His flat tone irritated me. "Have you got anything that didn't cost more than I earn in a month?"

"Your turn to judge me, is it?" Dom got out of bed, revealing that I was the only naked idiot, but he didn't wait for me to respond before yanking open a drawer and chucking a perfectly folded hoodie at me. Sweatpants followed, and then he stormed out of the room, leaving only anger I couldn't quite decipher in his wake.

I closed my eyes. However long I'd slept in his bed had been enough to clear most of the Valium fog, but I'd never been so tired in my whole life. When I was with Dom, it sometimes seemed like I'd only begun existing after I'd met him. That everything that happened in-between our secret encounters happened to someone else, but my worlds had collided now, and everything was still such a mess. Dom *didn't* know me, and I didn't know him either.

Could we fix it? Did either of us even want to? Doubt warred with a million conflicting emotions in my gut, but somehow I found myself at the edge of the bed, swinging my legs over the side. Dom had walked out on me, but I wasn't going to walk out on him.

TWENTY-THREE

Dom

I didn't expect Lucky to follow me. I wasn't even sure I'd wanted him to until he came up behind me and wound his arms around my waist, pressed his cheek against my spine, and held on for dear life.

Damn it, Lucky. I closed my eyes and leaned against the kitchen counter, hoping the cool marble would ground me.

It didn't. Lucky's touch had me flying no matter the shadows weighing us down, and it was all I could do not to sag against him. To spin around and hold him tight enough that he knew I'd never let him go.

As it was, I settled for picturing him curled up in a heap on icy concrete, and wondered how the fuck anyone ended up like that. *You privileged fucking arsehole.*

I sighed. Lucky knocked his head on my back. "I'm sorry."

"What for? You're right—I am the one who bailed. My life's still too screwed up to subject you to it, and all that's changed is now I know your life isn't too hot either."

"That's why you said you couldn't see me anymore? Because *your* life is a mess?"

In another world, I'd have thought Lucky seemed amused, but he had no right to laugh at me. Not when he had no idea who I was and what him being in my life could cost us both. "I don't want you to leave."

"That's not answering my question."

"I know." I turned around and grasped Lucky's wrists before he could retreat. "But I've been awake all night and I have to go to work in an hour to be the person the rest of the world thinks I am. I can't do that if you're not going to be here when I get back."

"You said nothing's changed."

"It hasn't."

"You look like shit."

I'd expected Lucky to legitimately ask why the fuck he should stay when it was highly likely I'd bail on him again the moment I got home, but his words hit me all the same. I looked like shit because I felt it, and I had no idea how I was going to last ninety minutes of the roughest domestic game of the year.

I pulled him impossibly closer and kissed the top of his head. "Can we go back to bed...please?"

Lucky stretched out beside me like a cat. He was still slower than I was used to, but at least his eyes weren't pointing in different directions anymore. "What do you want to know?"

"Whatever you want to tell me."

"If I had my way I'd tell you nothing. I don't want you to know what a disaster I am...I liked it better when I was a mysterious hook up."

"Did you?"

Lucky shrugged, conflict clear in his soulful eyes. "I don't know. Things feel so complicated now."

I slid down the bed so we were level. Pressure welled inside me, like a dam threatening to burst, but I fought the growing instinct to vomit my entire life at Lucky's feet, to lay it all out so he could judge for himself how privileged a wanker I really was, rather than taking my vague word for it. I stroked his face, scratching the soft stubble covering his jaw. "I wish I was better."

"Me too, Dom. Me too."

"Are you a drug addict?"

Lucky's hooded eyes widened. "What?"

"I'm not making any assumptions. It's just with you being wasted last night and what I found on the bathroom floor..." The force of Lucky's glare hit me. "What?"

"If you weren't making assumptions, you wouldn't say shit like that."

"So tell me I'm wrong. I want to be wrong, Lucky."

"You're a prick." The half-smile playing on Lucky's lips overrode any venom. "But to answer your question...no, I'm not an addict. I have bad habits I can't seem to quit when shit gets real, but I don't use anything when I'm happy and warm. If I am addicted, it's psychological, not physical."

"What do you use?"

"You know what I use...you flushed it down your bog."

I'd wondered if he'd remember that. If he'd wake up searching for it, needing it. "I know what Valium is, but not the other stuff."

"Drone," Lucky said absently. "It used to be a legal high."

"A what?"

"You're cute. What kind of bubble do you live in?" He laughed at a joke I didn't understand, his face briefly alive and as I remembered it. "Anyway, I didn't use for ages, but then I stopped sleeping, so I needed a little sniff to get me through the day, and Valium to take the edge off when I got home."

"Why aren't you sleeping?"

"I told you I moved into a new place, right?"

"When you're not at Jamila's?"

He shook his head. "I've never lived with Jamila—she lets me stay there sometimes when her mum's at work. It isn't my home...I've never had one, and I still don't, really."

"The new place fell through?"

"No, but it's probably not what you pictured when I told you I had my own place. It's the halfway house in Stoke Newington, the one behind the bus station."

"I don't know it."

"Why would you?"

I said nothing, because I had no defence. My employers supported city charities and occasionally sent players out to various projects, but it was sanitised, our appearances a photo op for Twitter. It didn't mean anything.

"Anyway," Lucky went on. "Before I scored that room, I slept out when Jamila's mum was home, and when things get rough at the halfway house, I still do. It's a devil I know, if that makes sense."

"It does. But what's so bad about where you live?"

Lucky shrugged. "It's not safe at night. The staff goes home, leaving the whole building to a couple of night wardens. My door's been bashed in, my stuff gone through, and someone set fire to the bathroom a few weeks ago, but that's not even the problem...it's more the anticipation of something happening. It reminds me too much of—"

"What?" I prodded gently when he broke off with a sharp intake of breath. "Is it your dad?"

"I s'pose so. I told you before that he stopped hitting me, but the threat never seemed to fade. When he was angry, I'd hear him stomping around downstairs, and I'd shit myself every time I thought he was about to come up to my room. I didn't sleep for years until I started smoking weed."

My heart ached for him. My childhood had been messed up too, but nothing like his. My angst had been my own, and for all my father's faults—that he'd loved me for someone I wasn't—he'd never laid a hand on me. I'd feared his disappointment, not his fists. "What are you going to do?"

"About what?"

"About your living situation. You can't carry on sleeping rough."

Lucky laughed humourlessly. "There's nothing I can do until my apprenticeship ends. After that, I can earn proper money, but it's six months away, at least, and that's if I don't do the extra bits."

"Do you need the extra bits?"

"If I don't want to be a grunt my whole life, yes."

"What about the night wardens at the halfway house? Surely they can do something if you feel unsafe?"

More toneless laughter. "Night wardens earn seven-fifty an hour, Dom. Do you think they wanna be anyone's hero?"

Desperation clawed at my insides. "You know I can help you, don't you?"

"No, thanks."

"Lucky—"

He pressed his hand over my mouth. "Nah. We're fucked up as it is without you playing sugar daddy."

I peeled his hand from my lips. Argument boiled in my chest, but I swallowed it down. Lucky was an adult, and no good would come from me forcing my money on him.

"Besides," he said when I didn't speak. "You were right when you said we shouldn't see each other anymore. You know my darkest secrets, even if you don't know *me*, but I can see in your face that you're not going to reciprocate."

"Lucky, I—"

"I know." He silenced me again, his hand firmer this time. "Whatever you're about to say, I fucking *know*, okay? But as long as you can't talk to me, we can't be anything real to each other."

How could something hurt so much? As I gazed at him and he gazed right back, pieces of me crumbled. My body cried out to yank him against me. My heart screamed at me to challenge him, to put something—*anything*—in motion to dismantle the iron curtain keeping us apart. But I did nothing, and now I had to leave him all over again. "I have to go."

"Uh-huh." Lucky leaned away from me, already shutting down. "Give me a sec to dress up in your huge clothes and I'll chip off too."

"You can wait for your clothes if you want. The machine is set to dry them as soon as the wash cycle is done."

"What?"

"Stay," I said even as I rolled off the bed, tearing my gaze from him to search out my phone and anything else I needed to take with me. "Rest, eat, whatever. I'll be gone all day, so there's no point in you rushing off."

"You want to leave me alone in your posh penthouse?"

"It's not a penthouse."

"You're still leaving a homeless bum in your place."

"I don't care. It's raining and I know I've fucked this up. I just can't—" I blinked hard as a fresh headache began to creep across my skull. "Just stay a while, okay? At least until the rain stops."

"And then what?"

I had nothing.

Lucky snorted and turned away.

"Whoa." Maldano's voice seemed far away as he yanked me off the bathroom floor. "Not you too?"

I stumbled sideways, wiping my mouth with the back of my hand. "Piss off."

"Not likely. If you're puking too that makes six. At this rate, we're not going to have eleven men standing."

I regained my equilibrium and tried to compute what Maldano was saying, but my head hurt too much. In fact, everything hurt.

Maldano gripped my arm and steered me out of the bathroom. He sat me on a bench and disappeared, only to return with one of the club's medical staff.

"What the fuck?"

The medic hovered nervously as I scowled at Maldano, who

shrugged and spread his hands. "We gotta know if you're fit to play, man. If you're not, they'll probably call the game off."

"Off?"

"Yeah. I told you already. We're six men down. Our bench is totally wiped out."

The medic kneeled in front of me. "When did you start vomiting?"

"What?"

"Jesus, Dom," Maldano muttered. "Wake the fuck up and answer the question, will ya? We ain't got time for this."

Reality finally crept into my consciousness. *You're at work, remember?* I tried to focus on the medic. "This morning. I puked as soon as I got here."

"Nothing at home?"

"No."

"And when did you start to feel unwell?"

I'd felt sick for months, and now the helplessness I'd carried since Lucky had carved his name on my heart was merging with whatever bullshit bug I'd picked up from the last place on earth I wanted to be. "I don't know."

The medic laid a hand on my forehead. "You're warm, but not as hot as some of the others. How do you feel?"

You look like shit. "Rough."

"Dizzy?"

"A bit."

"How long till kick off?" the medic asked Maldano.

"Two hours," he said, and they continued to talk over me while I stared into space.

Getting sick hadn't been on my radar, even though, with hindsight, I'd felt like death when I'd left the club the day before. Had I really become so miserable I couldn't tell the difference between the chaos of my personal life and legitimate illness? Damn, I was such a fucking basket case.

Maldano and the medic hauled me to the medical centre. An IV was hooked up to my arm, and electrolytes poured down my throat.

I was on my third round of throwing them back up when Fernando came to see me.

"It's your call, Dom. If you're fit to play, we'll go on, if not, we'll call it off."

I coughed and rubbed my chest. "Why's it down to me?"

"Because without you we have ten players to field."

Jesus. I'd heard stories about another London club who'd lost their place in Europe when food poisoning had blitzkrieged their starting line-up, but never dreamed it would happen again in my memory. "We can't postpone?"

Fernando shook his head grimly. "Believe me, we've tried, but the league won't have it. We play today, or we forfeit."

He didn't have to tell me what a forfeited game would mean for the club. The inquiry would find in our favour eventually, as there was no denying the team was in bits, but the points deduction would end the European dream everyone at the club had sacrificed so much for. A dream that wasn't mine, but just like everything else, no matter how much it hurt, I had to play on.

Besides, Lucky would be long gone by now, and the more I could delay going home to an empty apartment, the better.

I took a deep breath and reached for another bottle of electrolytes. "Let's do this."

TWENTY-FOUR

Lucky

I shouldn't have stayed in Dom's place when he left—I should've walked out before he caught me in the snare of his liquid-brown gaze—but even without his hypnotism, the trouble with being warm and safe when I knew how it felt to be otherwise, was that it was impossible to leave the sanctuary of his bed.

Also, his sheets really did smell like him. Once I was sure he was gone for real, I curled up under his duvet and breathed him in, knowing it would be the last chance I got. In his quiet way, Dom had been as all over the place as me, but I'd received his choked-up message loud and clear: *nothing's changed.*

Which meant there was still no place for me in his complicated life, a fact I'd been half-way to accepting until I'd come round from a Valium binge on his hardwood floor. And now? Shit. Now everything seemed so surreal I couldn't make myself move. Dom's bed was the last place on earth I should've been, but at the same time it felt so right.

I tried to sleep, but I had no zeds left in me, and drifting with my thoughts was pure fucking torture. Dom had gone for the day...and I knew where. Over the last few weeks, I'd found myself tracking his club, picturing him in all the cities they'd played: Liverpool, Manchester, and Burnley. Even Brighton. I wondered if he'd think of me when he was there today. Remember the tales of woe I'd told him, and ache for me like I ached for him.

Rubbing my chest, I poked my head out from under the duvet, and sat up. There was a digital clock built into the entertainment unit at the foot of the bed. Dom had been gone a few hours, and it was nearly time for kick off at the London derby the city had been gearing up for all week. Dom's club was playing its closest local rival. For years, I'd avoided football like the plague, but my hand reached of its own accord for the remote on the bedside table. Dom was right: nothing had changed except that he'd now seen the worst of me, and perhaps I could counter it by seeing the best of him.

The TV switched on straight to the game and the pre-match build up, and by a stroke of pure fate, Dom's face filled the screen, brooding and handsome, his eyes fierce, lips pressed in an expressionless slash, at least, it seemed expressionless to me when I saw him so differently in my dreams: smiling shyly, chiselled features twisted in pleasure.

TV Dom wasn't *my* Dom.

Still, I was transfixed enough by him not to take in what the commentators were saying about his team until the headline flashed up on the screen: *home side ravaged by norovirus will struggle to field a team.*

Alarmed, I sat up and pressed the volume button until the pundit's deep voice was booming out of the TV, explaining how more than half of Dom's team had been taken ill, and many of them were unable to play.

My heart pounded. I had vague memories of Dom growing paler overnight, but I'd put it down to stress—his and mine—lack of sleep, and the fact that he had to go and play the biggest match of the season when my bullshit had kept him up all night. So wrapped up in my own mess, it hadn't occurred to me that he was unwell, but his heated skin and bloodshot eyes now made sickening sense.

I glanced around the room. My bag was by the door. I got up and dug my phone out. It was on silent and nearly out of battery, twenty-four missed calls from Jamila and Dom clogging up the screen.

Dom's bedroom was swish enough to have charging points built into the wall, but they were for iPhones much newer than mine. I cringed as I opened a drawer, as though I could shield my gaze from parts of Dom's life that were none of my business, but when I looked down, the drawer was empty, and so was every other in the bedside table.

Unsettled, I got up and tried a few more in the chest by the door, but beyond the neatly stacked T-shirts and folded jeans, there was nothing to show a real person lived in the apartment—no tangle of mangled phone chargers, crumpled receipts, and odd socks. I'd always suspected Dom was a neat freak, but this shit was ridiculous. Soulless. An empty life he didn't deserve.

I padded out of the bedroom and paced the apartment, from the minimalist living room with its blank walls, to the spotless kitchen and its bare fridge. Disquiet clawed at my gut with every step, and even back in the bedroom—the only place I could reliably imagine Dom because I'd *seen* him there—I couldn't shake the sensation that despite everything he'd said—and everything he *hadn't* said—he needed me now more than ever.

Right. 'Cause you're just what he needs. But for once, I silenced the devil on my shoulder without synthetic assistance. Still as naked as when Dom had left, I stood in front of the TV, rooted to the spot. The game had started while I'd paced the apartment, and Dom was on the pitch, doing what he always did—slaughtering any foolish opposition who crossed his path—but every time the ball went out of play, he doubled over, one hand bracing himself on the icy grass.

It was painful to watch, even as the cameras made an obvious effort to avoid him after a while.

The commentators weren't so kind. They documented every

moment of his plain distress until the need to do something—anything—overwhelmed me. *Clothes, I need clothes.* The hoodie and sweatpants he'd chucked at me were on the floor. I stepped over them and hurried to the kitchen. The washing machine was hidden behind the last shiny white cupboard door I opened. As promised, my clothes were bone dry and scented with detergent that definitely wasn't the Daz I used at the garage.

They were warm too, but I didn't stop to enjoy it. I threw them on, and tore through the apartment gathering my shit—my bag, my boots, and Dom's hoodie, as my coat seemed to be MIA.

At the front door, I crouched to tie my laces and tap out a message in WhatsApp.

My phone died as I hit send.

Lucky: *i'm here for u*

Dom

Throwing up had never hurt like this—like my organs were clawing their way out of my body. I pretty much crawled off the pitch at half-time and slumped in the tunnel.

A medic crouched by my feet. "You need to come off."

"I can't," I said without raising my head. "There's no one else."

The medic was a sharp-featured blonde woman who rarely spoke, and I expected her to let me be, but she shook me instead, forcing me to look at her.

"You need to come off," she repeated. "It's down to me to declare you fit to play on, and I'm not doing it."

I stared at her, inexplicable panic merging with the relief that if I didn't protest, I could stay right where I'd fallen and die in peace. "They'll have to call off the game."

"They'll have to do that anyway if you collapse on the pitch. Besides, you're not the only one in trouble. I'm advising that at least three of you are admitted to the clinic for fluids and rest."

It took a moment for her stern words to compute. By then, Fernando had joined her at my feet, his expression grim.

"Jovic and Fulton are getting in the cars to go to the clinic. Go with them, Dom. We're forfeiting the match."

He walked off without awaiting my response. The medic looked at me expectantly, but I shook my head. "I'm going home."

"You're not," she said. "You need another IV."

"Right. You think the rest of the city is getting one when they chuck up a few times?"

"Mr. Ramos—"

"Fuck off," I growled. "I'm going home."

I hauled myself to my feet. Being upright again came with a wave of dizziness. The medic—Oli, I belatedly remembered—caught me as I swayed. "Look," she said. "I can't stop you leaving if it's what you really want, but at least come with me and get rehydrated first, okay?"

She was more persuasive than I deserved, considering she'd borne the brunt of my temper for the last few hours, and I let her tow me to the medical rooms. A few players were still there, hooked up to IVs, but I shook my head when Oli held up a saline bag. "I'm not sitting here for hours, mate. Just do your thing and let me go."

I won the IV battle, but Oli still confined me to a bed for an hour while she jabbed me with anti-emetics and waited for my stomach to settle enough to absorb the electrolytes she insisted I swallow before she'd let me leave.

"Anti-emetics can cause vertigo," she said. "If you're affected you shouldn't drive. Do you need me to arrange a car?"

"No."

"Sure about that?"

"Said so, didn't I?"

Oli rolled her eyes. Her mean mug had faded since I'd stopped puking on her shoes, and in another world we might've got on well, but the longer I was trapped in this damn fucking place, the more the panic crawling through my veins eclipsed the lingering nausea. The reality of facing my empty flat had me internally screaming, but I couldn't stay here. Playing, however horrific the forty-five minutes I'd spent on the pitch had been, had gifted me a welcome distraction. Without it, I was simply a prisoner in the world that had forced me and Lucky apart.

I blinked away the waver in my equilibrium and stood. My stomach rolled, but the urge to indulge it was dulled by the anti-sickness drug, and I found some hard-won composure.

Oli walked me to the car park, and her presence beside me kept everyone else away.

"Thanks," I said when we reached the side door of the grounds. "Sorry if I've been a git to you all day."

"It's fine. Believe it or not, I've had far worse. I would appreciate it if you went straight home, though, and stayed there until you're keeping food down."

The idea of eating nearly sent me to my knees, but I nodded anyway. "Trust me, I'm going home. There ain't nowhere else for me to be right now."

We parted ways, her contact card stuffed in my back pocket, and as I left the building behind and drifted to my car, the sensation of leaving something behind warred with what I'd already lost. It had been years since football had owned my heart, but my apathy seemed absolute now, despite the loyalty that had kept me playing today.

Wasn't loyalty, though, was it? You just didn't want to watch Lucky leave.

I hauled myself into my car. Habit had me unlocking the glovebox and retrieving my phone, but I barely glanced at it as I turned it on. The days of my heart skipping a beat with every WhatsApp notification were over.

My great escape was beginning to catch up with me. I tossed my phone on the passenger seat and started the car. My hand was on the gear stick when my phone chimed.

Expecting a rollicking from Fernando, I had half a mind to ignore it, but the masochist still alive and well in me picked it up.

Lucky: *i'm here for u*

Instinct had me punching the recall button, but five calls to him went straight to the automated message that his phone was turned off. It was so typical of our attempts to communicate that I found myself checking his message was real ten times over and not a figment of my desperate imagination.

I'm here for u. What did that even mean if I had no way of reaching him? Did I even deserve the sentiment?

My stomach twisted, reminding me of the pressing need to get home and away from prying eyes, to shut myself away from the world and die in peace. But Lucky's message haunted me, and I left it open on the passenger seat as I backed out of my space and rolled out of the car park. The driveway out of the club was lined with more paps than usual, with added TV crews hoping to cash in on the clusterfuck derby day had turned into. I pulled my cap low on my face—obviously, 'cause that was my answer to everything—and ran the gauntlet. Cameras flashed, and one dude jumped out in front of me, but I made it out without killing anyone, so I took it as a win.

Dazed, I turned onto the main road, frazzled and wilting under the weight of whatever microbe was wreaking havoc in my belly. I was considering pulling over to puke at the side of the road when a flash of sandy-brown hair caught my eye.

For the second time that day, I questioned my lucidity. Oli had warned me the anti-sickness shot could give me vertigo, but she hadn't mentioned tripping. *You're losing your damn mind.*

But when I looked again, the apparition had solidified. Lucky was sitting on the pavement by a phone box, blue eyes fixed on me.

And he was laughing.

TWENTY-FIVE

Lucky

I had no idea what I was waiting for until Dom's Lexus rolled out of the club, and then a missing link clicked into place: Dom's car was the first vehicle I'd worked on when I'd approached Jim's garage. Servicing it had got me the job. Oh, the fucking irony.

Dom rolled to a stop at my feet and his blacked-out window slid down like something out of a movie, but my amusement faded the moment I saw him. *Jesus, he looks half-dead.*

I sprang to my feet. "Move over. I'll drive."

He didn't argue.

I slid behind the wheel of his beast-mobile and pulled back into the traffic. The whole exchange had taken thirty seconds, but Dom was staring at me like the world had flipped upside down. "What?" I said. "I was worried you'd pass out at the wheel." More silence. I considered letting him be, but the pallor marring his usually tanned skin worried me enough to reach out and squeeze his unyielding thigh. "Seriously, it's okay. I've got a licence."

A gurgle of laughter escaped Dom and he shook his head. "Trust me, mate. That's the last thing on my mind."

"You're wondering how I found you?"

"I'm wondering a lot of things."

The bitterness lacing his tone startled me. I turned towards Greenwich and let my hand slide from his leg. "I guess I have some explaining to do."

"Yeah. If you wouldn't mind starting with how the fuck you know where I work, that would be awesome."

"Jamila told me."

"What?"

I repeated the statement as we eased to a stop at a red light and I leaned on the leather steering wheel. "I didn't recognise you, and I probably never would have, but she's had you pegged since the night you met her to give my phone back, and she told me. I know I should've said something, but I was scared you'd freak out and disappear on me...that you wouldn't trust me to keep your secret. Fucked up, eh? 'Cause it happened anyway."

Dom didn't say anything, and when I looked at him, he was staring out of the window, his gaze distant as he clearly weighed up what I was saying against whatever assumption he'd made—an assumption that clearly wasn't in my favour. *Damn, does he think I'm a gold digger, or some shit?*

I couldn't blame him. I tried, but the anger and indignation wouldn't come. I'd kept this from Dom for myself as much as him, and he was right not to trust me. How could he, when the dynamics of our relationship had been based on a reality he'd never known about?

His apartment building loomed into view. I chanced a glance at his narrowed eyes and set jaw. "Where do you park?"

"Hmm?"

"Where do you park?" I repeated. "I'm guessing you don't leave this bad boy in the street?"

Dom jerked his head at a side street. "Down there. It's underground."

I followed his directions to the type of car park that had been alien to me until I'd started work at Jim's garage. These days, delivering cars like Dom's to places like this were an everyday occurrence, but with him simmering beside me, twitchiness crept back into my veins. I hadn't given much thought to the drugs he'd flushed on my behalf, but I craved them now. Over the years, bad habits had become my only coping mechanisms, and fuck if I didn't need them as nerves merged with anxiety so deep *I* almost threw up.

The Lexus was so easy to drive it pretty much parked itself. I twisted in my seat to face Dom, but he was already getting out.

I scrambled to follow him. "Wait."

"What for? So you can tell me how you sold me out?"

"What?"

"Do you think I'm fucking stupid?" His yell echoed in the deserted car park, and he reared around to face me, abruptly all up in my personal space when he'd seemed so far away until this point. "Ten years I've been in the closet, and then you come along and my shit is suddenly on the desk of some tabloid hack. Tell me I'm a fucking idiot, Lucky, 'cause I damn well need to hear it from you."

"I don't know what you're talking about."

"Right." He turned away.

I caught his arm. "I *don't*. Yeah, I've known who you are for a while now but I haven't said anything. I'm a street urchin when my own bed scares the crap out of me. I'm not a fucking rat."

Rage finally filled me as I realised exactly what he was accusing me of, and my voice matched his in volume by the time I was done.

Breathing hard, I glowered at him, and he glared right back until something seemed to hit him and he flinched, a shaky hand coming up to rub his eyes.

I took a chance and released my grip on him to slide my arm around him. "Look, I don't know what the hell is going on in your life right now, but you're sick as a dog, so let's just get you inside okay? So you can shout your bullshit at me from your gold-plated couch, or whatever."

Dom's dead-eyed stare was lethal, but he didn't protest as I led him to the door of his building, or when I stepped into the lift with him. At his front door, he surrendered his keys, and I let us inside, and he didn't say anything as I steered him over the threshold.

I held his keys out, prepared to leave if he asked, but he shut the door behind him and leaned against it.

"I don't have a gold-plated couch, you stupid arse."

A hysterical giggle escaped me. "I know. Sorry. I get rowdy when I'm confused."

"What are *you* confused about?"

"What do you think? You just ripped me a new one for selling you out to the tabloids when you scraped me off the street less than twenty-four hours ago. Dom...do I look like someone who just made bank from a Premiership footballer?"

"You could've spent it on drugs."

"Only if they paid me twenty quid and a bag of weed. I *told* you —I'm not an addict. Just a loser with bad habits."

The fight seemed to drain from Dom as abruptly as it had arrived. His shoulders slumped, and he covered his face with his hand. "I don't know what the fuck's going on."

I pried his hand away and forced him to look at me. "Neither do I, but I can't figure it out if you yell at me. Come and lie down, and you can tell me all about it while I take care of you, okay?"

Dom's story made little sense to me. I already knew about his friend—who I now knew was his agent—hiding the fact that he'd known Dom was gay for years, but the tabloid dude threatening to expose him? That was next-level bullshit. "What a cunt."

Faint amusement flickered in Dom's tired eyes. He was curled on his side in bed, his head pillowed on his arm, and hadn't showed any sign of moving since he'd laid down an hour ago. "That's about where I am on it. I'm sorry you've been dragged into it, though. I honestly thought if I ever got caught out, it would be instant, you know? One strike and I'd be fucked."

I couldn't imagine what it was like to be Dom. "Don't apologise to me, I'm just glad you don't really think I was in on it."

Guilt darkened Dom's already fever-flushed cheeks. "Ugh. Don't remind me. I pretty much want to die over that. It's just I-I don't know. I've run out of people to trust, I guess. I've come round to the idea that Isha really was trying to protect me—and himself—but I don't have anyone else in my corner."

"What are you going to do?"

Dom sighed. "I don't know. Isha wants me to pay them off."

"But you don't want to?"

"It's tempting," Dom admitted. "But it wouldn't solve anything. Isha reckons he's got enough evidence to hard ball this dude right back if he resorted to full-on extortion, but I don't want to be mixed up in crap like this. I—" He stopped, like he had many times while we'd been talking, and swallowed thickly, clearly warding off nausea. "I'm of half a mind to fuck it all to hell."

"Call his bluff?"

"Whatever. I don't care much anymore."

I sat back on my heels and exhaled a long, slow breath. What Dom was implying was huge. Footballers rarely came out, and the ones who did, did so at the expense of their career. "Would your club support you?"

"Doubt it. My contract's up at the end of the season anyway."

"They'd drop you for being gay?"

Dom cracked a heavy eye open. "Not overtly, but they'd find a reason to let me go."

"How do you feel about that?"

He shrugged. "I'm trying really hard to feel anything."

It probably wasn't the best time to force the issue, but I couldn't seem to make myself let him be. "What about other clubs? Would they sign you?"

Another shrug. "I told you. I don't care. I've been over football a long time, I'm *tired*, and all the bullshit that comes with it means nothing to me."

"What would you do for money?"

"What do *you* do for money?"

I bit my lip. "I don't have any."

"Got a job, though, right? Don't you think it's time you told me what it is?"

"Um—" I cringed. "I'm an apprentice mechanic at Premier Autos in Tottenham."

Dom's bloodshot eyes widened. "The one behind the old-school record shop?"

"Yup. You found me there once, remember?"

"On the bench. Fuck. I took my car there."

"I know. I serviced it, though I didn't know it was yours until today, so don't go off on me again."

Dom didn't look like he had the energy to do much more than blink and mutter to himself, and I finally found the decorum to rein myself in.

I lay down beside him and stroked his face.

He moaned softly and closed his eyes. "I'm so tired, Lucky."

"I know, baby. I'm gonna let you sleep now."

His eyes flew open. "Don't go."

"I'm not gonna," I said. "Just rest, Dom. I got you."

He didn't believe me. I could tell by how long it took him to get his exhausted self to sleep, but he couldn't fight it indefinitely, and when he was finally knocked out, I tucked him up and slipped away to the kitchen with the iPad that apparently came with the apartment.

Dom had given me access to some posh online grocery service. I ordered Frosted Shreddies, eggs, milk, bread, baked beans, and two packs of Birds Eye Chicken Dippers. Inexplicably, the delivery ETA was an hour. *Do people really live like this?*

It was more than I could deal with, so I retreated to the bathroom to take a soak in Dom's tub, which I'd actually remembered, though it didn't feel quite right without him hovering in the doorway, or sitting on the closed toilet like an anxious monk.

Still, the relief at finally coming clean about what I knew was undeniable. Until I'd confessed, I hadn't realised how much it had weighed me down. I couldn't imagine how it had been for Dom this whole time—fuck, his whole damn life. A few months of secrets and I was a mess. I knew without doubt that I wouldn't have survived what Dom had been through. The fact that my life hadn't been a walk in the park either didn't seem to matter.

Restless, I abandoned the bath mid-wallow and crept back into the bedroom. Dom was awake and talking into the phone. "Listen," he said. "I need a couple of days to sort some personal shit. Can you do me a solid and swing it for me? I'd really fucking appreciate it."

He nodded as whoever he was talking to replied and obvious relief passed through him. "Thanks, Oli."

I tried not to be nosey as I slid onto the bed behind him, but glanced at his phone screen anyway. Whoever he'd been talking to wasn't listed as a contact and I held out for all of six seconds. "Who was that?"

"Team medic. She looked after me yesterday and she's pretty cool."

"Does she know?"

Dom scoffed. "Of course not. I've told you a million times, only Isha, you, and this hack twat know my business."

For now.

He didn't say it, but he didn't have to. I was used to the world tipping me upside down and dangling me over the edge, but even without being ill, it was clear how rattled Dom was. How his fingers tapped a nervous rhythm on his knee, and his gaze zoned out every couple of seconds. I wanted to—

A knock at the door startled us both until I remembered the grocery shopping. "Um, I suppose I shouldn't answer the door?"

Dom sat up with a heavy sigh. "Probably not."

He got up and left the room. I waited until I heard the front door open and close, and then joined him in the kitchen, where I found him bemusedly studying my beloved Chicken Dippers.

I snatched them from him. "Don't start. It's not my fault you live on macros and kale."

Dom started to roll his eyes, and then seemed to think better of it. "Do you think I even know what a macro is? I'm not a nutritionist. I eat what they put in front of me."

"That makes you sound like some kind of robot."

"Maybe I am."

I hopped up onto the counter and used my legs to draw Dom closer. "You don't have to be."

"I know. I'm working on it."

Dom buried his face in my neck and stayed there a while, rocking us slightly while he took deep and even breaths. The sensation was hypnotic, and I could've stayed that way for the rest of my life, but my stomach interrupted the bliss with a loud growl.

A chuckle rumbled out of Dom. He raised his head. "Hungry?"

"Are you?"

He blanched. "Not really."

"You should probably eat something, though." I slid off the counter, missing his touch already, and studied the gleaming built-in oven. "How about I cook some shit and you try?"

"What are you gonna cook?"

"Dippers, toast, and beans. Can't beat it, mate."

Dom relented and showed me how to use his gadget-rich kitchen. I cooked all the Dippers and ate about thirty to the five I managed to persuade him to eat.

I had more luck with the toast, though, and he seemed vaguely more human by the time we were done.

"Leave the washing up," he said. "I'll do them later."

"You don't have a housekeeper who does that stuff for you?"

"I have a housekeeper most days, but I don't expect her to do the dishes any more than I expect her to wash my clothes. What kind of arsehole do you think I am?"

"I don't think you're an arsehole. I just don't know much about how your life works." I pushed him away from the sink and turned the tap on. "Why don't you grab a shower while I do these, then we can chill, okay?"

Dom left the kitchen, and I buried my hands in warm soapy water and scrubbed the minimal dishes we'd used to eat. It was after midnight by the time I was done and I realised with a jolt that I had to be at work in the morning, a journey that would take me an hour on the tube.

The prospect of crawling out of Dom's bed when it was still dark depressed me. Then I pictured where I'd woken up for the last twenty-five years and gave myself a proverbial kick in the nuts. Even if I never made it into his bed again, I was already fucking blessed.

Dom was drying off when I drifted into the bedroom. I stared. He caught me looking and flushed, and I belatedly remembered that being naked around men who weren't die-hard hetero football players didn't come naturally to him.

To even the playing field, I stripped my clothes and folded them into an orderly pile to avoid stressing him out any more, then crossed the room and swiped his towel to finish blotting the water from his gorgeous skin. There was a fresh boot mark I hadn't noticed bruising his hip. I traced it with my fingertip. "Does that hurt?"

He shivered. "Nothing hurts when you do that."

God, he was fucking perfect, and the urge to push him onto the bed and recall what had drawn us together in the first place was so strong I nearly did it—nearly shoved him down and climbed all over him, taking what *I* wanted before I considered his needs.

Which was what people had been doing to him his whole life.

I took his hand and twined our fingers together. The simple gesture had always grounded me when his very presence set me on fire. "Can we get in your bed and watch TV?"

"Naked?"

"Yeah."

Dom squeezed my hand. "Of course."

Since we'd met, we'd spent most of our time together in bed in one way or another—eating, dozing, fucking—but right now, all I wanted was to be with him. To lay with him. To touch him. To feel his skin against mine and to know that he was real.

To show him *I* was real too.

We slid under the covers. Dom clicked the TV on, but neither of us glanced at the screen. I rolled onto my side, and he mirrored me, his arm tucked beneath his cheek. He still looked tired—and harassed by whatever was going on in his beautiful head—but the grey tinge had started to ease from his complexion.

I brushed light fingers along his jawline. "Do you feel better?"

"Actually, yeah. Maybe your chicken-butt nuggets did the trick."

"You can say what you want about them; you'll never put me off."

He chuckled. "I'm not trying to. I'm hooked on the little smile you get when you're eating them."

"If that's the only part of me you're hooked on—"

"It's not."

Dom leaned in for a kiss, and our lips met for the first time in—shit, I couldn't remember. Didn't want to remember, because it didn't fucking matter. All that mattered was the sensation of his kiss caressing me, and his tongue sweeping sweetly over my lips, gone before I could grant him entrance to my mouth.

He'd always been able to leave me breathless with a two-second embrace. It was like he tapped into a part of me I couldn't control and stole my ability to fill my lungs. Panting, I fell onto my back, kind of hoping he'd chase me down, but conversely relieved when he didn't.

When I'd composed myself, I faced him again to find him watching me, a tiny smile breathing life into his drawn features. "What?"

He shrugged. "Nothing. I'd just forgotten how animated you are."

"Animated? Like a cartoon or some shit?"

"No, mate. Just alive. I feel lazy sometimes watching you."

"You're the athlete. I don't even run for the bus."

"Bet you could, though. You're strong, I can tell." It was his turn to trace my body with his fingers, ghosting down my face, along my arms, and across my chest. "And your job is pretty hardcore, right? Lots of lifting and stuff?"

"It has its moments, but health and safety have us using machines for most things these days. It's not like my grandpa taught me with his old Avenger."

"Were you close?"

"To my grandpa? Yeah, but he died when I was ten, so I didn't get much time with him."

Dom nodded, offering nothing in return as always, a habit I wanted him to break now there wasn't much left to hide—perhaps wasn't anything, apart from the fact that I was possibly—*definitely*—in love with him.

"What about your family?" I said. "You've told me some vague stuff before, but I don't really know anything about you."

"What do you want to know? It would probably be quicker to google me."

I flicked his bicep. "Don't be a dick."

"Sorry. It's a habit."

"It's a defence mechanism, and you don't need it with me."

Dom sighed. "I know. It's hard when I've spent all this time telling half-truths and defecting attention. Even with you, it still feels wrong."

"How about I ask you questions? You can answer the ones you want and ignore the ones you don't."

"Are you interviewing me?"

"Nah, I'm just nosey as fuck."

"Noted." Dom grinned a little more. "And I guess it's my turn to share, though I'm really not that interesting."

"Where did you grow up?"

"Thetford."

"Where the fuck's that?"

"Norfolk. It's where all the Portuguese settle. My grandparents came over in the sixties."

"Whose parents were they?"

"My dad's, but he was born here, so he was as English as I am."

Was. I couldn't remember if he'd told me before that his father was dead, but Dom seemed to have a similar apathy for his family as I did mine, so I left it alone. "What would you have done if football hadn't worked out for you?"

"Dunno."

"Come on. There must've been other things you liked."

"I didn't have much time for anything that wasn't football. I've been playing full-time since I was sixteen."

"You never did anything else? Wow. That's sad."

Dom laughed. "It was what I wanted at the time. Football was a good escape for me, an outlet, especially when the position I play gave me plenty of opportunities to clobber people when I was in a bad mood."

"I read that about you."

"Yeah? What else did you read?"

"Not much, apart from that article about you snogging that model last month...the one with the pictures."

Dom cringed, and I regretted bringing it up. I already knew that Isha had planted stories about Dom with women to cover his tracks, but the pictures...he *had* kissed her. Or she'd kissed him. Whatever. I'd *seen* it, damn it.

Not that Dom owed me an explanation. I just wanted one, because I was a selfish fuck who didn't want anyone's lips on him but mine.

Like he'd read my mind, Dom kissed me again, light and sweet, before he pulled away with a sigh. "I met her in Manchester. I've been working up there a few days a week for the last couple of months. A friend dragged me out that night because I was moping around, missing you, though he didn't know that. We went to a bar where there were loads of wannabe WAGs. She came onto me, I told her I was gay, she kissed me anyway."

"You told her you were gay?"

"Yup. Ironic, huh?"

"What did she say?"

"She laughed. I don't think she believed me, so I'm hoping she hears about it when shit hits the fan so she knows I wasn't just trying to get rid of her."

I pictured the woman again, trying to recall anything about her that wasn't her lips on Dom, but nothing came to me other than the vague notion that she'd been a knockout.

"Hey." Dom touched my face. "Can we go back to talking about something real?"

"Like what?"

"Like, the fact that I helped on my uncle's building site for a while before I turned pro and I loved it. I mean, I didn't love pushing wheelbarrows of cement around, but I was fascinated by house building: the foundations, the brickwork, the plaster. I might do some more with property when this mess is done."

"You're not gonna be some cockhead landlord with sixty-five million houses while the rest of us can't afford a microwave, are you?"

Dom snorted. "No."

"Good. 'Cause you really would be a wanker then. Tell me something else about being Portuguese."

"I don't know much about being Portuguese. I'm English."

"Yeah, but you must've grown up with dual cultures. Jamila's grandparents are Grenadian. They cook the best chicken."

"You're obsessed with chicken."

"Nah. Just hungry."

"Already?"

"Sue me."

Dom shuddered. "Don't even joke about it. But staying on topic, you've had Peri Peri, right?"

"Like Nando's?" I lifted my head a fraction. "I like that shit."

"Yeah?" Dom was suddenly closer. Somehow he'd shifted while my mind had meandered to chilli-spiced chicken and lime mayonnaise. "What else do you like?"

We weren't talking about food anymore. Being naked in bed with him abruptly became everything I'd vowed I didn't need. I licked my lips. "You know what I like."

"Remind me."

TWENTY-SIX

Dom

My existence was a blur of everything and nothing, but the moment the prospect of being inside Lucky again hit my brain, it was all I could see.

I covered him with my body, pinning him down the way he seemed to like; my chest to his chest, our dicks rubbing together with a friction so hot I half-expected to see sparks when I dared to glance between us. "Jesus."

Lucky laughed. "You're feeling better then?"

"Shut up." I kissed him roughly to make sure he did, and something I couldn't describe sluiced through me, setting fire to every scrap of dry tinder I had left. *I need him.*

But it didn't matter how hard I kissed him, how deep I took him down my throat, it wasn't enough. I needed *more.*

Lucky rolled us over. His hands were everywhere, digging into my skin, fingers squeezing around my cock—his palm cupping my balls, and then sliding lower.

I arched against him, remembering with perfect clarity how his fingers had felt inside me that very first time. How I hadn't known how deeply I craved it until it was happening. It was different now—so different—but the shot of pain-laced pleasure as he slid a slick finger home was just the same.

"Oh fuck, Lucky."

He grinned evilly and scooted his knees closer to nudge my legs further apart. It felt natural to hook my hands beneath my thighs and hold them wide, granting him better access. Vulnerability was a distant memory and all I wanted was *more.*

Lucky finger-fucked me for what seemed like hours, edging me closer and closer to a precipice I didn't want to come back from. He found my prostate and grazed it over and over, drawing louder, longer moans from me until I was shuddering, and drenched in sweat.

"Do you want me to fuck you?" he whispered. "It's okay if you don't...I can ride you."

God, I wanted him to ride me, but the alternative was everything I'd dreamed of, and my soul screamed at me to make it reality. "Fuck me...please."

The strangled sound I made as he slid his sheathed cock inside me was indescribable, and the stretching burn melted every nerve. Him on his knees, me on my back, still clutching my thighs as I held them open. My dick was rigid and weeping. He began to move inside me, easing in and out with growing purpose, and I was going to come without touching myself. The only question was how loud he could make me scream.

Lucky leaned forward and drove in and out of me, one hand on my chest, the other gripping the pillow beneath my head, fisting the fabric as he thrust harder. "Oh god, Dom. I've dreamed about this, I fucking swear. You're so hot."

I'd never felt that hot when I'd bottomed before. Despite the pleasure, I'd always felt scrappy and undignified, but this was nothing like that. *Lucky* was nothing like anyone I'd ever been with, and his every touch, every drive of his hips, injected me with liquid sex.

He dropped his torso down to press against me, and his taut

abdomen slid along my sweat-damp skin. My legs found their way to his shoulders and there wasn't an inch of space between us.

I buried my face in the silky hair that had escaped from the messy knot at the nape of his neck. His cool scent grounded me briefly, but then urgency stole over me, a frantic need I was almost afraid of. I was so full, and consumed by Lucky, I could hardly cope, and pressure built inside me until something snapped, and a crazed yell burst out of me. "I'm gonna come."

Lucky growled and fucked me harder, any caution he'd started with all but gone. He pounded me against the headboard, moaning filthy words in my ear, but somehow, it wasn't quite enough.

Out of my mind, I gripped his arse and pushed him deeper into me, and his cock scraped my prostate. I saw stars, and agonising pleasure broke me in half. Everything I had spilled out of me, spurred on by Lucky hardening and pulsing inside me.

"Dom—"

But I barely heard him, my mind fixated on one thought only: *he's coming inside me*. He was wearing a condom, but the thought of him filling me up still sent a fresh jab of heat rocketing through me. "*Fuck*."

Lucky dropped his head and groaned, his rhythm faltering, slowing, and then easing entirely before he pulled out of me. "You really do like that shit, huh?"

"What shit?" I slurred with my eyes closed.

"Getting fucked. It takes you somewhere."

I cracked an eye open, and then two when I caught his smirk. "*You* take me somewhere. It wasn't like that when—well, before. You know what I mean."

"It's okay to have fucked other people, Dom. We ain't nuns."

A rough laugh bubbled out of me. "You're ridiculous."

"So?"

I had no answer to that. His ability to challenge me in the simplest ways had built the foundations of my affection for him—

affection and desire that had fast become an inability to live without him.

There'd been no doubt in my mind for a while now that I was head over heels in love with him, but as the minutes ticked by and we grinned daftly at each other, something changed between us. Like him fucking me—owning me—had reset a balance we needed to move forward. I didn't understand it, and probably never would. All I knew was whatever happened next, there was no going back.

Isha paced my living room, tapping his fist against his lips as he processed what I was asking him to do. "This is insane."

"Is it?" I said blandly, my gaze flitting to the closed bedroom door. Lucky was in there, pretending to be asleep after his crack of dawn awakening to go to work, but I knew he felt awkward as fuck about being around while I discussed setting a bomb under my career and blowing it to pieces. Like it was his fault it had come to this.

I wondered how many times I'd have to tell him it wasn't before he believed me.

"Dom?"

I blinked at Isha. "What?"

Isha narrowed his eyes. "Come on, mate. I need you to focus if we're going to pull this together. This is huge. I can't do it on my own."

I was lucky he was considering doing it at all and not running for the hills, so I pulled my thoughts away from the beautiful boy in my bed, and gave Isha my full attention. "How soon can we sit down with Fernando?"

"As soon as we've figured out what you want to say to him."

"You know what we have to say to him—the truth, man. I'm done hiding."

"Hiding from who, though? When this gets out, the whole world will know, and they'll all want a piece of you for a while. Are you ready for that?"

Of course I wasn't, but I'd come to realise that I never would be, and I was done wasting my life pretending otherwise.

Isha came to a stop in front of me and sat on the coffee table. "This is so sudden. When did you decide this?"

I shrugged, as clueless as him. Clarity had come suddenly, but the path to it had been long and muddy. "Does it matter?"

"If it's a knee-jerk reaction to something, then yes. You can't take this back, Dom. It's gonna change your life."

"Fuck off," I snapped. "Don't you see? I have no fucking life like this. What do you want me to do? Stay closeted and celibate till I'm dead?"

"No—" Isha stopped, conflict marring his handsome features. "Of course I don't want that. I never have. I want what's best for you, and I'm worried this will hurt you just as much as staying quiet has."

"You have no idea what's best for me."

"Then I'm sorry I'm a shit friend, okay? Just tell me what you need and I'll see that you get it."

But it wasn't as simple as that. A sit-down with Fernando would do nothing but confirm my near certainty that he'd drop me like a stone, and doing it before the end of the season was a clusterfuck no one needed. Could I wait till the summer, though? With a target on my back from the tabloids, I doubted it.

Hours later, Isha left with a meeting with Fernando nailed down for the next day. Drained, I double locked the door behind him, messaged Constance to give her a few more paid days off, and let myself be drawn to the bedroom like a tired moth to a bright new flame.

Lucky was by the window, staring out over the city.

I came up behind him and slipped my arms around his waist. "Why are you peeping round the curtain like that?"

"I didn't want anyone to spot me."

"They'd be hard pushed to see up here."

"Not if they were in that building over there." He pointed to the bank headquarters opposite. "I can't see through the windows, but that doesn't mean they can't see us."

I'd never given much thought to whether anyone was spying on me from across the road. My apartment was far from homely, but despite being higher up than I could deal with elsewhere, I'd always felt safe.

I wanted Lucky to feel safe too. I drew him away from the window and turned him around. "It's starting not to matter if someone sees us. I'm speaking to my manager tomorrow."

"Fernando Rodriguez?"

I rolled my eyes. "That's the one. Isha and me are meeting with him in the afternoon after training."

"And telling him everything?"

"Telling him the truth," I said, ignoring the echoes of my conversation with Isha. "I don't know what will happen after that, but I'm going to tell him I'm gay and roll with it."

Lucky grabbed blindly for the nearby dresser and leaned heavily on it. "Dom, that's huge."

"So people keep telling me."

"You don't think so?"

I knew so, but for some reason, I didn't feel it. Forced apathy had become a numbness I couldn't explain, and all I wanted—apart from Lucky—was to get it over with. "I need to talk to you about something else."

Lucky's expression didn't change. He gestured for me to continue, but I didn't want to have this conversation with him in my bedroom. Since I'd brought him home a few days ago, the space was sacred to me. I didn't want it tainted by this ugliness.

I hustled him into the living room and sat him on the couch. "Even if I manage to take control of revealing my sexuality, Isha thinks the tabloid rat will run any information he has on you because it's all he'll have left. Best case scenario is that he doesn't have much, but I honestly have no idea how far this is gonna go when it blows up."

Lucky reached forward and claimed one of the bottles of water from the coffee table. "What's the worst case scenario?"

"That he knows everything about you, prints it, and the paparazzi hound you for the rest of your life."

"I meant for you, Dom. I don't care about me."

"Why not?"

He shrugged. "Habit."

"Yeah, well, quit it."

"I will if you will."

"*Anyway.*" I grasped his shoulders and shook him slightly without meaning to. "Shit. Sorry."

"It's okay."

It wasn't. I dropped my hands and chased my racing thoughts in search of a coherent sentence. "Listen, this is going to blow up in my face however it goes down, but I want you to know that I'm gonna do everything I can to keep you out of it...and, um..."

"Um? And?"

"And I don't expect you to stick around through any of it, okay? If you want to bail, I totally get it."

I wasn't sure what reaction I was hoping for from him, but a burst of his infectious laughter caught me off guard, and then irritated me enough to lean away from him and narrow my eyes. "The fuck you laughing at?"

Lucky struggled to compose himself and slapped a hand over his mouth, sucking in deep breaths through his nose. When he was done, he reached for me again. "Don't get pissy. I'm not laughing at you... I'm laughing because I've spent all night worrying that *you're* gonna bail on *me*."

"What?"

"You heard. I know you're not doing any of this *for* me, Dom, but I heard that Isha guy say my name, and thinking that he was trying to talk you out of whatever foshizzle is going on between us had me kind of freaked."

"Foshizzle?"

It was Lucky's turn to glare. "I've told you before—I'm inarticulate when I'm hungry. You know it's practically midnight, don't you?"

It was barely eight, but I took his point. Food was the last thing on my mind, but I hadn't hoofed it to Tottenham and back, or done a full day's work.

Lucky had.

I confined him to the couch and retreated to the kitchen to make beans on toast. He seemed mollified when I delivered it, and I took my chance to bring the conversation back to my original point.

Lucky's position remained unchanged. "They can hound me all they like. I'm a slippery fucker, they'd soon get bored."

"It's not funny."

"I'm not laughing." But he schooled his features all the same. "Seriously. Don't fret, okay? If they find me, so be it, but you don't have to worry about me giving you up, Dom. I'd never say a word. You know that, don't you?"

I knew it like I knew water was wet. We had much to learn about each other, but our unspoken loyalty was absolute. "I'm hoping the rag hack will scrap anything he's got on you in exchange for an exclusive interview or some shit."

"You'd do that?"

I suppressed a shudder. "Not if I can help it, but if I had to...yeah."

"What would you say?"

"Pure facts. That I'm gay, I've always been gay, and it ain't gonna change."

"You know they'll push you harder than that."

"Uh-huh."

"*Dom.*"

"What?"

Lucky was suddenly in my face, his eyes wide, and his soft, pillowy lips twisted with concern. "It's okay to be scared."

"I'm not scared."

"I don't believe you."

"So?"

He shook his head. Knocked it against mine, and kissed my cheek. "Fine. Have it your way. But can I give you something?"

I expected another knock, or maybe one of the sweet kisses that bellied his sharp tongue, but Lucky rolled up his sleeve and unknotted one of the bazillion bracelets he wore around his slender wrist. It was plain dark brown and wonderfully weathered. He dropped it into my palm and I brought it to my face to smell leather, smoke, and Lucky.

"Wear it," he said. "When you're not playing, anyway. It's an old one...it's been with me from the start."

"From the start of what?"

"From the start of being me."

Fernando slow-blinked, his sleek white eyebrows coming together as he struggled to piece together what I'd just told him. "You're gay?"

"Yup."

"Since when?"

"Since forever. I told you, man. I've carried this all along."

Fernando pushed his chair back and came around his desk. He stopped in front of me and stared down at me like he was trying to figure out if I was taking the piss. If Maldano was going to burst in at any moment wearing a tutu and screaming April Fool.

Except it wasn't fucking April, and this was my life.

"You're twenty-six," Fernando said.

"What's that got to do with anything?"

He shrugged. "You have a few years left. Why do this now?"

"Are you asking for my benefit or yours?"

There was no guilt in his gaze as he scowled at me. "The Premiership found in our favour over the derby game and didn't deduct points. If the season plays out as we expect it to, we'll make Europe. Are you telling me we'll be doing it without the lynchpin in our defence?"

It was my turn to shrug. "My contract is up."

"You were about to be offered another three years."

"So? That doesn't change the fact that I've got an axe hanging over me. If things were different, I might've played on a bit longer, but this is going to come out one way or another—"

"Does it have to come out?" Fernando cut in. "Is there nothing we can do?"

"If you're talking about a super injunction." Isha spoke for the first time since I'd broken the news. "It's a possibility, but the horse has bolted. Dom's right—it *will* come out."

Fernando sat down heavily in the chair beside me. His reaction had surprised me, though I don't know why. The bloke had always been all about the game, first and foremost. It was what made him such a successful manager. Single minded. Ruthless. Thoughtful in a crisis without wasting energy on anger. "You really want to retire because of this?"

"Not just because of this. I probably would've considered it anyway."

"Why?"

"I want to do other things." My gaze wandered to my wrist. The bracelet Lucky had given me was barely visible, but my heart quickened regardless. *This is really happening.* "I want to be myself."

Fernando said nothing for a long moment, and then he nodded slowly. "I think perhaps we should go for the injunction anyway. It might buy us some time."

Isha's intense stare flickered to me before he shook his head. "We only need time to prepare statements. Delaying anything else isn't fair on Dom."

Fernando sighed. "Very well. I'll make the calls."

He disappeared. Isha and I stared at each other, but didn't speak. What was there to say? We knew where we were going, and what we'd face, and I was thankful that I still had him on my side. That he hadn't figured out that *I* was the judgemental arsehole who'd turned on him without facts. "Isha—"

"Don't," he said. "Let's forget the past, okay? We don't have time to dwell on it. I should've told you, and you should've believed me when I explained why I didn't. We're both wankers."

"If you say so."

"I do, Dom. I do."

In need of a distraction, I left him in the office and returned to the dressing room to retrieve my training gear. It was deserted, but as I gazed around I felt the presence of every man I'd ever played with. For the first time since this mess had truly opened up, I wondered how they'd look at me when it all came out. When *I* came out. There weren't many I cared about, but I couldn't deny that rejection from Maldano and Micah would sting.

I sat down on a bench, slipped my phone from my pocket—for some reason, I hadn't been able to bring myself to lock it away in my car today—and opened my message threads. Lucky aside, they were all, without exception, about work and business. There was the occasional joke from Maldano, or snaps of his kids that I'd rarely responded to, but all the warmth in my life from the last decade had come from a few months of interactions with Lucky.

What kind of shit was I that something huge was only just occurring to me?

Fuck, I don't even know his real name.

It was the second time the realisation had hit me like a train, but Isha knocked on the dressing room door before I could come to terms with it.

"Dom? The board are meeting now. Sit tight, they'll call you in soon."

Lucky

Dom kept coming at me with serious conversations, and all I could think about was curling my body over his and fucking him. Of his wild eyes and ragged moans when he'd come, and his contented exhaustion when it was all over. I'd watched him sleep for hours before I'd laid my head on his chest and dozed off.

"Lucky? Did you do the brake inspection on the NX?"

I swung my gaze to Jim. He was hovering over me with his favourite clipboard. "Which NX? There's two in today."

"Damn it. Blowed if I know. Whichever one you were working on this afternoon."

I took pity on him and slid off the shelf I'd perched on to drink my seventy-five-millionth cup of tea. "The black one didn't need brakes. It was the craptastic gold one that came in for an inspection."

"Did you finish it?"

"Of course. I wouldn't be bunking off over here if I hadn't. I'm waiting for Cash to come back with the new filters."

"Good lad, good lad. Oh...talking of Cash, do you think you could pin this up in the staffroom? He asked me this morning, but I'm like a bucket with a bleeding hole today."

Jim handed me a scrap of paper and disappeared. Lacking anything better to do, I took the paper to the staffroom, and pinned it to the noticeboard I rarely looked at. I didn't pay much attention to goings on in the garage beyond the cars and the state of the shower, but even then, not in the last few days 'cause I'd been using Dom's bath—

Stop it.

I caught myself before my imagination went off on another sex tangent and focussed on the note Cash had scribbled on the paper. It was an ad for a flatmate—a house share, seven-hundred quid a month, all bills included.

Seriously? I blinked. That was less money I was paying for a single room in a fucking hostel, and unheard of in London. *Must be a shithole then.* But though Cash was a bit random, he didn't seem the type to live in a sty. *Nah, mate, that's just you.*

Damn my brain today. Staying up all night gawping at Dom was really fucking with my ability to string coherent thoughts together. I finished pinning the ad up and returned to the parts cave to find Cash.

He was waiting for me, his messy dark-blond hair making mine look tidy. "Filters aren't coming till tomorrow. Go home if you want, mate."

I eyed him suspiciously. Most blokes at the garage were pleasant enough now they'd got bored with the hair jokes, but Cash had always been kind to me. Looking me in the eye, asking my opinion on things most people around here assumed I knew nothing about. *Maybe he's a plant from that tabloid—*

Jesus Christ, I needed a nap.

Cash frowned. "You okay?"

"Yep."

"Sure? You look spaced, man."

"Piss off," I snapped before I remembered the piece of paper on the staffroom wall. "Is that ad for your place?"

Cash's frown deepened before he seemed to catch on to what I was talking about. "Shit, I'd forgotten about that. Yeah, it used to be my uncle's place, but he sold it to me on the cheap so he could fuck off to Thailand with his new bird. I'm fixing it up before I flip it, but I could do with a flatmate to help me out."

"So whoever lives with you has to help with repairs?"

"No, I meant with the cost. I bought the house with some inheritance money, but I've run out, so some rent would help me get going again. Why? Know someone looking?"

"No."

Cash cocked an eyebrow. "Sure about that? You seem kind of curious."

Curious wasn't the word. I'd bite any hand that offered me a way out of the halfway house, but for some reason, I couldn't bring myself to say so. To nod and admit that I wanted more than anything to push for something that could make my life better.

"What are you two gossiping about?" Jim reappeared, still brandishing his clipboard.

"We're not gossiping," Cash said with a grin. "I'm just asking Lucky if he wants to rent my spare room."

Jim grunted. "Good idea. It's only up the road, lad. Just the ticket when you like to get here at the arse crack of dawn, eh?"

I scowled as he wandered off again, though I had no right to. Jim had turned a blind eye to me being all over the place for the last few weeks, even bringing me breakfast when I'd been too buzzed to remember to eat. If he thought I should rent Cash's room, chances were he was right.

Taking a deep breath, I turned back to Cash. "Is it really seven-hundred quid?"

Dom opened his front door and pulled me inside, pushing me up against it as soon as it clicked shut. "What's your name?"

"What?"

"Your name," he repeated fiercely. "And don't say it's Lucky or I'll lose my fucking mind, I swear."

I almost laughed, but the obvious anxiety in him tempered my amusement. "My full name is Luke Coleman, but my granddad called me Lucky 'cause I was born on the day he won big at the bingo."

"Your name is Luke?"

"Yeah, but only my parents and teachers ever called me that, so don't even think about it."

Relief seemed to pour out of Dom. He sagged against me, but I didn't question it as I held him. What was the point? His world had gone mad, and perhaps I needed to do better at anchoring him.

If he wanted me to anchor him. After all, we'd come this far, but still had no defined end game.

I didn't know how I felt about that.

I didn't know how I felt about anything while Dom's entire body was pressed against me.

He sighed and pulled away, his lovely face unshuttered again. "You look happy."

"Do I?"

"Yes. What's happened? Something good?"

"Um...I think so."

Dom kissed my cheek and tugged me away from the door, and into the apartment. "You don't have to tell me if you don't want to."

"Why wouldn't I want to tell you?"

He shrugged. "I don't know."

I laughed, couldn't help it, even though it was clear he really didn't know where he was going with this. "I want to tell you, but I'm freaking out about it a bit. You know when something seems too good to be true?"

"You mean like being a rich-bitch football player?"

"Something like that." I dropped onto the couch, kicked my boots off, and tucked my feet beneath me. "A bloke at work has a room to rent. It's in his house, so it's not some shitty HMO, and it's super cheap with bills included."

"HMO?"

"House of multiple occupancy—you know, like twelve people crammed into a two up two down?"

"Oh."

I could tell by Dom's face that he was struggling to put a picture to my words. "I don't know the bloke that well, though," I added. "He could be a serial killer for all I know."

"So could I have been when you first met me." Dom stretched his muscular legs out in front of him. "Does anyone else know him?"

"I think so. He's quiet sometimes, but friendly enough with most of the guys."

"And they like him?"

"Yeah."

"Do you?"

I chewed it over and nodded. "Yeah, he's sound."

"So what's the problem? He's not a creep and you can afford it, right?"

"Yeah. I mean when I said super cheap, I meant for London, not for my budget, but it's the same as I'm paying now."

Dom took it all in, and I could pretty much see him trying to get his head around stressing out over a few hundred quid. He was the most down to earth fella in the world, but he hadn't worried about money in years.

Eventually, he gave up, kissed my cheek, and left the room. He came back with a takeaway pizza box and a couple of beers. "I met with my manager today."

I blew out a breath. "Wow. How did that go?"

"As expected in some ways, and completely off the wall in others."

"Meaning?"

"Meaning the reactions of individuals were as expected, but the board surprised me. They've accepted my retirement at the end of the season, but they're going to back me all the way, and speak out to let other queer players know the club is a safe place for them."

"What?"

"I know, right?" Dom rubbed his face. "I was pretty flipped by it, but it doesn't really change things for me. I *want* to retire, not be some poster boy for gay footballers."

"They asked you to do that?"

"Not exactly, but that's what will happen if I stay, and I don't want that. I want to get back to living, and actually, knowing the club is gonna do the decent thing with or without me makes that easier."

I opened the pizza box and forced myself not to get distracted by barbecue chicken. "So...you don't want to be a poster boy, but you don't want to leave knowing the next queer player would have it just as hard?"

"Something like that. It sounds better in my head. And to be honest, the poster-boy thing isn't about being gay. I've never liked that shit—I don't do press or endorsements, and I made damn sure I never signed a contract that obligated me to."

"I can't imagine you doing a Head & Shoulders advert."

Dom snorted and snagged a slice of pizza, though he didn't take a bite. "I never did that stuff because no money in the world seemed worth it, but I don't judge the guys that do—it's just not me. Thing is, though, I never knew what *was* me until the last few days."

"What's changed?"

"Nothing. Everything. I don't really know. I just—" He dropped the pizza back in the box. "It's ridiculous, but I feel like something's shifted in me. Like seeing you on the ground and thinking you were dead showed me what my life really was...and what the future held for both of us if things didn't change."

"I hate that you saw me like that."

"I don't," Dom said. "I mean, I hate that you've been in so much pain, and I'll do anything you need to help you get better, but I had to see that reality, Lucky—*your* reality—or what we have wouldn't mean anything."

"What do we have?"

Dom speared me with a stare that warmed me from the inside out. "I don't know what you'd call it, mate, but I fucking love you, if that helps."

My face split in a grin a mile wide. "Are you serious?"

"Am I funny enough to pull off a joke like that?"

"Probably not." I abandoned the pizza box and slithered like a drunken chimp into his lap. "But I've never loved you for your wit."

"No? What have you loved me for?"

"For everything, Dom. You're everything to me; you know that, don't you?"

He smiled. "I do now."

EPILOGUE

Six months later...

Dom

"I still can't get used to strangers knowing my name," Lucky said. "I thought all the attention would've fucked off by the time I finished my apprenticeship."

I glanced up from my phone. Lucky was staring after the young girls who'd approached our table in the Tottenham cafe and greeted us both by name. "It's that bloody gossip rag. They love you."

Lucky cringed, but—thankfully—humour danced in his lively gaze. "They only love me because they get off on the idea of a weed like me taming a stud like you."

I snorted. "There's nothing weedy about you."

"They don't know that."

"Why should they? Fuck them."

"I don't want to fuck them—literally, or metaphorically. They were nice."

Most people who approached us were, and it still felt surreal. The shitstorm of hate I'd expected when the club's team of publicists had carefully managed my coming out had never come. An injunction had silenced the tabloid hack who'd stalked my meetings with Lucky, giving me time to play out the season before I'd retired from the game. I'd come out two weeks later, but the impact had been softened by a bigger sporting scandal, and I'd got off lightly. Paps still followed me around from time to time, but I was mostly too boring to warrant much attention.

At least, I had been until the lighter gossip magazines had caught up with Lucky. After that, we'd somehow ended up as a hashtag for cute queer relationship goals, and most days I wondered if I was living a dream.

Not that having my life mapped out in mushy memes on Snapchat had ever been my dream, but if it outweighed the occasional batch of hate mail from disgruntled football yobs, I could dig it. "Are you still getting girls coming by the garage?"

Lucky drained his tea mug and wiped his devilish mouth with the back of his hand. "Every day. It freaks Cash out a bit, but the other guys love it. Don't think half of them get to talk to women otherwise."

"What about Jim?"

"He don't care as long as the work gets done."

Sometimes I envied Lucky's ability to live such a normal life. How he wore his pansexuality like a second skin. I had so much to learn from him. Still, his smile kept me alive, like it always had. I reached across the table and brushed my fingers over his. "Can we go home?"

He grinned. "My place or yours?"

"Yours."

We walked home to the house Lucky shared with a fellow mechanic from Premier Autos. Cash was somewhere downstairs, hitting stuff with a hammer. I liked him. He was sharp enough to be interesting, and mellow enough to keep his nose out of my shit—the perfect combination. And he was a dude to Lucky, so he was pretty much my fucking hero.

Still, the fact that he was preoccupied making a whole lot of noise somewhere else was a relief as I tugged Lucky upstairs to the bedroom that made him so happy. Bright and airy, with huge bay windows, it was a rare day I didn't wake up to find Lucky grinning at his surroundings like he couldn't quite believe they were real.

His bed was awesome too. It was the only thing I'd asked if I could buy him, and I was fairly sure the fact that he knew my motives weren't entirely selfless had swayed his decision to let me.

The bed was big and white, covered with too many pillows, and finished off with a duvet as thick and squishy as a fucking marshmallow. It wasn't my thing, but it was everything Lucky had never had, and on the nights we spent apart, knowing he was safe in his Lucky-scented cocoon made me happy.

And, the nights we did spend together, the duvet was so warm we had to sleep naked: winner.

Lucky threw himself down on the bed in question. "You look like you're plotting something."

"Plotting? You think I'm that kind of man?"

"Nah. I just meant you've obviously got something on your mind, and I'm hoping it involves locking the door for the rest of the night."

Heat rushed through me, like it always did at the mere thought of having sex with Lucky. Gone were the days where my desire for him —or any man—came with a hefty dose of shame. I couldn't pinpoint when it had left me, or even why, but I never forgot it.

I locked the door and joined Lucky on the bed, kicking my shoes off on the way. Just lying with him was enough, but he clearly had other ideas. He yanked impatiently at my clothes until I was bare, and set to work slowly driving me mad.

Sometimes it shocked me how fast we'd moved from a sordid Grindr hook up in Dalston, to bareback love-making in Tottenham, but on days like these, when I rolled onto my stomach and gave myself up to him, time ceased to mean anything.

Lucky moved like magic inside me, his slick cock nailing my prostate with every slow, deliberate thrust. "You know what else I can't believe?" he whispered.

"Tell me," I gritted out.

"That you love me doing you like this more than fucking my brains out. I had you pegged for a monster top when we first met."

"I do love fucking your brains out."

"Yeah, but you love this more."

I couldn't deny it. Fucking Lucky was a ride I couldn't describe, but having him inside me, turning me inside out like I was his most precious thing—fuck, it was everything.

The time for talk faded. Lucky drove into me with more purpose, harder, faster, and his hands were everywhere—roaming my back, my neck, his fingers twisting in my hair.

I lost myself to sensation, and the coiling pit of pleasure in my gut, as I moved with him. Frantic need drove me to my knees, and I gripped my dick with a desperate hand, jacking myself in time with Lucky's thrusts until I choked out his name, and orgasm hit me like a shit ton of bricks.

Behind me, Lucky cried out. Wet warmth pulsed where we were joined, and he slumped against me, panting. "Damn, I've never come so hard before."

A chuckle that was more of a gurgle rumbled out of me. "You say that every time."

"'Cause it's true." Lucky rolled off me and landed in a heap of long limbs and pale skin.

Grinning, I left the bed briefly to clean up, and then returned to lay my head on his abdomen.

He combed his fingers through my hair and brushed his thumb over the faint scar on my wrist he'd never questioned. "Can I ask you something?"

I forced a heavy eye open. "Of course."

"Are you happy?"

Now there was a question. Before my sordid closeted life had carried me to him, I hadn't known what happy meant. I'd had the glory and riches of top-flight football, and the bone-scraping lows of self-loathing, but never the pure joy I felt when I woke up in the morning to find Lucky beside me. Or when I reached for him in a public place without giving a shit who saw me. When I was *proud* to be seen. Proud to love him. Proud to even know him.

And proud of my fucking self.

"I'm happy, Lucky. Are you?"

His answering smile set me free.

Lucky

"You're a bit of a dick to Isha," Jamila remarked from her perch on Dom's kitchen counter.

"That right?" Dom didn't even look at her. "How do you know he isn't a dick to me?"

Jamila hopped down and came to peer over his shoulder. "Because he's almost as in love with you as Lucky is."

I snorted into my drink. Jamila had pegged Isha as a closet case the moment she'd laid eyes on him, and enjoyed terrorising Dom about it, even though he largely ignored her.

His silence usually wasn't enough to shut her up on its own, but today, whatever he'd been doing on his iPad for most of the morning since his meeting with Isha piqued her curiosity. "What's this?"

"New project," he said.

She rolled her eyes. "I can see that, but what *is* it? It looks like that hellhole Lucky used to live in."

"That's because it is." Dom's gaze flickered to me, wary for the first time in months. "The charity running it dissolved last month and the centre shut down, so me and Isha were thinking of taking it over."

"The charity?" Jamila dropped onto the stool beside Dom. "Or the building?"

"Both."

That was news to me. Dom had used his retirement so far to build a property business that would shore up his already ridiculous finances, but he'd never mentioned fucking with the halfway house I could still smell when he wasn't lying close enough to me.

Dom caught my frown and beckoned me closer. I scowled harder, but my nosiness got the better of me. I claimed my place at his side and flicked through the drawn-up plans on the iPad. The centre was unrecognisable to how I remembered it.

"Why?" I asked, sharper than I meant to. "You could throw money at anything. Why this?"

Jamila silently slunk away. Dom waited for the front door to bang, and then turned so he was facing me and pushed the iPad away. "Because I haven't been able to get the place out of my mind since you told me you'd rather have died on the street than go back there. It's supposed to be a safe space for people who are trying to recover from homelessness, but it wasn't fit for purpose."

"So? What do you care?"

Dom sighed. "Seriously?"

"Yes. You don't have to change the world for me. I'm doing just fine."

"I know you are, and that's because you're strong as fuck, even if you think you aren't, but what if you weren't? What if living in that place had derailed everything you'd achieved up until that point? If you'd lost your job? Or been hurt? I know I can't change the world, Lucky, but I need to do this."

I didn't get it, and I didn't have time to argue with him. I had an appointment at the addiction clinic I'd signed up to when it had become clear that being head over heels in love with Dom wasn't a cure for all my bad habits.

Still glowering, I left him alone, and stomped to the tube. My appointment was in Tottenham, which had become my base for just about everything—home, work, play when Dom and I forced ourselves to go out. And of course when I drifted to the clinic, my brain still wrapped up in Dom's plans, I had to pass the very shithole in question.

Except it wasn't a shithole. It was a sanctuary that had been underfunded and badly managed. In the right hands, perhaps it *could* change the world—or, at least, a small slice of it.

It amazed me how it sometimes took me so long to find common sense. I said as much to the kindly woman who had guided me through the addiction course.

"Logical thinking isn't easy when it's a subject close to you heart," she reasoned. "Didn't you say Dom didn't always make sense when he was struggling with his decision to come out? That you didn't understand because he seemed to think so simply about everything else?"

I kind of hated this woman, but only because she was always right, and that meant I regularly had to go back and adjust my thinking. "I suppose I just figured that part of my life was done with."

"Nothing in life is ever done with. We learn and move on."

"That's not done with?"

"You tell me."

Bitch.

I left the clinic and walked back to Cash's house. I'd last seen Dom in Greenwich, but he was waiting for me, naturally, sitting on the front steps.

"Miss me?"

"Of course," he said with a grin. "And I was worried I'd freaked you out."

"Nah." I helped him up and unlocked the door, still half-awed that I called a house like this home. "You know me—snap before I think, just like my dad."

"You're nothing like your dad."

"I know."

"So why say it?"

"'Cause I'm a dick."

Dom didn't argue. Just shut the door behind us and trailed me to the kitchen.

I opened the fridge and pulled out the pasta I'd stashed the night before—tomato and chilli, 'cause Cash was a fucking vegetarian nut and wouldn't have meat in the house. It was the only downside to living with him, so I couldn't complain, but I did, all the time, much to his amusement.

"*Lucky.*"

I blinked to find Dom had crossed the kitchen and invaded my personal space. He took the pasta dish from me, set it aside, and lifted me onto the counter.

He inserted himself between my legs and forced me to look at him. "Nothing is set in stone. I can back out at any time if you're not comfortable with it."

"I am comfortable with it."

"Really?"

"Yes." I nodded slowly. "But, Dom, you've got to do it right. That place needed double the night wardens, and better security, and—"

Dom pressed his hand over my mouth. "I know all that. And Isha is hiring people who know how this shit works better than we do. My role is to make sure the project has the funding it needs to set up properly, and Isha will see it becomes self-sufficient enough to continue. I would like you to consult on it, though? If you can?"

"Consult?"

"Yeah. Basically tell me everything we're doing wrong so we can fix it. It's a real job—you'd get paid."

"Paid?"

Dom rolled his eyes. "Yes. And don't go thinking I'm creating a job for you because I love you. If you don't do it, we'll find someone else and pay them the same."

"But I have a job."

"I know. This would only take a few hours a week."

There was no part of me that wanted to refuse, but still I found myself unable to say yes. Would I ever learn to reach for the things I truly wanted?

"Tell you what," Dom said when my silence stretched out. "How about you look over the preliminary plans in a couple of days? See what you think? Lucky—look at me."

I hadn't noticed my gaze drifting from his. I stared up at him now and lost myself in the kind eyes he'd never quite been able to hide, even in the beginning. "What?"

Dom smiled and shook his head. "Nothing, mate. I'm just happy to know you."

"I'm happy to know you too...and, Dom?"

"Yeah?"

"I'll take the job."

Before he could react, I wrapped my legs around him, and then my arms, and held him so tight he grunted in surprise, but I didn't let him go. Couldn't. Wouldn't. Never. He told me often that loving me had set him free. That I got to love him in return? Damn. I learned every day that lucky didn't even come close.

THE END

NEWSLETTER

For the most up to date news and free books, subscribe to my newsletter HERE.

This is a zero spam zone. Maximum number of emails you will receive is one per month.

PATREON

Not ready to let go of Dom and Lucky? Or looking for sneak peeks at future books in the series? Alternative POVs, outtakes, and missing moments from **all** Garrett's books can be found on her Patreon site. Misfits, Slide, Strays...the works. Because you know what? Garrett wasn't ready to let her boys go either.

Pledges start from as little as $2, and all content is available at the lowest tier.

CASH – EXCERPT

(Coming January 2019)

Cash

"I'm not getting it." I pointed the kitchen knife in Lucky's general direction, ignoring Dom's overprotective glare. "The only idiots whoever knock at the side door are twat-hound reporters looking for you."

It was true. As the man Dom had given up a premiership football career to be with, the press loved Lucky, a fact he indulged to keep them away from Dom. And me, when he wasn't being a dick.

"Put it this way," I said when he didn't move. "You ain't getting dinner otherwise."

I knew it would work. That boy was a slave to his stomach, and I enjoyed feeding him, even if the two minutes flat it took him to clear his place reminded me that it wasn't so long ago he'd had nothing and no one.

Lucky slid off his kitchen stool and sloped off to answer the door. I promptly forgot all about it and went back to chopping veg for dinner.

He surprised me when he reappeared a moment later, smirking. "It's for you."

"What?"

"You heard." He hopped back into his seat. "Some moody hottie who whole named you."

I froze, knife in hand. My name was no secret, but there was no one round these parts who'd use it on my doorstep. Everyone called me Cash, even the damn postman.

Trepidation rippled through me. Lucky didn't seem to notice, but I felt Dom's gaze on me as I left the kitchen. That fucker saw everything.

I slipped down the hallway to the side door we never used. It was open a jar, concealing who was on the other side, and my heart jumped again. Chances were it was some market research bullshit and they'd got my name from the electoral role. That he was, in Lucky's words, a hottie, was a bonus, right?

Life was never that simple. I eased the door open. At first, I saw no one, then a slim figure stepped out of the shadows, his expression grim until recognition seemed to hit him. And me. *Jesus Christ.* Dark hair, moody eyes, beard, and perfect skin, dear-fucking-God, it was Rae.

Heat rushed me in the same moment suspicion shut me down. I stepped outside and shut the door behind me. "What the fuck are you doing here?"

ACKNOWLEDGMENTS

Love and thanks as ever to my husband and cubs for their unending patience when I'm grumpily glued to my computer.

Also to Con Riley for having my back with every book I write, and Rachel at Signal Boost Promotions for her tireless work on my behalf.

ABOUT GARRETT LEIGH

Bonus Material available for all books on Garrett's Patreon account. Includes short stories from Misfits, Slide, Strays, What Remains, Dream, and much more. Sign up here: https://www.patreon.com/garrettleigh

Facebook Fan Group, Garrett's Den... https://www.facebook.com/groups/garre...

Garrett Leigh is an award-winning British writer, cover artist, and book designer. Her debut novel, Slide, won Best Bisexual Debut at the 2014 Rainbow Book Awards, and her polyamorous novel, Misfits was a finalist in the 2016 LAMBDA awards, and was again a finalist in 2017 with Rented Heart.

In 2017, she won the EPIC award in contemporary romance with her military novel, Between Ghosts, and the contemporary romance category in the Bisexual Book Awards with her novel What Remains.

When not writing, Garrett can generally be found procrastinating on Twitter, cooking up a storm, or sitting on her behind doing as little as possible, all the while shouting at her menagerie of children and animals and attempting to tame her unruly and wonderful FOX.

Garrett is also an award winning cover artist, taking the silver medal at the Benjamin Franklin Book Awards in 2016. She designs for various publishing houses and independent authors at blackjazzdesign.com, and co-owns the specialist stock site moonstockphotography.com

Connect with Garrett
www.garrettleigh.com

facebook.com/garrettleighauthor
twitter.com/garrett_leigh
instagram.com/instagram

ALSO BY GARRETT LEIGH

Slide

Rare

Circle

Misfits

Strays

Dream

Whisper

Believe

Crossroads

Bullet

Bones

Bold

House of Cards

Junkyard Heart

Rented Heart

Soul to Keep

My Mate Jack

Lucky Man

Finding Home

Only Love

Heart

What Remains

What Matters

Between Ghosts

www.ingramcontent.com/pod-product-compliance
Lightning Source LLC
Chambersburg PA
CBHW030545310726
48979CB00010B/2044/J
9781913220013